G. J. DAILY

STRANGE CHILD

First published by Blossom & Paige 2022

First edition

ISBN: 979-8-9868553-0-1

Cover art by Aleksandar Milosavljevic Alek

This book was professionally typeset on Reedsy.
Find out more at reedsy.com

To Karen,
For always believing.

To Rick,
You always inspired us.

STRANGE CHILD

Chapter One

1941

A seven-year-old Marvin walked down a dry Alabama road kicking up small tufts of light tan dust as he carried his little brother on his back. Two small feet stuck out from underneath his arms, one on either side.

Moses, only four years old, gripped Marvin's neck as tightly as his little arms could muster so that his brother didn't drop him.

"Where are we going Marvin?" the tiny voice asked, just behind Marvin's head.

Marvin grinned large and hoisted Moses up higher on his back because he kept sliding down as they walked. "I done told you it's a surprise. I ain't sain' till we get there."

"I like sus-prises," Moses replied, bouncing up and down as Marvin walked.

Finding the bend in the narrow country road Marvin had been looking for, he pushed aside the long branches of a magnolia tree with its dark, waxy green leaves. Most of the thick white petals of the magnolia's flowers had already fallen to piles of withering brown detritus on the ground, but the rich perfume of those few still holding on would forever paint his memory of the day.

A sign nailed to a tree trunk read NO TRESPASSING, but neither of the boys could read, so they, like many of the other children in town, ignored the sign as Marvin made his way across the blanket of brown and white petals.

"Marv, do you think momma 'll give us a bite of that sweet pote-a-toe pie when we get back?" Moses asked.

"That's for church tomorrow," Marvin replied, now thinking about his favorite dessert and making him realize he had grown hungry on their long walk from their small wood-paneled home. "I'm tired. You gotta walk now. We're almost there anyway," Marvin said, kneeling so that his brother could climb down off of his back.

As they walked, the ground began to slowly slope downwards until they came to a rocky outcropping where the two boys could look out over a large pond where a wooden platform bobbed in the center of the cool, azure-blue water that lightly dipped and jostled from the slight afternoon breeze.

"I brought you swimming!" Marvin exclaimed, holding both of his hands over his head with excitement.

"We can't be here," Moses said, leaning over one of the large rocks and looking out onto the water.

"No one will see us if we're here for just a while. Besides, all the town kids are in school."

Moses scrunched his face and sat down on the ground behind the rock. This was one of the many places their parents expressly forbade them from going.

"Don't you want to go for a swim? Even if we just splash around a bit to cool off before we go back? It'll be our secret. A brother's secret!"

Moses sat up on his knees and looked out over the water a second time. He liked that: A brother's secret. "It's so hot."

Marvin nudged him with a smile. "I bet I'm a faster swimmer than you."

Moses looked at him. "I'm faster!" He hollered.

"Besides, how'd you get to be such a good swimmer?" Marvin asked, knowing how to convince his brother to come along with him on his little adventures.

"I don't know," Moses replied, slowly taking Marvin's hand and stepping around the large rocks. Marvin gripped it tightly. "Go down sideways," he said as both boys carefully shuffled their way down the steep embankment of loose gravel and shale. Once they made it to the bottom, Mavin pulled off his loosely-fitting button-up shirt and broken brown leather shoes. Then he helped his little brother strip down so that both boys stood on the water's edge in their discolored underpants.

"It's cold!" Moses hollered, dipping a foot in the water.

Marvin splashed out and dropped down to his chin. "Don't be a baby!" He laughed and began to swim back and forth. "You'll get used to it. See, it doesn't feel cold to me!"

Moses always dove head first into whatever Marvin was doing, whether Moses was big enough or experienced enough, or ready. None of that mattered to him. If it was good enough for his big brother, it was good enough for him. Thankfully, this had made Moses a fairly respectable swimmer, even at his young age, mainly from when their father had taken the boys out fishing with him along the Tombigbee. So, Moses set his reservations aside and stepped out into the cool water, trusting his older brother to keep him safe.

At first, Moses wanted to stay along the edge where he could feel the slime-covered stones beneath his reaching toes, but Marvin kept circling around him and swimming farther and farther out towards the wooden platform.

"Don't go so far!" Moses exclaimed.

Marvin swam back to him and took his hand. "I'll swim with you."

"Look, Marvin! A fwog!" Moses yelled to him, pointing to a small bump of a head protruding from the pond water at the tip of a V-shape growing behind the frog as it swam. "That's because fwogs are green!"

Marvin smiled. "Yep. Frogs are green. Hey! Why don't we swim with it!"

"Yeah! Wet's swim wiff it," Moses replied. And both of the boys, hands held tight, left the safety of the shore, both fascinated by how the small green-brown creature so casually kept its head safely above the water as it kicked its long legs out behind it.

The day was hot, but the water was cool, and Marvin loved being with his little brother. Marvin always felt strong and capable around Moses, almost like he was a grown-up. To Moses, Marvin was as strong as Samson in those Bible stories their momma told them before bed each night.

When they reached the platform in the center of the pond, Marvin leaned his elbow up over the rough wood edge and pulled Moses towards him. The platform dipped towards them just enough for Moses to pull himself up out of the water, and Marvin pushed on his bottom so that Moses fell forward onto his chest and rolled onto the platform. Both boys laughed, and Marvin pulled himself up out of the water and rolled onto his back alongside his brother.

Together they laid there in the afternoon sun, letting the

cold water slowly evaporate off of their skin.

"Marvin, what you fink this is here for?"

"I don't know. Probably boats or fishing or something."

"Why doesn't papa let us come here every day?" Moses asked. "I like this."

"The townies swim here usually, and they don't like us very much," Marvin replied.

"Why?"

"We don't look like them, I guess."

Marvin had heard his parents whispering other reasons at night; reasons he didn't know how to put into words his baby brother would understand.

Just then, Marvin heard laughter from high up near the rocky overlook where they had been earlier, and he quickly sat upright and shielded his eyes from the bright sun.

Three boys, older than Marvin but not by much, pushed each other and started crawling over the rocks. It was clear they hadn't seen Marvin or Moses yet, but they would soon, so Marvin whispered to Moses: "Quick! Get into the water!" and pointed to the side of the platform opposite the hill where the boys began to slide down the steep bank. Moses rolled and slid quietly into the water after his brother, and both boys held onto the edge of the platform and listened to the sound of laughter and tumbling rocks.

"What's this?" Marvin heard one of the boys ask. "Someone left their clothes."

Marvin squinted in frustration and bit the edge of his lip. They had found their clothes. How long would it be before they found them? What would they do when they did? Marvin knew well that grown adults had killed boys like him and Moses for offenses much less than swimming in forbidden waters, but these were kids. Would they care? Could they be as mean? Marvin knew they could.

There was a splash, and the boys laughed. "Throw the others in!" One of them said.

Marvin slowly swam to the corner of the platform, wordlessly motioning Moses to stay where he was, as he peeked out to see the boys throwing his shoes into the pond. Then a second boy, with great flourish, threw their clothes in a spray of fabric onto the water.

Marvin scolded himself in the voice of his father. How could he be so foolish? And he wasn't the only one in trouble here. He had brought his brother right into it with him. But maybe it wasn't so bad. The boys on the shore thought that whoever the clothes belonged to were gone. Perhaps if he and Moses just stayed out of sight on the platform's edge, they could wait until the boys left, and no one would be the wiser.

Then there was another splash as one of the three stripped down to his underpants and jumped off a small rock into the pond. He splashed water up at his friends, who chided him for getting their clothes wet as they pulled off their shoes and pants as quickly as they could and jumped in after him. It didn't take long before all three were casually swimming toward the floating platform.

Marvin looked back at his brother, who hung onto the edge of the platform with a look of fear and confusion, only four years old. Marvin had to protect his baby brother and knew that his brother was looking to him for that very protection. He wasn't their father, but he knew he needed to find some of that courage he had seen in his father, like the night the man who owned their property stumbled onto their porch drunk and asking about his momma. But no one had ever told

Marvin how to have that kind of courage. Besides, maybe it wouldn't be so bad. Maybe the boys would be friendly.

He took a deep breath. "Stay here until I come and get you," Marvin whispered to Moses. Moses nodded. "Promise?" Marvin asked. Moses nodded again. "Brother's promise?!"

Moses thought about that for a moment and nodded with greater flourish and a smile.

That moment, that big I-know-my-big-brother-just-figured-out-how-to-save-us smile would stay with Marvin for the rest of his life.

Marvin nodded in agreement, took the deepest breath he could muster, and dipped below the water.

As he swam beneath the platform, not unlike the frog they had followed out into the pond, he opened his eyes trying to see where he was going, but all he could see were the streaks of sunlight piercing through the murky water. He swam as far as his lungs would let him before popping his head up out of the water, trying to put as much distance between him and his brother as he could.

All three boys flailed in the water, startled at the sight of Marvin coming up out of the pond and swimming past them to the shore.

"Hey! Who's that?" One of them asked.

"Who are you!"

Marvin didn't respond. He just kept swimming until he made it onto the muddy beach, rose out of the water, and sat on the rock the boys had jumped from. Then he leaned onto his knees, catching his breath and watched as the three changed course and swam towards him.

"Where'd you come from?" a slender boy with red freckles and a green gob of snot dripping down his lip asked.

Marvin took a breath. "Up the hill," and pointed at the outcropping.

"What are you doing here?" a fat boy with a large scar on his shoulder asked.

Marvin ignored the question for the obvious answer and asked them instead, "Why'd you throw my clothes in the water?"

The three boys turned and looked at the clothes lying on the surface of the still water, then turned back to Marvin.

"You can't be here!" The fat boy said.

"Who says?" Marvin calmly asked, still breathing heavily and not looking at them but out over the water.

They looked at each other. None of them knew who made these kinds of rules, but people like Marvin couldn't be swimming where town children swam, and they all knew it; Marvin knew it even better than they did though he also knew that distraction and a little confidence were his only defense at the moment.

They shrugged. "We say!" The fat boy retorted. "And we say you have to get out of here."

Oh, how Marvin wanted absolutely nothing more than to do just that, but he couldn't leave his little Moses hiding in the pond like the biblical baby in the basket his momma had told them both about by the light of an evening fire as she took turns rocking them.

"No." The word slipped past Marvin's lips before he had any time to think about it; the word above all other words that no one like Marvin was allowed to ever say to anyone from the towns. "I can swim here if I like."

"No, you can't!" The third boy said, shorter than the other two.

"Yes, I can." And Marvin stood. For the first time he looked each of them in the eye.

"No, you can't," the boy with the scar said, pushing Marvin, who wouldn't have fallen if he had remembered how close he was to the stone behind his legs, but because he hadn't, he stumbled backward, both feet flying up over his head.

Marvin's knees and hands sank into the mud as he tried standing to his feet when a sudden, sharp pain jabbed into his shoulder. It was a rock. A second and third stung at his chest, and he flinched and tried guarding himself with his arms and shielding his face with his hand, but it didn't do much good.

The freckled boy pitched a stone the size of a baseball at Marvin as hard as he could, striking him just above his left eye and spinning him around. Marvin fell to his knees.

The boys paused at the sight of the blood that flowed quickly from Marvin's forehead, and Marvin tried to use the small boulder to stand. But he quickly became so dizzy that he vomited before dropping to the water's edge, the cold soil and grass pressing against the back of his shoulders and head as he lost consciousness.

It was nearly dark when Marvin awoke to the tickle of a harvestman spider crawling across his cheek and the water lapping against his leg and left arm. His head hurt worse than he could ever remember it hurting. At first, he couldn't remember where he was or why he was so wet.

He sat up and touched the sharp pain above his eye, which stung even more when he touched it. The soil where he had landed had somehow helped to stop the bleeding, and all he saw when he looked at his fingertips were crusts of dry red.

In a daze, he looked around. The pond was quiet. What was he doing here?

Twigs dug into his knees as he slowly rose and sat up on the cold soil.

His clothes still bobbed on the surface of the water, and seeing them, he slowly and painfully began to remember the three boys who had come down the hill and attacked him.

And all for what? Swimming in a pond? Was it their pond? He didn't know whose pond it was.

Then he looked out to the wooden platform resting still and quiet across the water and remembered his baby brother.

He immediately ran as far as he could before diving into the water and swimming around to the back of the platform.

But there was no sign of Moses.

"Stay here until I come and get you," he had told his little brother. "Brother's promise!"

He spun around in circles, water splashing into his face, scanning the glittering surface, trying to see any sign of his little brother through the growing darkness.

Then panic began to set in.

He swam around the platform three, four, then five times. But there was no Moses.

Where had he gone? Had he left? Did he try to hold on until he couldn't any longer? Maybe he just walked home without Marvin?

Marvin took a deep breath and dove beneath the surface.

As hard as it was to see through the algae when the sun was high, it was now impossible to see anything deep in the murky water, but the pond wasn't more than a few feet deep, so he came back up for another breath and dove back under, this time frantically trying to feel around in the muck and mud and sticks and leaves that pile the bottom of a pond like this several inches deep. But, even though he felt something about the size of his hand swim away from his grappling fingers, he didn't feel any indication of his brother's tiny arms or legs. The legs that had bounced under his arms as Marvin carried him through the magnolia forest, the arms so small they had clung to his neck for safety, what felt to Marvin like just minutes ago.

After three more attempts to find Moses beneath the water's surface, Marvin finally cried out: "Moses!" "MOSES!" But only the sound of his voice echoing back at him from the steep shale embankments could be heard. He spun again and again in the water crying out, but nothing but his deep and venomous panic responded.

His arms began to burn, and his legs grew tired from treading water, so he swam back to the bank where everything had happened and splashed violently through the grassy edges, as the growing darkness made it hard to see what he was stepping on, causing him to trip and fall to his knees in the muddy quagmire more than once.

The faster he ran along the water's edge, looking for any sign of his baby brother, the more Panic enshrouded his every sense of reason.

Then he stopped.

There, in the blue light of the harvest moon, where a small creek fed into the large pond, lay a tiny arm.

Marvin stumbled and crawled up to Moses and slowly pulled his baby brother's wet and water-logged body out of the muddy water where he lay face down. Then Marvin screamed a scream that might have awoken long-dead ancestral spirits—if any such thing existed—as the talons of Panic flayed his reality open in front of him.

"Help! Someone help me PLEASE!" Marvin shrieked in

terror and anguish into the night like a wounded animal. "MOSES!" He pulled the limp body close to his chest and rocked him back and forth like their mamma would do with them in the chair his father had made for her. But instead of a soft warm blanket of wool, Moses' tiny body lay in Marvin's arms wrapped in cold mud and leaves. And there upon that dreadful shore, Marvin cried so bitterly that words came out of his mouth in languages he didn't recognize; Sounds like those of a mongrel animal beaten nearly to death. Pain and anger and confusion poured out of that seven-year-old boy that night in a way that would have broken the hearts of even the coldest kings or the hardest princes or even the heart of the Great and Mighty God of all of heaven.

There Marvin cried until he had no more tears.

He screamed until his voice went flat and hoarse, and all the while, he just kept rocking his baby brother, his baby Moses.

That's what his mother had called him the day she put the wrapped bundle in Marvin's arms. She didn't want Marvin to be jealous of the new child, and to avoid that, she had instilled in his heart from the beginning that this was his baby. His little baby. And now that baby was gone.

Sometime that night, Marvin, only seven, gave up caring at all if he would get up. He gave up caring about anything and resolved himself to simply hold his brother until time ended, when an image began to rise in his adolescent mind.

He blinked, his eyes burning from the dirt and tears. He didn't know if he had been sitting there for minutes or hours. He did not care. But, the single thought of his mother and father losing both him and his brother in one night sparked a light in his mind. Not a great fire, but just enough of an ember that he felt his arms twitch.

His legs had gone completely numb, beyond that needle tingle of sleep to a complete loss of any feeling at all. He couldn't even feel the cold water or mud beneath his naked legs any longer, though he sat sunken far enough into the bank of the pond that his legs had nearly disappeared in the mud.

But there again, he felt his arms twitch to life, and he unclenched the fists that he had unknowingly clenched so tight that his nails had cut bloody puddles into his palms.

He knew then that he had to stand. He had to rise from the mud and filth and somehow get his brother home. The spark of this purpose began to grow and warm him and give him vision. He still couldn't feel his legs, but he refused to set his brother back onto that unholy soil, so he gripped Moses' body tight, screamed in pain, and swung his head as he tried desperately to push himself up on the useless poles that were his legs.

He took one step forward, then another, as he paused and tried to wait for his legs to wake up beneath him. He knew he wasn't taking his brother anywhere without them.

He watched the reflection of the moon on the water and pulled Moses' body closer to his own. Then he rose to his feet and began walking.

But, he just couldn't do it. He didn't have the strength to get Moses up the embankment.

They had nearly fallen down the loose gravel and shale, and he barely had the strength to carry his brother's body back around to this side of the pond.

Only, there was no other way out with the thick bramble and trees surrounding the pond on all other sides.

He slumped down on the large rock and shifted his brother's body so that he could lock his fingers together to avoid dropping him—the strength in his arms now completely gone.

He kissed his brother's cheek. "I'm so so sorry. I'm so sorry. I just wanted to surprise you. You always was the fastest swimmer." And he looked with helplessness at the embankment rising like a monolith in the moonlight before him, which now looked five or ten times higher than it had when they slid down.

He rested his head against his brother's cold and lifeless body, with barely the strength to sit upright when another thought came to him out of the cold quiet darkness. If he had carried his brother into these woods on his back, he could carry him out.

He carefully slid onto the muddy ground and leaned his brother's tiny body so that it gently sat on the rock, leaning forward, with his help as he turned and draped his brother's arms over each of his shoulders and leaned forward to rise.

And rise he did.

But the embankment gave him no help, and he slid backward after just a few steps, causing him to drop onto his hands and knees, holding his brother's wrists in one hand and crawling with the other as he slowly and carefully inched his way up and out of the steep shale pit.

The smell of the magnolia blossoms was thick in the air, and more than once the branches of the magnolia trees clawed and scrapped at his face. Still, he was unwilling to shield his face or protect himself for fear of dropping his brother's tiny lifeless body, sure that if he did he may never have the strength to pick him up again.

So, step by belabored step, he left that forest and began walking the narrow country road that had brought them to that wretched place until small pin pricks of head lamps from a car far down the road began approaching him, and in the middle of the dirt path he dropped to his knees and pulled Moses' body tightly to his chest, unsure of whether the approaching car was going to help them or finish them off.

Chapter Two

Present Day

The rain picked up, and Marvin, now 87, kicked up his collar against the back of his neck, squinting into the darkness as he crossed the parking lot.

He was so tired, he felt like he was in a waking dream. Tired physically. Tired emotionally. Tired of taking his endless pills. Tired of being poked by doctors. Tired of the same old reruns and the same old songs. Tired of seeing that old man looking back at him in the mirror every morning, even though he still thought of himself the way he looked when he was thirty-five. And now he could see the solution was so very simple.

He would never have admitted it to Margaret, but he'd always been afraid of death, afraid of endlessly falling. He didn't know where that idea came from, but most of those fears that grab ahold of us and never let go aren't strictly rational. Now, only minutes from closing his eyes forever, the scratching echo of his doubts and fears were so completely silent it startled him.

Arthritis in his knees shot fingers of pain up his back as he crossed the parking lot when long grey feathers blew past his feet.

He lifted his face against the rain as water ran down the back of his neck, making him shudder.

Then he saw blood.

Matted grey feathers mixed with blood looked like something had caught a large bird and torn it to pieces. Loose feathers shifted and swirled in eddies of wind and rain. Blood dripped down the brick wall in front of him, still very red and glistening in the sideways light cast by two lamps across the parking lot. There was so much blood he could smell it mixed with damp trash and wet street.

The damp and filthy mound of torn bird covered a naked body, which he overlooked until he saw a small foot—a leg.

It was a child!

He quickly stepped over to the child lying curled tightly like an unborn fetus painted dark with the devil's brush.

Oh no! He's dead, Marvin thought.

He bent down, wondering what horrible event had taken place here. He had just come this way. Could he have been so lost in himself and Margaret's death that he hadn't even noticed a child lying dead on the sidewalk? Or had this just happened?

He looked around but didn't see anyone. All of the homes were dark and locked up against the harshness of this part of the city at night.

He quickly turned back to the pawn shop he had just come from, looking for help, hoping to use a phone since he didn't carry one, even though he and Margaret had talked about getting one of those pocket ones.

He buzzed the door, but there was no answer. He looked in through the bars but didn't see the owner. He buzzed again and again. Nothing. He looked back across the parking lot but couldn't see the child from here. It was too dark and too far removed from the red glow of the pawn shop sign. He tried next door, but the liquor store was already dark and closed for the night, so he came back and buzzed the pawn shop door again. But again, there was no response.

He took his cap off and rubbed his forehead. He didn't know what to do.

He went back to the child. Should he cry out for help? Would anyone hear him? Would anyone come even if they did? He had always quipped that the police didn't come to this part of town anymore unless there was a body on the floor. Now there was.

Only a few blocks from home, he could call the police from there, but he didn't want to leave the child alone. How could he leave this tiny, retched body lying on the side of the street like a piece of trash?

Then, an echo of a memory.

He felt like he had seen something like this before, but where?

He froze.

The long slender legs, doll-like hands, and contorted body.

Marvin fell to his hands and knees, overwhelmed with the emotional memory of finding his baby brother in the mud. Memories buried in the same Alabama soil they had used to cover his brother's body more than half a century ago. His stomach cramped and his throat went dry. He couldn't breathe. He pulled at his collar trying to get some air, but it wasn't working.

He couldn't even tell if it was a boy or girl, but whoever they were, they were only seven or eight.

Then the child moved.

Chapter Three

Earlier that Day

Peter stood in front of the olive-green gun safe in his designer jeans, holding a small saucer in one hand and a cup of espresso in the other. He looked like an Olympic swimmer, blonde and clean-shaven, standing in the large bedroom he had paid an interior designer nearly $6,000 to put together for him. Plush Egyptian cotton sheets. A Tibetan dresser. Hand-painted modern art from an artist he knew nothing about.

In the corner of the room stood an antique, green gun safe—a gift from his father.

He set the small cup and saucer aside, drew the blinds, and dialed in the eight-digit combination that was his mother's birthday on the large, saucer-like dial set into the front of the cold steel door. The dial spun smoothly, but he could feel the faintest texture of fast ticks from the tumblers beneath the metal surface. Then a muffled click, and the door slightly opened.

A row of rifles, antique and modern, stood on their butts. There was a well-polished 1910 Fox Sterlingworth double-barrel shotgun, an all-black Sako TRG bolt-action sniper rifle, and an AR-15 assault rifle with a tactical flashlight on the end. On a small shelf sat an array of handguns, some antiques that would never fire again and others that looked mean and modern like SWAT team kit, such as the Glock 26 with its double-stack magazine and laser sight.

Beneath the shelf of handguns were three more shelves, each stacked with boxes of ammunition. Four of the largest read Winchester USA centerfire cartridges 5.56mm.

He took one of these three off the shelf, pushed the safe door most of the way shut, and set the box on a small glass table next to his bed. The metal container was about the size of a toaster with pealing hunter-green paint and a lid that lay across the narrow top and latched on one side.

This was his little treasure chest, and if his apartment burned to the ground, the items contained herein would be the only things he would care to keep from the fire.

Peter pulled up a plush office chair in front of the small table, rolled back his shoulders, savoring the moment, and took a deep breath.

He carefully opened the box.

Inside were stacks of sealed plastic bags.

He gently removed the first one and laid it on the desk. Then he pressed his hand flat against it. It contained a swirl of long blonde hair and a photo of a young girl who looked maybe fifteen or sixteen.

Then he carefully opened the bag and took in a deep breath of the fading fragrance that the lock of hair still captured.

He sat back in his chair and closed his eyes, remembering who the hair belonged to. He said her name to himself and remembered the night he met her, which was the last night anyone ever saw her. He then resealed the bag and set it aside.

He gently removed the next bag, this one smaller. It contained a green and blue earring, and he said her name to himself and remembered.

He laid the eight bags out on the desk one by one and remembered who they belonged to. Each was increasingly important to him; each increasingly potent. Some of the bags stored photos, and others only a small trinket or memento. But each had a story, and every one of them were *his*.

Then the alarm beeped on his phone.

He carefully returned the bags to the box, latched it shut, and put the box back in his safe before stepping over to the navy-blue uniform he had carefully laid out on the bed before having his espresso.

On each shoulder of the shirt was a blue and yellow embroidered patch that read: Boston Police.

THE YOUNG WOMAN'S PHONE BEEPED and began drawing her out of her sleep. Cold enveloped her face, and she pulled her blanket up over her head as low-lying hunger pains twisted her stomach. Problem number one. She also really had to go to the bathroom, problem number two.

She wanted normal problems. She wanted bacon. *Oh god, bacon sounded fantastic.* She wanted a shower. Her scalp was starting to itch, and she felt gross.

Most people don't realize just how itchy you begin to feel everywhere when you haven't showered in weeks. She tried to keep herself clean, but there was nothing in the world like a hot shower. She had once broken into a hotel room just to take a hot shower and then a quick three-hour nap between the clean, pressed sheets.

The young woman sat up in bed and rubbed her eyes. The cold stung her shoulders and made the hairs on her arms stand on end.

She rubbed her hands together and blew into them, trying to warm them just a bit. Then she pulled a worn black backpack over to her, unzipped the front pocket, and removed a small pouch. She found and tore open a white packet with green lettering that read: Wet Nap moist towelette, her last one.

The towelette was cold as frozen coins.

She held it between her hands and blew into them again, trying to warm the towelette, but it was like trying to warm a thin shard of ice.

She unfolded the still cold cleaning cloth and vigorously wiped her arms, hands, back of her neck, and her armpits before squeezing it back into its foil and paper packaging.

She pulled on a black hooded sweater she regretted not having fallen asleep in and pulled her long black hair back into a rubber tie. Then she slipped on her shoes and folded her blankets.

She set aside the backpack for a moment and reached for a canvas, reusable grocery bag sitting next to her bed and rummaged through it, looking for something to eat but only found a Gatorade bottle with a few swallows of sweet liquid and the last remnants of a snack-sized bag of pretzels she had bought a couple of days earlier. They had gone soft and were now nearly flavorless, but they would have to do because the rest of the cloth grocery sack was empty.

She double-checked that she had everything she needed, then pulled aside a sheet safety-pinned to the ceiling above her bed and climbed onto the passenger seat of her rusting-orange car. As she rose out of the car through the passenger seat, she closed the door behind her and double-checked the lock with her key four times when she noticed a yellow slip of paper tucked beneath her windshield wiper. It was a second parking ticket with a notice to move her vehicle in twenty-four hours or be towed. Problem number three, and the day hadn't even begun yet.

She crumpled the parking ticket into a ball and tossed it into the dumpster she walked past on her way to her bus.

Chapter Four

The morning was mostly quiet.

A street sweeper trundled along the edge of the wide road, trying to whisk away filth from the previous night as the dangerously slender young woman scanned the bus shelter timetable and bit at her cuticle. She was seventeen, with chipping black fingernail polish, short black frayed shorts and a pair of filthy Chuck Taylor's. Rings of silver and turquoise adorned her fingers, and a tattoo of a moth fluttering around a branch of coffee beans decorated her left arm. A single key hung from her wrist by a blue and white cotton thread.

She checked her watch. The number thirteen would be around in about twelve minutes, so she sat on the cold metal bench.

Without thinking, she tore a piece of skin off her finger large enough to make her finger bleed, and she flinched at the sharp pain. She sucked off the rising droplet of blood and pressed it against her shorts, then started nibbling at her lip.

She hated riding the bus, but Clifford was out of gas.

Once and only once, she made the mistake of falling asleep on the bus, and she awoke to the cold and dirty touch of some guy sliding his hand up the front of her shirt.

She shuddered at the cold and blew into her hands, trying to warm them, then swung her bag around to her lap. A small purple lock with round dials secured the main compartment. Three of the four tiny dials sat at zero, but the fourth sat at one, which made her wince. Four zeros made her happy, not three. Always four. She dialed the one to a zero, slid her finger over the numbers and sighed. Then she dialed in the correct combination and took out a small coin purse with a broken zipper.

She counted off the $1.25 she needed to get to Happy Grocery, dropped the tiny, nearly empty pouch back in her bag, and locked the backpack shut with a small purple dial lock, careful to ensure all four numbers lined up to zero.

As the thirteen pulled up, she stood and looked in through the windows.

No. This won't do at all. There are too many people on this one.

She stepped up onto the first step and looked in to double-check.

"Are you getting' on or not?" the driver asked.

She shook her head and started to get off but stopped. The next one wouldn't be around for another twenty minutes, and she couldn't be late again for her shift at the Blue Bonnet, so she cautiously turned back to the driver, one finger in her mouth, tentatively dropped her coins into the mouth of the metal machine and walked to the back of the bus as it lurched forward.

The taste of iron whispered across her tongue, and without thinking she wiped her finger on the back of her shorts again.

She sat across from a middle-aged woman with thick glasses and a little girl wearing an orange dress printed with black cats. The little girl pressed into the woman's side and peeked out from underneath the woman's arm as the young woman smiled a gentle smile and waved her little finger at the little girl, who smiled and waved her little finger back.

The young woman remembered her own Halloween dress she had when she was the girl's age. It had had a small tear along the hem at the back, but her mother stitched it with black thread making it as good as new. A fun find on a trip to the Goodwill with her mother.

She took a pair of headphones out of her bag, put them on, and pulled the black hood of her shirt over her head. Of course, her headphones didn't work, and they weren't plugged into anything, but she liked wearing them and running the cord into the front pocket of her hooded shirt giving her a plausible reason to ignore anyone who might want her attention.

She checked her watch. Eight minutes. She started biting at a different cuticle.

Happy Grocery was large enough that she could just disappear into it. She would pick up a few supplies and use the toilet—she really needed to use the restroom. Public bathrooms and running water should be a fundamental human right. Still, nearly all bathrooms in and around Boston were for "paying customers only," and she couldn't afford a $12 burger to use the restroom, no matter how amazing a $12 hamburger sounded. She often thought about how locked bathrooms were simply cruel to someone in her situation.

She had a hard time doing nothing with her hands while she waited.

She opened the lock again and removed a purple cloth-covered journal and a black hair tie that she squeezed into the palm of her hand. She had begun the book the night she moved into Clifford, and now, even though she wrote small and filled every inch of blank space, the book had only two empty pages left.

She let the book lay open on her lap as she slowly fingered through photos of a young girl with charcoal hair and a bright smile. One of the photos was of the girl at a park with her mother. Another was a classroom portrait of the girl, now slightly older, wearing a small sea turtle pendant with a mother-of-pearl shell. There was a third photo of the girl in high school with a muscular, olive-skinned man on a beach. Surfboards stuck into the sand next to them.

The purple book was the young woman's plan to kill Savannah Georgia and get back to the life she thought she deserved, but she was running out of time.

If she didn't kill Savanna soon, she'd never get home.

Chapter Five

Hunger drives good people to madness.

Watching the excess of the world when you cannot afford a sandwich distorts your view of reality. You stop thinking about your future and start trying to simply survive. You begin saying things and doing things you never thought you would do until, one day, you don't recognize yourself.

The young woman sat on the bus, trying to remember who she was—or who she once was—but the lines were beginning to blur.

She took a deep smell of the cloth hair tie and flipped to the back of the purple journal.

Yesterday's entry read:

"I can't get Clifford to start. I've been here four days trying to move him with no luck. I got a ticket yesterday saying that I had 24 hours to move him, so I'm going to call Mike tomorrow. He's got to help. If he doesn't, I don't know what I'm going to do. I've moved some of my stuff to the unit, just in case, but I can't lose Clifford. I just can't."

$37.14 was written in the margin.

She wrote today's date on the first blank line, calculated

$37.14 minus the cost of her bus fare, and wrote $35.89 next to the date.

She closed the journal, slid it back into her bag, and took out a small flip phone to check her balance of minutes.

"Your balance is zero minutes. Please visit your nearest Nextel representative to purchase additional minutes. Thank you," the mechanical voice on the other end told her.

She clicked the phone shut, dropped it and the hair tie back into her bag, and relocked the purple lock making sure to line up all four dials to zero.

The bus stopped in front of a large sign with an orange smiling character that waved at customers and read: Happy's Grocery.

Today she was a "paying customer," unlocking resources she didn't regularly have access to.

She stopped by the front entrance and changed her camouflage from moody teenager in black hood who couldn't be bothered by anyone into upstanding young woman casually shopping for groceries.

She shoved the black hooded sweatshirt, dotted with gold pins of rock bands, and her non-working headphones into her bag. Then she dropped her bag into the bottom corner of a shopping cart and started casually cruising to the fountain drinks at the back of the store by the restrooms.

Every step she took was calculated and intentional. Not just here but everywhere she went.

The world was open to paying customers and entirely off-limits to people like her. As a paying customer, she had access to all the complementary resources the store had to offer. She shouldn't have trouble with anyone asking questions as long as she followed a well-choreographed rhythm of avoidance.

She'd use the restroom first so that no one asked why she was in the bathroom with items in her cart. Then she'd leave the restroom and put a few things in her cart so no one thought she was loitering. She'd make her way to the fountain drinks and condiments by the salad bar, taste some free samples on offer to "paying customers only," and go back to the discounted items by the fulfillment doors where there were no cameras.

Finally, on to check out before anyone could ask any questions. In and out in less than ten minutes, with plenty of time to get back to Clifford to drop off her things before work.

She thought through her grocery list, trying to decide which items were the most critical and which could wait until payday. Wet wipes. Ramen noodles. Kool-Ade packets. A phone card. That stupid phone card was expensive, $15, but she had to have a phone.

She bit the edge of her lip.

Maybe she'd get lucky and there would be some day-old muffins or bread on the clearance shelf she could grab for a couple of bucks, which would be fantastic because those could stave off hunger for at least a few days. As long as they weren't lemon. Last month all they had on offer were packs of lemon muffins, so she took two home with her. Unfortunately, she found herself without anything else to eat except those lemon muffins, morning, noon and night, for nearly three days until she got so sick and tired of them that she pitched the last two in the bin deciding that she'd rather starve than eat another lemon muffin.

She clicked on the light in the women's restroom, bent down to check beneath the stalls to see if she was alone, and locked the door behind her.

She turned on the water to full hot and leaned against the sink. How long was she going to have to live like this? She missed hot showers. The feel of shampoo running down her back. The smell of cocoa butter body wash. Had it been six months? The next time she'd get to take a shower, she was going to turn it on as hot as she could stand and just stand there until she fell asleep.

There was a lot that she missed, but showers had to be one of her top five; showers and a refrigerator full of food and her own bed. She missed the soft swoosh of clean sheets as she pulled back the covers and ran her hand across her pillow.

She pulled off her shirt.

She pushed the black hand soap dispenser on the wall, but only a dot the size of her fingernail came out. She tried again and pushed it hard, but it was empty. She slapped the side of it in frustration. *I just need an inch*, she thought and looked down at the tiny dab of green gel. At least she had hot water.

She cupped her left hand, filled it with hot water, and sudsed her hands together into as much of a lather as she could. She leaned over the sink and washed her armpits, her arms, and the back of her neck, dipping her hands underneath the steaming faucet to rinse herself off. Then she washed her face and let down her long dark curls to rinse them underneath the flowing sink. It was the closest thing to a bath she had had in nearly two weeks.

She needed to change her bra and underpants, but she only had two clean pairs left, so that would have to wait until tomorrow. She'd have to work her shift tonight before she could afford to do laundry, which cost her the ridiculous price of $4.75. $5.75 if she bought soap.

A couple of handfuls of the coarse brown paper towels dried her arms, face and hair. Then she pulled open her pants and, with the damp pile of paper towels, wiped clean between her legs and tossed the pile into the trash.

She reached into her bag for a different shirt, not fresh, just fresher than the one she was wearing, and took out her stick of deodorant, nearly gone. She rolled it onto her underarms and the smell of "gentle spring rain" lifted her spirits. It didn't smell like gentle spring rain of course, but it still smelled clean.

There was a tug on the bathroom door.

She quickly finished up and went back out to the store, trying to avoid the look of the woman with a little boy who had been trying to get in to use the restroom.

Feeling a little better, she cruised the aisles for the items on her mental grocery list and made her way to the fountain drink area. A can of beans, a small bag of rice, and a handful of snickers bars vanishing into her bag as she walked, quick and quiet.

The row of free condiments for salads and sandwiches was like a buffet of free food, and she picked up four packets of each item they offered. Always four. She didn't know why, but four made her happy. Four ketchup. Four Mustard. Four mayo. Dropping each little bundle into her bag as she went down the line. Four croutons. Four sugar packets. Four single portions of non-dairy creamer. Three packets of grated Parmesan cheese.

She stopped.

There were only three packets left of grated Parmesan cheese, which were meant to be used on Cesar salads.

She looked around the buffet for another packet, perhaps a stray misplaced, but she didn't find one.

Three, not four.

Three wouldn't do at all. Three was wrong. There had to be one more lying around somewhere.

She pulled at her eyebrow and put the eyebrow hair that came loose into her mouth.

A male employee stood behind the counter packaging sushi.

She could live with three, couldn't she? Did she *really* need four packets of Parmesan cheese? What would she even do with Parmesan cheese? One, two, three. She counted them again. Three was wrong. She needed four.

"Excuse me," she said, walking up to the sushi counter.

The slender man with a blue mask over his mouth looked up. He had a small tattoo of a schooner on the inside of his arm and held a long, curving, slender blade with a red handle.

"You're out of Parmesan at the salad counter."

His eyes smiled at her over his mask. "Thank you," he nodded, then went back to carefully slicing a large fillet of salmon.

"Do you have any more?" she asked.

He looked up at her again. "Sorry. Yes. One moment, let me get some from the back." And he slipped behind a shelf of organic bread.

She looked around.

She didn't want to lose time waiting for him, so she went to the soda fountain and took an empty Gatorade bottle out of her bag.

Sugar packets were free. Water was free. Soda costs something. So she tore the tops off four packets of sugar, poured them into the wrinkled, clear-plastic bottle, and filled the bottle with water from the fountain.

Then the employee walked back over to her. "I am sorry. It

looks like we are out."

"What? You don't have one more packet behind the counter somewhere?"

His face turned from cheery and helpful to concerned and questioning. "I'm sorry. No. We are out," he replied.

"That's fine. You know what? That's fine. I've got some other shopping to do anyways. Thank you," she said.

He nodded and went back to slicing his salmon.

The young woman spun the lid back onto her Gatorade bottle, shook it a few times, and slid it into her bag.

She only had one item left to grab on her way out, but now she needed to make a detour.

She walked down the salad condiments aisle, scanning the shelves for…there it was. Salad Parmesan, single portion packets.

She looked around.

The aisle was empty.

She tore the box open, took out a single packet and put the box back on the shelf. Now she had four packets. This time it wasn't her fault, she told herself. They should have had enough cheese at the salad bar.

The first time she visited a grocery store without money, she spent a week trying to find something to eat but hadn't found anything anywhere.

She bitterly hated stealing, but her stomach forced her to rationalize bending the rules like a bowstring.

At first, she was just hungry. But then she started lusting after food. She'd spend hours at the library looking at cookbooks making lists of what she'd prepare the next time she had money.

She avoided restaurants because of the smell of cooking

food and once sat for forty-five minutes staring at a half-eaten cookie in the trash in front of a cafe, trying so hard not to pick it up and consume it on the spot that her hands began to shake.

Then one morning, she drove past Happy Grocery with its fifteen-foot sign of a chubby boy holding bread, and she thought about how there was just so much food at the grocery store. So much they throw away every day. So much waste. So much excess. And she imagined a few day-old items disappearing off the shelves without anyone ever noticing.

The first thing she ever stole was a wrapped sandwich from the cold case, which she took to a park bench and sat and wept while she ate it.

Savannah Georgia was a thief; she wasn't a thief.

But the sandwich tasted so good, and her stomach cramps subsided.

It became easier after that. Little thefts of opportunity here and there. A muffin at a cafe when the barista was distracted or a candy bar from a newsstand, but after a while, she began to realize that if she took something of cash value, she could live off of that cash for a week or more and not have to steal as often—less chance of getting caught.

Fewer people hurt.

That day in the park, she made a promise to herself. She would record every item she stole and pay it back one day. Purchase what she could, take what she had to, and pay it back. And in this, she learned to do whatever it took to survive.

The young woman approached the discount shelf at the back of Happy Grocery and saw it had already been well picked over. Wilting flowers, bug spray, and tins of cat food marked down to .25 were all that remained. She was hungry, but she wasn't *that* hungry. So, she grabbed a $15 phone card from a kiosk by the front checkout lanes and waited in line to pay for her few items.

"Can I get a ten-pack of the five-dollar scratchers please?" the woman in front of her asked the clerk.

"Diamonds Galore or Billions of Gold Bullion?"

The woman thought for a moment, her long purple fingernail resting on her chin.

"Oh goodness lord, I can't decide. Why don't you go on and give me ten of each," she laughed and looked back at the girl standing behind her. As she glanced at the young woman's dirty shoes and tattered shorts, her smile fluttered away, and she took a half-step to the side.

An emerald and diamond ring sat in a large cluster on her finger, gold bangles piled halfway down her forearms and a Louis Vuitton handbag hung from her elbow.

"Here you go ma'am," the clerk said, handing the folded pile of lottery tickets to the woman.

"I never win at these things, but the good lord showed me in a dream that I will one day," she told the clerk, as she quickly glanced at her rhinestone-studded smartphone and dropped it back into her handbag.

The young woman laid her wet wipes, crackers and phone card on the black conveyor belt behind the mound of ranch dressing, diet soda and steaks piled three high that the clerk swiped and put into plastic.

Elizabeth Arden's Red Door perfume was so thick in the air it made the young woman's throat burn.

"$172.94," the clerk said, and the gaudy woman laid open a wallet full of rows of credit cards. She pulled out a black one and handed it to the clerk. "I also need a five-dollar gift card."

The clerk swiped the gift card and handed it to the woman, along with her receipt.

Then the gaudy woman turned.

"If you don't need it, give it to someone else," she said, handing the card to the young woman, who was surprised even though $5 wouldn't buy much.

Then the woman smiled at her, took her groceries and left.

The clerk raised an eyebrow but didn't say anything as he scanned the young woman's items.

"Do you want to use that to pay?" he asked.

"Uh, yeah."

She wanted to go back to the food aisles and get a few more groceries, but she was out of time and had to get to work.

As she made her way to the front door, a stout security guard with thinning red hair walked toward her. She glanced away to avoid eye contact, but he sped up and stepped in front of her before she could leave the store. "Ma'am."

She stopped and looked up at him from her shoes.

"I need you to come with me."

Feigning confusion, she replied: "What? Why? I have to get to work."

He reached out and touched her elbow, but she jerked it away. "Don't. Touch me," she spat at him with disdain as though he had touched her somewhere profoundly inappropriate.

His brow creased with seriousness. "We saw you take the food out of the package in aisle 12."

"I don't know what you're talking about," she said.

He held up the open box of Parmesan Cheese.

"Oh, that?" she asked, laughing it off. "You were out of Parmesan by the salad counter, and I needed another packet."

"You can't just open boxes without paying for them. Besides, did you even buy a salad?" the guard asked.

A $7 salad? she thought to herself. *Who could afford that?*

"You know what?" she asked, opening her wallet. "How much was the *stupid* Parmesan? Three bucks? Here! Here's your three bucks," and she pressed three dollar bills into his chest, which fell to the floor as he looked at her with surprise, and she turned and left the store before he had time to object.

Three. Bucks. That hurt. She scolded herself as she shoved everything into her backpack and nearly ran across the large parking lot to the bus stop.

She was about halfway across the lot when she saw the thirteen sitting at the stop. She burst into a run and waved her hand, but it didn't help. The bus slowly began to pull away. "Hey, HEY!" She yelled, running up to the side and slapping the back door, but the driver either didn't notice or didn't care because all she could do was watch the bus pull away without her.

She ran a hand through her still damp hair and spun around, looking for options. There were none. The following bus wasn't coming for another thirty minutes, and she couldn't afford an Uber.

She quickly checked her watch. Her shift started in less than fifteen minutes and was across town.

She pulled another two hairs from her eyebrow and put them in her mouth.

Having no other options, she gripped both straps of her bag and started jogging.

As she ran, she tallied the cost of her trip to Happy's. Groceries were $12.62, the calling card was $15, and that stupid cheese was $3. Those three dollars may as well have been $30. This left her with only $5.27.

She was glad she had a shift tonight. Her tips would give her a quick influx of cash, and it would be another shift on her check she could look forward to in a little over a week. But she could NOT be late again, so she broke into a sprint.

After a few blocks, she sat down on the stone steps of the red brick Faneuil Hall Marketplace to catch her breath. She took out her Gatorade bottle of sugar water and took a big drink. Water ran down her chin she wiped away with the back of her hand.

She flipped open her phone, dialed in the code on the back of the phone card to refill her minutes, and called her friend Mike.

"Hey Mike," she said through heavy breaths.

"What do you want?"

"My car won't start again."

"Okay, what's it doing?" he asked.

"It just clicks when I try to turn it over."

"It's probably the starter."

"How much is that?"

He took a breath. "A new starter is $175 plus my time," he replied.

$175! She thought to herself.

She quickly tried to estimate what her first paycheck might be worth.

"Come on, Mike. I can't afford that," she said.

There was silence.

"Mike?"

"Why are you calling then?" he asked.

"Because I can't start my car, Mike."

"That's not my problem. I have a business to run. I can't

keep dropping the paying work to come and fix your car for free. How am I supposed to keep the lights on?"

"I know I'm not asking for charity. I just need a little help until I get paid. I've got a shift tonight and can get you some money in a couple of days," she said.

"Then call me in a couple of days," he replied.

"I can't wait that long, Mike. They're going to tow my car if I don't move it."

"I've *already* helped you as much as I can. Now I have to go."

"Mike. Please. I just need to get through this week, and I can get you some money," she said.

There was a long silence.

"Even if I didn't charge you for my time, which I *should*, you still need to pay for the part. My cost on a new starter is $130."

"What about a used one?" she asked.

"You don't want a used starter Savannah. It's just going to…"

"I don't have a lot of options here, Mike. How much is a used one?"

"I don't know. I could call the yard and see if they even have one for your car, but there are no guarantees."

"There never are. Can you just guess?"

There was a weighty sigh on the other end.

"$75. Maybe $80. But…"

"Thanks a ton, Mike. I know I've said this before, but I owe you. You're an angel," and she hung up before he could say anything else. Then she clicked shut her phone and started running again.

Chapter Six

"It's not too hot, is it?"

There was no answer.

Marvin, slender with nearly no hair and hands that shook, carefully cut off a piece of the microwave enchilada and touched it to his lip. "No. That feels okay," he said, reaching the forkful of food towards his elderly wife.

Margaret slowly leaned forward in her wheelchair and took the bite without looking at him.

Police sirens screamed past their ground-floor window, sending red and blue flashing lights across their floral wallpaper, but neither of them paid any attention.

For the next fifteen minutes, Marvin alternated between feeding himself and feeding his wife. A rhythm well practiced, during which time no words were spoken between them. Then his watch vibrated.

He looked down at the scratched face. "Do you need the restroom? It's almost time for your shows," he told her, holding up a plastic cup of Guava juice so she could take a last drink. Then he wiped her mouth with a napkin.

She nodded.

"Alright. I'll tidy this later."

He wheeled her down the hall to their small bathroom, pushed her up next to the toilet, and helped her hand to the steel bar he had installed some years ago to steady herself. Then he locked the chair's wheels in place and lifted the arm of the wheelchair between her and the toilet. "Together on three, my love," he said, leaning down and putting his arms around her waist the way the nurse had shown him. With careful steadiness, he helped Margaret drape an arm over his shoulder.

"One. Two. Three," and he strained as he rocked her forward onto her feet and into a standing position. It had been months since he felt help from her, and it was getting harder by the day for him to hoist her up and down onto the toilet, out of bed, or into and out of the shower. The nurse was only coming by half-days three times a week now, and he was slowly running out of strength to lift her, but his strength had not failed him yet. Maybe next month, but not yet. And he'd never say anything about it to her. He would simply press on until the very moment he absolutely could not press on any longer, and that's all there was to it. What else was there?

His knees ached as he knelt to pull down her elastic-waisted pants and beige padded underwear, trying as best as he could to offer her some modicum of decency, turning his head away from her nakedness. Then he sat her down on the toilet and stepped away to let her do what she needed. After she had finished, he cleaned her up and rolled her back down the narrow hall, past a small locked door connecting their kitchen and bathroom to their bedroom.

There used to be a couch in their tiny apartment, where they would watch nightly news and reruns of I Love Lucy together, but they got rid of that when Margie was past the point of being able to get herself from her wheelchair to the couch. Now only a small table sat next to Marvin's favorite armchair, and the wheel marks rubbing the carpet threadbare where he parked her in front of the television for his news and her shows. At least they were still there together.

He often watched her tap her finger to the opening tune and sometimes grunt out a smile at the jokes, and she used to even reach for his hand if he forgot to take hers after sitting down, but that hadn't happened in a long long time.

The long, dark shadow of time had slowly crept up and finally overcame them both, leaving behind only a reflection of the lively, beautiful young woman he remembered her being from their youth. Even now, when he looked at her, he could sometimes still see that energetic young woman beneath the unerasable marks of age.

She had been a math teacher when they met, the daughter of a pastor. He had tattoos and smoked, which might sound like nothing worth mentioning but seventy-some years ago in a small town in Minnesota, cigarettes and sailor tattoos were more than enough to keep the young daughter of the town preacher from dating this sinner, as her father called him before they had even met. But she was so down-to-earth and beautiful and smiled at him and accepted him for who he was beneath all that nonsense that he absolutely lost himself whenever she was around. Her fragrance was like a drug to him that he became so addicted to that he could recognize it when she had been in a room long after she had left. The way her hair reflected sunlight. The freckles on her arms. The way she wrinkled her nose when she laughed at, or along with, one of her students. He *lost* himself in these and so many millions of other little details that would punctuate the story of their life together.

Now, the rich color was gone from her hair, and he couldn't remember when he had last heard her laugh like that, but he could still, just barely, see the freckles on her arms, and she still was and always would be the love of his life.

The opening tune of Margie's show struck up, and Marvin cringed. He loved being with her, and he didn't mind most of her shows, but he couldn't stand the constant bickering back and forth of this one, so every night from 7 p.m. to 8 p.m., he stepped out to have a piece of pie at the Blue Bonnet Diner down the street. He knew she wasn't going anywhere, and this was an hour a day for him to breathe some fresh air and lift his head out of the hum-drum of his day and see that the world was still alive and thriving around them, even if he would never really be a part of it again.

She started tapping her finger to the tune, and he smiled. He kissed her cheek.

"I'll be back in an hour. Don't go on any walks without me," he told her and smiled. Then he went to the door, took his brown jumper and cap from the coat hooks and stepped out onto his small front porch, one of the last in a neighborhood that had turned into mostly brick project housing. And as he turned to lock the door behind him, he paused for a moment and looked in on her one more time. She just sat in front of the electric light of the television, tapping her fingers.

When they had bought their apartment on the ground floor, the building was new, and the neighborhood was full of young Norman Rockwell-esk families. His commanding officer from his sailor days even lived on the corner for a while. But, as the community grew older, those who could, moved out and Boston began subsidizing some of the housing, which pushed more middle-income families out and more subsidies in. There were a lot of good people still living in the neighborhood, a few who had been here almost as long as he and Margie had, but people with free housing tend to care little about taking care of it, and now most days the police didn't even bother responding to calls in the neighborhood unless there was a body on the floor.

Marvin no longer had the energy to dwell on such things anymore. He chose to remember the neighborhood the way it had been when he and Margie had moved in. As one of the "old timers," most of the more dangerous residents in the neighborhood actually looked out for him and Margie in a way that he could only attribute to some strange attempt at recompense for the life choices that they were making that hurt everyone else around them. So, every night on his walk to get a piece of fresh pie, he would pass through the valley of the shadow of death and fear no evil.

Dusk was settling in as the electric blue of the Blue Bonnet Diner sign flicked on, the BL staying dark as he walked past an overflowing dumpster and stepped over a stream of some fragrant liquid flowing out from the alley. *"Don't step in liquid,"* he thought, repeating to himself the words his father had said to him the first time they visited the city a lifetime ago.

"Hey!" A stout waitress with a yellow bunny keychain hanging from her pocket said to him as he walked through the door. She was balancing a row of plates full of food on one arm, from her shoulder to her fingertips, and carried a half-full pot of coffee in the other hand. "There's a booth open in the corner. I'll be over in a minute. Let me just drop this order."

"That'd be fine," he said, taking off his cap and jacket.

The Blue Bonnet was mostly quiet at this time of night: A young couple, pierced and tattooed, sat in a corner where Marty, with nails as long as her fingers, asked if she could get the couple anything else. A police officer sat at the bar a couple of stools down from two women, and the cook leaned over the flat top behind the counter, looking over tickets.

"How you doin' tonight Marv?" Marty asked, as he sat down.

"Ohhh, everything's doing just fine."

"And how about Margaret? We haven't seen her in here in a while."

He looked up at her from the list of pies on the menu. "She's good." He nodded. "Maybe next week." It pained him to lie to her.

"Whatcha thinkin?"

"What's good?"

The same questions. The same answers. Every night.

The Blue Bonnet had the same four options of pie all year, except for Christmas: German Chocolate, Lemon Meringue, Pecan, and Apple. From November first to January first, they added Pumpkin.

"Franky just took the Apple out of the oven. And we have some fresh ice cream if you want it a la mode."

"That'll be fine, and I'll take half a cup of coffee with it if that's alright."

Just then, a young woman with curly, partially damp black hair burst through the front doors of the diner, tying her apron behind her back.

She saw Marty dart her a look of frustration for being late from across the dinner, but she ignored it. It wasn't Marty she was worried about, and she didn't have time to fuss. The two women and the cop were in her section, and she really needed the tips, so she didn't want them to wait any longer than they already had. She was looking forward to a half-priced meal on her shift and a little cash in her pocket at the night's end.

Marty looked at her watch and then shook her head.

"That Savannah?" Marvin asked.

"Mmm hmmm," Marty said. "And she's late for the third night in a row, and this time by twenty minutes. If she can't be bothered to show up on time, she shouldn't be bothered to show up at all." Then she whispered: "But I suspect Susan will nip that in the bud. And right quick."

He wondered what that meant but didn't ask.

"Cream and sugar?" she asked without writing anything down. She never needed to write anything down.

He nodded and handed her the menu.

The young woman came out from the back.

Sitting next to the coffee station was a bin of dirty dishes. At the top of the stack was a small plate with two pieces of wheat toast that looked like they hadn't been touched. Glancing around, she bent down like she was getting something from under the counter and slid one of the pieces into her apron pocket before rising to help her customers. A half-priced meal was all well and good, but stolen morsels of food here and there also went a long way.

"Good evening," she said to the two women as she filled their mugs of coffee. "Have you had a chance to look over the menu? Our pork roast is especially good."

She caught a half smile from the attractive, blonde police officer who sat up straight and looked down at his plate. She knew what that smile meant.

"We're ready to order," one of the women told her. She took a breath and looked back at them to take their orders.

She couldn't ignore the officer even though she had been trying. He had come in every night this week, always sitting in her section no matter where her section was. He even moved his food and coffee across the diner to where she was serving a couple of nights back when she had to switch sections with Marty.

"You're late," Marty whispered with venom, both women standing with their backs to the bar.

"I know! I'm sorry. I missed the bus."

"Well, that cop's been here for near 45 minutes just nursing that pie. He's already had four cups of coffee. You'd think he'd have somethin' better to do than hang around here for you."

"What do you think he wants?"

"Darlin, I think he wants your number," Marty told her.

He was cute and all, clean-shaven with clean-cut blonde hair. She even thought he had lovely blue eyes and was handsome in his navy-blue uniform. But he must have been ten years older than her. She knew she looked older than she was, which was often an advantage in her situation, but the very last thing she needed in her life was a cop coming around, asking questions or not.

"If you don't talk to him, he'll be here all night," Mary said.

"Well, it's not like we need the table," she replied.

Marty shot her a look of disapproval.

"Okay, okay. I'll pour his coffee and say hi."

Marty pulled a small box of candles out from a drawer under the bar, pressed one into a piece of pie and lit it.

"Whose birthday?" she asked Marty.

"Your number thirteen, that's who!" Marty harshly whispered to her, and Savannah glanced over her shoulder at Marvin, who sat quietly alone, watching the television that hung on the diner's back wall. The elderly man always looked so proper, like someone's grandfather, with a buttoned-up, collared shirt and button cap sitting next to him on the table. He didn't look wealthy, but he always tipped well, and he had always been courteous to her, calling her ma'am, which she liked, even if she was far too young to be a ma'am. And then there was that antique watch with its peculiar brown leather band that looked like it could be snakeskin.

Marty handed her the pie, lit the candle and shewed her over to Marvin's table.

"Happy birthday, Martin!" Savannah said with a big smile.

He looked up at her with astonishment. "It's Marvin, actually. But how…"

"Oh, a friend remembered, that's all," she said, trying to move past getting his name wrong.

"To be perfectly honest, I had forgotten myself," he told her, not sure what was more bewildering, the fact that this waitress had remembered his birthday without being told or that he had forgotten it himself. Truth be told, he wasn't entirely sure what day it was anyways, which probably contributed to his lapse.

He blew out the candle as he noticed her looking nervous and cagey.

"How *you* doin' tonight?" Marvin asked her.

"Oh, you know…"

"Why don't you pretend I don't," he replied.

She shook her head. "I'm having a little car trouble and missed the bus. That's all."

"I'm sorry to hear that. Do they have any idea what the trouble is?"

She looked around but didn't answer. "Can I get you

anything else?"

Maybe there was car trouble, or maybe there was more. He suspected there was more. Every time he saw her, she looked like a scared animal running from something, and he had seen her eat food off someone else's plate a few nights earlier, just as he was leaving.

She hadn't realized anyone was watching.

"It's Savannah, isn't it?" he asked. "Are you in some kinda trouble child?"

For a brief moment, her face changed. And there it was. He saw her let her guard down, but then she put it back up as quickly as it had dropped. "Let me know if I can get you anything else," she told him, then turned and walked away.

Savannah returned to the coffee pot, picked it up, and turned with her best got-to-earn-my-tips-whether-I-like-it-or-not smile.

The police officer moved his silverware around nervously and smiled at her as she walked over.

"How are you tonight, officer?"

"I told you last time, call me Peter. I could use another cup, but I'm good. I'm good." He nodded.

Another cup? You've had four, she thought to herself, but only smiled and poured.

"How about yourself?" he asked.

She set the pot down on a towel. "I missed my bus. Late the third time this week."

"Oh, I'm sure they won't notice."

Right. Not notice. Susan looked like she would strangle me with her bare hands, she argued to herself, her smile not fading.

"Were you eating anything this evening?" she asked him.

"I heard the pork roast is good."

Her smile grew, which made him smile back at her.

"Do you want mashed potatoes, corn, or green beans with it?"

"Mashed potatoes, please. And your number."

She looked up at him from her order pad.

He leaned forward, and she could smell the spruce and juniper of his cologne. "I thought maybe we could grab a bite together tomorrow night," he said in a lowered voice. "Marty said…"

Then she started to laugh but caught herself and put her hand over her mouth, and a second quick chuckle snuck out before she turned and walked away.

His charismatic, cover-model smile vanished, and he looked away. He wasn't expecting her to laugh at him.

She walked down the side hall to her bag and took out a tissue. A tear streaked down her cheek, a mark of laughter and sorrow at the absurdity of having a police officer ten years older than her flirting with her.

"I need to see you," Susan said from the door of her office.

Savannah's demeanor quickly changed. "I've got tables."

"NOW!"

Savannah wiped her eye with the tissue and went into Susan's office.

Back in the dining room, the officer sat for a minute, looking down at the phone number he had written on a napkin for her earlier in the evening. He had imagined several ways the conversation might go, but in none of them had he ever imagined she'd laugh at him—and right here in front of everyone!

He squeezed the napkin into a ball and pushed it down into the remaining coffee in his cup. Then he took a ten out of his wallet and dropped it on the table.

He felt Marty watching him as he left the diner.

The memory of her laugh tightened his chest as he stopped to look back into the glowing light of the diner.

The Blue Bonnet was on his beat, and he ate here occasionally. He thought the food was pretty awful, but the pie was decent, even though he had to work it off with an extra twenty minutes on the elliptical every time he came, *and for her?*

He turned to go back to his black outfitted Ford Explorer, then stopped.

In a Gaussian haze of blue from the diner's neon sign sat a little orange and red hatchback with balding tires and a coat hangar holding the driver's door shut.

On several occasions, he had seen the young waitress pull up to the diner in the tattered hatchback when he began memorizing her work schedule.

He walked up to the orange car and flashed his light through the front windows. The seats were torn with yellow foam turning to powder and protruding from under the white webbing of threadbare covers. He looked back at the diner. There was no sign of her. He shone his flashlight into the back windows but couldn't see anything through some sort of black plastic taped to the inside. He then walked around the car, noting the rust on the bumper and a crack in the bottom corner of the windshield.

A cracked window is not really probable cause, he thought to himself. *Plastic over the back windows? No.* Then he returned to the rear of the car and shone his flashlight onto the license plate. Her registration tag was curling in one corner.

He bent down, flipped open a black tactical pocket knife and carefully pulled at that curling corner. The tag peeled off easily, leaving a residue of yellowing glue on top of another tag from last year beneath it. He'd seen this before. Tag thieves cut the corner off of license plates with current tags, steam the little metallic sticker off and glue it over their expired ones. They did this when there was something about either their car, their insurance, or their license that wouldn't pass registration, and it was definitely probably cause.

He stood and clicked the radio on his shoulder.

"Central, this is bravo 3-18, over."

"Bravo 3-18, go ahead."

"I need history on an orange Gremlin hatchback, plates Henry, Adam, seven, one, two, niner. VIN: Adam, 3, Mary, 7982-153-559, over."

There was static for a few moments before the dispatcher called back: "1975, orange Gremlin hatchback, registered in Boston to a Susan Wilkins, aged 47. The registration is expired, and there is a 14-Lincoln outstanding."

"A request to move? When?"

"9:30 tomorrow morning."

He thought for a moment and looked at the peeled tag he was holding. He had to give a reason for the plate check, but he liked the idea of having an excuse to talk to her again, having some leverage.

"Repeat: 9:30 tomorrow morning?"

"That's correct, Bravo 3-18."

"Then someone must have called it in already. Over and out."

"If you're done there, Bravo 3-18, there's a 4-11 just up the street from your location that just came in."

"I'll check it out, Central. Over and out."

He clicked shut his knife and squeezed it in the palm of his hand as he stared back at the diner. He knew she'd be off her shift at 2 a.m., and he'd approach her about the registration then.

Back in the diner, Susan, a heavy-set woman with thick pink lipstick and three hairs growing out of a wart on her chin, plunged her cigarette butt into the ashtray sitting on the corner of her desk, spilling old ash onto the desk and the floor, which she swept off her desk with the side of her hand before pulling another Virginia Slim from an open pack and lighting it. A mix of stale and fresh cigarette smoke that had no way of escaping the closet-sized back office burned the young waitress' eyes and throat as she came in.

"I know I'm late," she said, sitting down on a pea-green cushion that was hard and flat as boards beneath her.

"Save it." Susan coughed up a ball of phlegm that she swallowed back down again. "You're fired," she said, showing no emotion.

"What? I missed…"

Susan held up the hand, still holding the cigarette and showing off two yellowing fingers from countless years of wielding the little cancer sticks. "Three strikes and you're out, honey. Simple as that."

"I'm sorry. I need this job. I really need this. I'll cover the graveyard, whatever you want."

Susan looked up at her. "Get out before I call the cops."

Savannah sat there stunned. She knew she was in trouble, but she thought she might just get yelled at. She'd never been fired before.

"Can I at least finish my shift?"

"Marty'll cover your tables. Leave your apron on the counter, get your junk and get out. I don't want to see you in my restaurant again."

Savannah stood up and knocked the aluminum chair over with the backs of her legs, sending a loud clang echoing down the hall and out into the diner.

"You know what? Whatever!" Savannah barked back, untying her apron and throwing it into the waste bin next to Susan's desk. Then she left the small, smokey office.

"I don't *need* this right now! You can wait your own tables," she hollered to everyone in the dining room as she kicked the front door open.

Marvin looked up from a spoonful of ice cream he had been dipping into his coffee. *"Nipped it in the bud*, he thought to himself.

Marty walked over to him and handed him his ticket. "I knew that child was nothin but a hot mess from the moment I laid eyes on her. Can I get you anything else, darlin?"

He shook his head.

"Well, you be safe out there," Marty told him.

"Yes, ma'am," he replied, then he took out a pen from his inside coat pocket and wrote a short note on a napkin that he slid underneath his coffee cup along with a twenty-dollar bill.

Then he stood, put on his jacket and button-bill cap, and left the diner.

THE HUMID EVENING ENVELOPED Savannah as she walked to her car and fumbled for her keys. She had begun her shift hungry and tired, and now she was falling into despair at the thought of having no cash and no food.

She put her key in the ignition and tried turning Clifford on. Click, click, click. Nothing. Tears streamed down her face in frustration. "Please, God. Just a little help," she whispered under her breath and tried again. Click, click. The light inside the cabin dimmed as she tried to get Clifford to start, but he would not.

In futility and desperation, she turned over the ignition until the clicking became a low sputter. Then she threw her keys against the window and pounded the steering wheel with both hands.

She had always been a bright and cheery child. In third grade, she was the youngest recipient of a scholarship to a music conservatory for brilliant young minds, and life was beautiful. But now, that life felt like a photo in someone else's frame, and every time she thought she might find a foothold, the world would pour in like quicksand and swallow up her resources, energy, and hope.

This wasn't her life. It couldn't be her life. It was Savannah's life.

If she could just find a way to get through the next few weeks, she would get rid of Savannah and return to the life she loved. But she was running out of resources, ideas, money, and favors.

She leaned over the passenger seat and opened the glove box looking for a tissue to wipe her face, but there weren't any, so she pushed the glove box shut, but it fell open. She slammed it, but it opened again.

She screamed and pounded the steering wheel.

Just then, a warm light cut through the blue haze of the diner sign as Marvin, slightly hunched forward as he walked, left the restaurant and made his way home.

Savannah watched him through bleary eyes and thought about his kindness, how well he had always tipped...and his watch.

Chapter Seven

As he walked, Marvin's thoughts were on the young waitress. *No one that young should look like they were running from something,* he thought to himself. And what would make someone eat from someone else's plate like that?

He remembered the rows of homes with white picket fences that used to stand where a liquor store and 24-hour pawn shop now stood. "Honest Johnny's Fast Cash, No Questions Asked!" glowed red from a neon sign.

Marvin couldn't remember how long the pawn shop had been there. Before the pawn shop was a thrift store, and before the thrift store was a hardware store where he used to buy hooks and wire to hang Margie's photos.

Why did they tear the houses down? he wondered, but the memories poured through his fingers like sand; he could not keep hold of them.

However, he did remember the Smiths, who lived on the block back when he and Margie bought the apartment. Susan and Margie had both been teachers, and he had always thought Susan was attractive but not in any way that would make him question his marriage. She was like a beautiful ornamental rose you admire from a distance without needing to pluck. And Jack Smith was a neighborhood police officer for years before they moved from Boston back to Pennsylvania to be with his ailing mother. He told Marvin, quietly during beers once, how the city council had given up caring about certain "less prestigious" neighborhoods, which broke Jack's heart because he loved the community as much as Marvin and Margie.

"I'm home, love," Marvin said as he hung up his coat and cap. "There and back again."

A rerun of The Dick Van Dyke Show danced across the television.

"You're never going to guess what Marty did for me. Would you believe she lit me a birthday candle and put it on my pie?" He paused and shook his head. "I had completely forgotten it even was my birthday."

He took off his shoes, set them side-by-side on the rack next to the door, and walked into the living room, where Margie sat quietly.

He gently touched her shoulder, kissed the top of her head, and sat down in his reading chair next to her.

"How was your show?" he asked, surveying the conversation between Buddy Sorrell's and Barbara Britton's characters. "Do you need a bathroom break?" he asked, glancing at her.

There was no response, so he looked back at the television and leaned back in his chair.

"Can you believe that? Marty remembering my birthday like that? I asked her how she knew, and she said she remembered you wishing me a happy birthday last year when we were in together. I wish my memory was that good. I can barely recall what I ate for breakfast, much less someone's birthday I heard once a year ago." And he shook his head again.

Then he had an idea and sat up. "What's say you and me, we celebrate? Nothing fancy now." He rose out of his chair, went to the record player that didn't get much use anymore, and flipped through their small collection of records.

"Now, there it is! Ms. Billie Holiday!"

He lifted the tiny needle, gently laid the vinyl onto the turntable, set the needle in place, and flipped the switch.

The music made him feel young again, younger at least, as the deep melodious voice of Billie Holiday filled the apartment, and even if it only lasted for a few minutes, he wanted to share it with the love of his life. He knew not to squander little bursts of joy and energy like these at his age.

Billie started singing I'll Be Seeing You as he began swaying with the music.

It was his and Margie's song. The one he had asked the band to play on their first date and then again for the first dance on their wedding day.

He lifted his hands and swayed his hips with the slow, rich tones, showing off for her in that playful way couples do who love each other beyond words; love each other in a way that creates a language only they understand. That way that senses each other's slightest movements and subtle body language across a restaurant or in the pitch darkness of a bedroom.

His smile grew, and he raised his eyebrows, laying on thick his little flirtation, then he slowly turned in anticipation. Maybe a smile? A raised eyebrow? She always got a kick out of his little flirtations.

Only, she sat motionless.

She sat unblinking at the television like he wasn't even in the room. Like there was no music. Like he had never mentioned his birthday or the kindness of the waitress.

He stopped swaying and went to her.

"Margie, love?" he asked, his knees protesting as he knelt beside her and took her hand.

It was cold.

"Margie?" he asked again, but there was no response.

He reached up and touched her cheek, which was also cool.

Every part of him went numb, from the tips of his fingers to the crest of his sanity. He slowly took in what was happening. Then the back of his throat started to burn, and his eyes welled up with tears.

"Margie? Talk to me, love. Talk to me, baby," he said, leaning forward and pressing his cheek against hers. "Talk to me, love. Talk to me, baby."

And he began to weep.

"Please. Just squeeze my hand. Don't leave me. Don't go on. Not yet. I'm not ready." He took both of her hands into his and filled them with his tears.

Her skin so soft it felt like velvet. Her fragrance like summer afternoons. Her always laughing at his jokes, even his worst ones. He could feel it all leaving, slipping through his fingers like forgotten names of old friends.

He looked up at her through his burning, puffy eyes and touched her cheek again. Then he gently closed her eyes and laid his head in her lap. His throat tightened and burned as his ears rang. And just like that, he reverted all the way back through the decades and countless chapters of his life to that little boy—sad, scared and lonely—fawning for a gentle touch.

He lifted her hand and laid it on his cheek.

It had been a long while since the effervescent woman he

was so infatuated with had cooked him breakfast or helped him paint a railing, but there were days. Days when she could still smile at him as they looked through photo books together or when they'd watch Kids Say the Darndest Things Thursday nights at 4 p.m. before dinner. Now, all that sat in front of him was the cooling husk of his life-long friend.

Their song had ended. It had played long, and it had played true, but it still felt to him like it had ended in the middle of a beat.

Next to her was a place where he didn't feel alone, but alone he now was, and the sudden loneliness was so vast, it echoed.

The apartment felt both vast and as small as a coffin at the same time. The home he had known for decades felt like a stranger watching him through the harsh electric light of the television.

He had to call someone, but who? The nurse aide wouldn't be around for another two days.

They had no family. Margie's brother was the last, and he died more than three years ago.

Margie had always been the one to handle these sorts of things. Not him. House sorts of things. Paying bills, updating their insurance.

Should he call a funeral home? The doctor? The police? 911? There was no emergency. It was clear they couldn't help her.

Then another terrible thought came to mind.

If he had to call someone to get Margaret, there would be strangers coming into his home. Strangers with their dirty shoes, asking him prying questions like what she had eaten lately, what medicine she took, and had he remembered to give her her nitroglycerine after dinner. They'd put their hands on her; people she didn't know. Strange men tearing at her clothes, trying to resuscitate her, plying her with needles and instruments.

No one other than the two of them had crossed the threshold of their apartment since 1983 when the Franklins came over for their last roast dinner before moving back to Atlanta.

Now the thought of strangers walking through his home gave Marvin heartburn and made him cross his arms over his chest and start rubbing his shoulders like he was cold, even though the temperature was at its constant 71 degrees.

He imagined her lying alone in the basement of some hospital, cold and uncared for. It was too much for him, just too much.

He shook his head. No, he couldn't have any of that. She wasn't ready to see anyone yet. He couldn't let all those strangers see her without at least helping her put on her face first.

Yes. That's what he'd do.

They were going to have company, and he needed to help her prepare.

Chapter Eight

arvin's back began to ache, and even though Margaret's hand lay on his cheek for several minutes, it did not warm.

"Margie, Luv, we're going to have some people over," he began to say, but his voice was dry and raspy and the words caught in his throat. "But don't you worry about anything. I'll take care of everything," he whispered. Then he slowly used the strength of her wheelchair to help him rise, and he wiped his face.

He pulled back the small metal handle that locked the chair's wheels in place, clicked off the television, and wheeled her back to their bedroom.

He stood in front of their closet, looking at a long crack in the mirrored door, remembering how many times he had promised to fix it for her. His reflection now on one side of the crack and hers on the other.

As he slowly slid the door to the side, her fragrance stepped forward from the closet and embraced him; his legs shook.

He closed his eyes and steadied himself.

"We're meeting some important people, but nothing formal," he said in a low voice, walking his fingers along the plastic hangars. "Which are you thinking?"

This is the last dress she will ever wear, he thought.

"What about the black one?" he rolled its fabric between his thumb and forefinger. "No. I don't think so. I always liked it, but I know it's not your favorite." Then he took out a red dress with small white flowers and turned to her. "How's this one? I got it for your birthday last year, and you haven't had a chance to show it off yet. What do you think?" He looked it over. "I think this will do just fine."

He laid it across her lap and wheeled her into the bathroom. "Now, I know what you're going to say. It isn't your day for a shampoo, but I think we can make an exception for our guests. I know you want to look your best," he told her.

He slowly knelt before her and began unbuttoning her blouse, the beginning of a carefully choreographed ritual practiced twice a week for nearly eight years, a number he had never let himself dwell on.

As he folded her hands onto her lap, he considered their shape. Hands he held in the park. Hands so young when they met, now curved and twisted by age. But he loved these hands. These were the hands that he danced with on their wedding night. Hands that touched his daughter's cheek and combed her hair.

He lifted them both and kissed them softly.

He folded her blouse and laid it on a small table between the toilet and shower, then lay each of the items she was wearing in a neat pile before unbuttoning his shirt and removing his trousers.

He clicked on the shower head and let the cold water slowly warm over his hand. Then he pulled her as close as he could to the edge of the shower basin.

This is the last time I will ever do this, the last time anyone will ever clean her, he thought.

He slowly lifted her arm and laid it over his shoulder. "On three Luv. One. Two. Three," and he strained to lift her onto the shower seat built into the wall, her cold skin against his.

They were close enough now that his body knew this wasn't her anymore. Oh, it looked like his Margaret, but it wasn't. She was heavier. She was limp. Her skin was cold and losing its supple quality.

Then he stopped.

Before setting her down on the shower seat, he held her.

He pressed his nose into a tiny freckle on a small patch of soft skin just behind her ear that he had always thought of as his little hiding place. A site he loved to kiss. A place he nestled into as they fell asleep at night. His silent oasis from the violent world. Somewhere he wanted to say goodbye to.

Tears streaked down his cheeks and onto her shoulder as he kissed that freckle one last time.

He tore open a vanilla white package of French soap she bought years ago and never used and gently washed her, scanning all of the shapes and patterns of her skin he knew better than his own. He laid her head back and washed her hair, careful to keep the soap out of her eyes as he always had.

Then he stepped out of the shower, dripping wet in his underwear, and walked through the house looking for every special occasion soap she had ever bought and brought the small pile back to the bathroom where he peeled away each of their onion-skin wrappers and wax-covered boxes and washed her again and again, leaving a floating pile of small pastel soap bars circling the drain of the shower.

After drying her off, Marvin moved her back into her

wheelchair and pulled her red floral dress down over her head and arms.

He told her how much he loved her and how blessed he was that she was in his life as he heated the iron, curled her hair, and did her makeup. A dance he became proficient in as her condition worsened over the years.

He told her how he remembered the night they went together to tell her father they were getting married, with or without his blessing, and how he would miss her French toast in the mornings and her hair tickling his face in the middle of the night.

Tears fell from his cheeks and onto her hair as he also told her how very sorry he was about what had happened to Ellie.

"You were such a wonderful mother. Always so patient with her," he said, leaning down and looking at her in the mirror.

He returned her to their bedroom, pulled back the covers, and moved her from her chair onto the bed.

He pressed the wrinkles out of her dress with his hands and reached for a small bottle on her nightstand. "I think we should use the good stuff," he told her, dabbing a drop of perfume on either side of her neck, just below her ear, just how she liked it. Then he set the small bottle aside on her nightstand, turned out her light, and lay on the bed next to her.

"Our guests will be here soon," he told her. "I just need to rest a spell. It has been such an honor being a part of this life with you."

He laid his arm across her chest and fell asleep crying.

MARVIN AWOKE to the vibration of his watch.

Why did his head hurt so bad? Where were his glasses?

He sat up.

The kitchen light was on.

He sighed. He must have dozed off.

His hand groped for his glasses, which he found, and he looked down at the glowing hands on his watch—10 p.m.

He needed to get up and make sure Margie was ready for bed. Pills for him and pills for her. Brush his teeth and take hers out, dropping them into their cup to soak. Get them both in their evening clothes. Both go to the toilet. He ran through the list in his mind, not remembering that his life had forever changed just a few hours earlier.

"Margie, Luv, I think I dozed off," he said loud enough for her to hear him from the living room. Then he felt her body lying next to his, and his hands quickly swept across the covers looking for hers. But when he found one, he found it cold and stiff.

He gasped and pulled away.

Then he remembered: His birthday candle. Their song. Her motionless in front of the television.

And the crescendo of loneliness crashed again.

He still had to call someone.

He slowly pulled himself out of bed and went to the bathroom sink to wash his face, leaning against the basin as he looked at himself in the mirror. He could see her silhouette in the mirror, outlined in the faint glow of kitchen light he had forgotten to turn off.

He was so tired, and his back ached from lifting her.

Walking into the kitchen, he put the kettle on. Then he took two cups and two tea bags out of the cupboard and realized he only needed one. He took a deep breath and put the second one back. *How am I going to do this?* he asked himself, looking down at the single cup and the single tea bag. *I'll look for the nurse line in the morning*, he thought, waiting for his tea to steep—*no need for anyone to fuss tonight.*

Once the tea finished steeping, he dutifully dropped the bag into the bin, stirred in a drop of cream from the fridge, and walked to the bedroom, where he pulled up a chair and sat down next to his now forever-sleeping wife.

There was silence.

From now on, it would be tea for one and it would be breakfast for one. One microwave dinner instead of two. How would he even make half a sandwich? What would he do with the other half of the can of soda at lunch? Who would sit with him in the community garden down on Roosevelt? Her clothes. Her makeup. The house would be dead without her things scattered about. An empty bed. Empty nights. An empty life.

For forty-five minutes he sat next to her, holding her hand and nursing his now cold cup of Darjeeling that didn't even taste as it should. *Flavorless tea; flavorless life*, he thought to himself.

Is there a sedative for loss? A tranquilizer for loneliness? he wondered, *and it had only been two hours.*

He rubbed the stubble on his chin and made a decision.

"I think I know what to do, Margie dear. You'd be proud of me," he told her, squeezing her hand. Then he returned his cup to the sink, rinsed it out, and went back to the bedroom, where he took a small jewelry box from the top drawer of her dresser.

From the box, Marvin retrieved a small key.

He pulled up a chair in front of their closet that he could

stand on, reached up behind a box of papers on the top shelf, and removed a blue zipper pouch with a heavy brass lock.

The pouch was so heavy and awkward that Marvin almost dropped it taking it down from the closet. The tiny key popped the lock and released the zipper.

"I need to step out for a few minutes, Luv, but don't worry. I'll be back soon," he said, returning the small key to the jewelry box. Then he quietly closed the bedroom door, slid on his button cap, and put the zipper pouch into the pocket of his thin jacket.

Chapter Nine

Savannah sat behind a tree in the park across the street from Marvin's apartment, slowly pulling a long curl between her lips and watching the street. There were predators in this part of town, especially in the Commons after dark, and she didn't like being here, but she was absolutely out of options. She could think of no other way of coming up with the cash she needed to get Clifford fixed, and if she lost Clifford, she'd lose everything.

She planned to wait until a couple of hours after the lights went out, pop the lock on Marvin's front door, quickly look for anything she could find of value, and get out. She wouldn't take more than she had to, and she'd pay him back. Somehow, someday, she'd pay him back.

She bit her lip and glanced at the park, watching the wide-open Commons as much as the tiny apartment.

Why is he living in such a crappy part of town? she wondered. Then the front door opened, and Marvin stepped out into the night.

She sat up.

What's he doing out this late, going for bread? She thought he had fallen asleep, but it didn't matter. All she needed was three minutes.

Savannah watched Marvin as he disappeared around a corner, then quietly but quickly crossed the street, unscrewed the glowing bulb above the front door, and took a small leather roll of locksmith tools out of her back pocket.

She had learned nimble ways of getting in and out of tight places and locked spaces in her six months of living on the street. She hated stealing, but she had become good at it.

She watched the street as she slid two thin toothpick-like tools with curved and jagged tips into the lock, ready to feel the faint movement of tumblers, but the door was slightly ajar.

She paused.

This didn't feel right, especially in this neighborhood. Had she just gotten lucky?

She tucked the tools away and slid in through the open door without a sound.

The smell of DHMSO was tannic in the air, a scent she knew from visiting her grandfather in his retirement home as a young girl.

Now it felt like she was stealing from her grandfather, a thought she pushed away.

Photos of Marvin and his family filled the walls of the narrow hall she now stood in, and they watched her as she crept into the living room where a small, old-fashioned television, with foil on the antenna, sat in front of shelves of books. Hand-written papers lay in piles on beige filing cabinets. Faded stacks of black and white composition notebooks stood floor to ceiling.

Even though she was far from an invited guest, it was nice to be in someone's home again. The last time she had been anywhere this nice was before she and her mother left their small house in the suburbs and moved into the motel.

The kitchen was tidy and quiet.

For too long, she had been eating on paper plates and plastic cups, using plastic forks and knives that broke if you pushed them too hard. But this place had real plates, real cups, and real silverware. It smelled old, and everything was out of date by at least forty years, but she didn't care. Little round magnets held scribbled drawings in crayon to the front of the fridge, drawings that had gone brown and curling from age. This was someone's home. Someplace solid and stable.

She opened the freezer and rummaged around, hearing somewhere that people sometimes hide their valuables in the freezer, thinking thieves won't bother to check there. No luck.

A closed door stood down the hall, past the photos of Marvin's happy life.

She gently tried the handle, but it was locked, so she decided to return if she couldn't find anything of value elsewhere.

Then she went into the bathroom and felt around the back of the toilet seat, carefully and quietly lifting the lid on the tank. Her mom used to hide a little cash in a zip bag in the toilet, but she had no luck there either.

She bit her lip in frustration. She had to find something she could sell, and she was running out of time.

Only two rooms left. The back bedroom and whatever was behind the locked door in the hallway.

MARVIN WALKED DOWN THE STREET past a smoke-filled SUV playing something with a heavy beat as a television flicked late-night news through one of his neighbor's living room windows. He and Margaret knew better than to ever be out this late in the neighborhood, but tonight he had business.

He made his way six blocks down Lincoln Avenue to the 24-hour pawn shop, where the row of white houses used to stand, as it began to rain a light, sticky rain that made the night feel heavy with humidity. Then he pushed a broken button next to the locked pawn shop door.

Johnny Dukes heard the loud buzz and looked up from his paper at the eighty-seven-year-old man standing outside his painted glass door and creased his brow, wondering what this was all about.

Johnny's gift was observing people very carefully. When someone walked through his door, did they make comfortable eye contact or avoid it? Were they carrying something they wanted to sell, scanning the shelves for something to buy, or acting nervous? Cops also visited the shop twice a week, like clockwork. If they came in off schedule, they had something specific to ask about. And every item, in or out, was recorded and documented in one of two books, the official books or the unofficial books. He told himself that there was none of this cliche, one shop up front and another in the back business like you see in every cop show on tv, but realities were different. Johnny had two kids to feed at home, and buying stuff someone didn't want and reselling it to someone who did was the best way he knew to do that. And sometimes, an opportunity would present itself he could not ignore.

Now, this grandpa walking through his front door at 11-whatever o'clock with a hallow look on his face was more than a little unusual. If the guy were 25, Johnny would be reaching for the Glock 9 he kept loaded for just such a look, but it's hard to suspect grandpa, so he pushed the unlock button beneath the counter and let him in.

"How you doin?" Johnny asked, chewing a blue plastic straw.

Marvin didn't respond. Instead, he moved slowly down a center aisle.

Johnny left his barstool and followed Marvin to the glass cases at the back of the shop. Johnny could see the old man had something heavy in his pocket he was babysitting with his right hand.

"You looking to buy or sell?" Johnny asked.

Marvin scanned the glass cases, past the jewelry and electronics, stopping when he found the guns.

Johnny tilted his head and slowly followed the old man, trying to get a read on him and figure out what he was babysitting in his pocket. Then he noticed Marvin's Submariner Rolex, a late 70's model with what looked like a custom leather strap—a bracelet as it's called in the jewelry business. It was pretty beat up, but with a new bezel and some polish, Johnny figured he could get a fast $4,000 or slow $5,000 for it, maybe even $5,500 if it was one that one of his collector clients was looking for.

Marvin stood motionless, looking through his reflection into the glass case. *Maybe there is a sedative for loss,* Marvin thought to himself as he looked over the pistols laid out beneath the glass like miniature works of art.

He was a good shot back in his youth, but that was when Truman was president, and there were no semi-automatic pistols back then.

He moved on to the simpler and, what he thought would be, more reliable selection of revolvers.

"Looking for a little home defense?" Johnny asked.

"How about that one?" Marvin pointed to a very short pistol with a wood-grained handle stained black. "Rhino 20DS, .357 MAGNUM, Made in Italy" was etched on the side.

Johnny whistled through his teeth. "There's a reason why there's a rhino etched on the side of that one, pops," he replied. "This might be a little easier for you to control," and he pulled a black satin board out from underneath the counter and laid a matte black .38 on top of it.

"I'd like to see that one, if you don't mind," Marvin retorted with more attitude than Margaret would have appreciated.

Johnny took a breath, put the .38 back into the case, and took out the .357 MAGNUM. He checked that the safety was on, opened the cylinder, confirmed the empty chamber, and laid the pistol on the mat.

Marvin slowly picked it up and felt the weight of it and its cold, thick steel press against the frail bones in his hand.

He could see his reflection looking back at him in the highly polished nickel plating.

"That one there is $675, and I can toss in a box of show stoppers for ya'. I'd just need to see some picture ID for a background, and you can pick it up first thing Thursday. Just make sure you understand what you're getting into with that one. It's got enough of a kick you could break your wrist trying to shoot it."

"Good," Marvin said without meaning to.

At that, Johnny slowly reached for the gun, took it back, and laid it on the mat.

"But I need it tonight," Marvin replied.

Johnny shook his head. "I can't give it to you tonight. It takes at least a couple of hours for background check to come through, but the system locks us out after 8, so no one comes stumbling in drunk and crazy in the middle of the night. You ain't drunk or on somethin, are you pops?"

Marvin chuckled at the thought. He often drank in the Navy but gave that all up for Margaret long ago. Although, a drink might help. Maybe he'd stop by the liquor store on his way home—no reason not to anymore.

"I'll give you fifteen for it right now," Marvin said, not looking up at Johnny.

Fifteen? Johnny wasn't expecting that. People usually try to negotiate the price down, not double it.

"You're not planning on hurting anyone, are you? Because I'd hate to have to answer a bunch of questions tomorrow mornin."

"Just a little self-defense, like you said," Marvin lied.

Johnny looked around. There was no one else in the shop. The security cameras didn't have audio, but he knew one was watching him overhead.

He shook his head and said quietly: "I can't help you. I have to do a background check. It's the law. But since we don't have business, I may as well take a smoke break 'round back. Now, if you decided to leave the watch on the counter, I wouldn't report this stolen for at least 48 hours." Then Johnny put the pistol back in the case and reached behind the counter like he was going to lock it but purposefully neglected to push the lock shut before going outside.

When Johnny returned, the pistol was gone, and the case was shut and relocked. A box of .357 MAGNUM shells sat open on the counter, missing a single round. However, there was no watch.

Instead of the watch, a crisp stack of $100 bills sat on the velvet mat wrapped in a mustard yellow bank band with

$10,000 printed on the paper wrap.

THE YOUNG WAITRESS quickly calculated that the closest store open this late at night was either the liquor store or the grocery down on 26th. If Marvin had gone to the liquor store, he would be back any minute, but if he had gone to the grocer, she still had ten minutes. He had also been walking slowly, which she figured would buy her at least another couple of minutes, but that was still starting to cut it a bit close. She hadn't come this far to leave empty-handed. Maybe she could still find that watch.

She didn't touch the door as she slipped into the dark bedroom.

As she crept to the nightstand, a soft blue light from the moon pushed through clouds offering enough of a gentle kiss of luminescence to help her get around the room.

She felt around the top of the small table but didn't find anything other than a pair of glasses, a box of tissue, and a paperback book. Then she went around to the other side of the bed.

As the moonlight through the window slowly shifted from behind clouds, the room brightened just enough for her to catch the presence of someone lying in bed suddenly, and she froze.

Marvin's wife! Why hadn't she considered the possibility that there might be someone else in the apartment?

She squeezed her eyes shut and held her breath. After a moment in the quiet darkness, hearing nothing but the beating of her own heart, she slowly opened her eyes.

Margaret lay on top of the bed covers, fully dressed with

her shoes on, her hands folded neatly in her lap.

Get out before she wakes up, she screamed at herself in her head, but something wasn't right.

Savannah watched Margaret closely for a minute, then two. Margaret didn't look like she was moving, but it was dark.

She moved cautiously closer.

Margaret wasn't moving at all.

Even in the darkness of the room, Savannah could sense something was off. The way Margaret lay there was wrong. The way Margaret was fully dressed was wrong. And why was she wearing shoes?

She carefully and quietly lifted an empty glass from the nightstand and held it beneath Margaret's nose.

There was no breath.

Then she set the glass down and touched Margaret's hand. It was cold. This might have frightened someone else, but it did not frighten her.

She had found the body of a homeless man once, who had fallen asleep on the courthouse steps and had never woken up. When she found him, she felt deep sorrow that he had died alone, so she sat with him all night, holding his hand until the police came the next morning, always wondering who he was or if he had family somewhere who missed him. She also thought about how easily it could be her if she didn't get back to her life, and she remembered thinking just how much she wished someone would sit with her and hold her hand if it was her there, leaning against those cold marble columns that November night.

Now, here was this woman lying in this dark shroud of moonlight. But this woman was not alone, was she? She had died in this lovely home around people who loved her, and here she was stealing from her.

Just then, the front door of the apartment banged open.

Chapter Ten

Marvin was so tired, the world felt like a waking dream as he walked across the parking lot, kicking up the collar of this coat against the rain and squinting into the darkness. He was tired physically. Tired emotionally. Tired of taking his endless pills. Tired of being poked by doctors. Tired of the same old reruns and the same old songs. Tired of seeing that old man looking back at him in the mirror every morning, even though he still thought of himself the way he looked when he was thirty-five. And now he could see the solution was so very simple.

He would never have admitted it to Margaret, but he'd always been afraid of death, afraid of endlessly falling. He didn't know where that idea came from, but most of those fears that grab ahold of us and never let go aren't strictly rational. Now, only minutes from closing his eyes forever, the scratching echo of his doubts and fears were so completely silent it startled him.

Arthritis in his knees shot fingers of pain up his back as he crossed the parking lot when long grey feathers blew past his feet.

He lifted his face against the rain, as water ran down the

back of his neck making him shudder.

Then he saw blood.

Matted grey feathers mixed with blood looked like something had caught a large bird and torn it to pieces. Loose feathers shifting and swirling in eddies of wind and rain. Blood dripped down the brick wall in front of him, still very red and glistening in the sideways light cast by two lamps across the parking lot. There was so much blood he could smell it mixed with damp trash and wet street.

The damp and filthy mound of torn bird covered a naked body, which he overlooked until he saw a small foot—a leg.

It was a child!

He quickly stepped over to the child lying curled tightly like an unborn fetus painted dark with the devil's brush.

Oh no! He's dead, Marvin thought.

He bent down, wondering what horrible event had taken place here. He had just come this way. Could he have been so lost in himself and Margaret's death that he hadn't even noticed a child lying dead on the sidewalk? Or had this just happened?

He looked around but didn't see anyone. All of the homes were dark and locked up against the harshness of this part of the city at night.

He quickly turned back to the pawn shop he had just come from, looking for help, hoping to use a phone since he didn't carry one even though he and Margaret had talked about getting one of those pocket ones.

He buzzed the door, but there was no answer. He looked in through the bars but didn't see the owner. He buzzed again and again. Nothing. He looked back across the parking lot but couldn't see the child from where he stood. It was too dark and too far removed from the red glow of the pawn shop sign. He tried next door, but the liquor store was already dark and closed for the night, so he came back and buzzed the pawn shop door again. But again, there was no response.

He took off his cap and rubbed his forehead. He didn't know what to do.

He went back to the child. Should he cry out for help? Would anyone hear him? Would anyone come even if they did? He had always quipped that the police didn't come to this part of town anymore unless there was a body on the floor. Now there was.

Only a few blocks from home, he could call the police from there, but he didn't want to leave the child alone. How could he leave this tiny, retched body lying on the side of the street like a piece of trash?

Then, an echo of a memory.

He felt like he had seen something like this before, but where?

He froze.

The long slender legs, doll-like hands, and contorted body.

Marvin fell to his hands and knees, overwhelmed with the emotional memory of finding his baby brother in the mud. Memories he had buried in the same Alabama soil they had used to cover his brother's body more than a century ago. His stomach cramped and his throat went dry. He couldn't breathe. He pulled at his collar trying to get some air, but it wasn't working.

He couldn't even tell if it was a boy or girl, but whoever they were, they were only seven or eight.

Then the child moved.

"Oh my God in heaven, you're alive!" He said, quickly taking off his jacket and laying it over the child's naked form as the pistol he had just illegally acquired at the pawnshop fell out of his pocket and clattered against the pavement.

He picked it up out of the blood, wiped it on his trouser leg, and put it back in his pocket as the rain carried creaks of blood and feathers down the sidewalk, into the drain.

Marvin gently touched the child's face, causing the child to flinch. Then he carefully lifted the jacket, looking for wounds, but he didn't see any. Where had all the blood come from? He had never seen so much blood. Had the child bled from their mouth or ears? This might mean the child had some sort of internal trauma Marvin couldn't see.

He would not, could not, leave the child alone, and if the child didn't get help and soon, they may not survive.

He wrapped the child up in his jacket, hoisted them in his arms, and carried them home.

Even though he was eighty-seven, lifting Margaret in and out of bed all those years had helped Marvin maintain his lean, taught strength, and possibly even improved it a bit. Compared to her, this child felt like barely a whisper of nothing, especially with his sense of urgency salted by high levels of adrenaline and fear.

He tried to shield the child from the rain with his body as much as he could, soaking his shirt so that it clung to his narrow frame.

Dirty water from rooftops and draining gutters splashed over him, stinging his eyes as he walked.

His thoughts jumped from Moses to his daughter, and he couldn't ignore how close this child was in age to Ellie when she died. Had she cried out or lay silent like this one? Had Ellie called for her mommy, or him? How many times had he wished he had been there to help *her?* To pick her up and carry her home. To hold her, and reassure her she wasn't alone?

After the police found her, they wouldn't let him or Margaret touch her body. He never had the chance to kiss her cheek and say goodbye.

The thought that he hadn't been able to do anything to help her, or Moses, interrupted his sleep throughout the years more than any other. That was the seed that grew into a vine of bitterness that absolutely choked to death the joy in his life, a vine he felt powerless to ever cut back or break free from.

But, he could help this child. He had to help this child.

Why was this child *not* crying?

He walked faster, nearly breaking into a run, but his knees fought him.

When he finally made it home, he nearly dropped the child, fishing around in his pocket for his keys when the front door swung open, banging the wall behind it.

The loud bang startled Savannah who was still creeping through the darkness in Marvin's bedroom.

Marvin's back! How long has it been? Maybe he had just gone to the liquor store, she thought to herself, frantically opening dresser drawers, looking for anything of value when she suddenly she found a small jewelry box.

The child hadn't moved, at least not in any way Marvin could perceive, which made him increasingly fearful.

The worry he might wake Margaret streaked across his mind until he remembered her lifeless body lying in bed.

He leaned against the wall, trying not to drop the child who hung low at his hip, his arms burning from exhaustion. He hoisted the child up, dug deep for his last few ounces of strength, and carried them into the living room.

Now he wished he had a couch to lay the child on, but since he did not, he slumped down in his armchair, not knowing what else to do.

Marvin's head was pounding, his back screamed, his arms burned, and frankly, he had no idea why his legs hadn't given out halfway home. The two of them were an absolute hot mess of bloody rainwater soaking into his armchair.

He had hit that place of extreme exhaustion where his body was now pulling sugar from his brain just to keep his heart pumping and his muscles moving, making every thought a struggle.

He stared with numb confusion at the beige rotary phone hanging on the wall in the kitchen, but he didn't see any way to reach it. Exhaustion was transitioning to dizziness, and he could feel himself starting to pass out. He had to call someone.

Then the child shivered.

Marvin looked down at the small face hidden in the folds of his soaking wet jacket and wiped his face with the back of his hand, but his hands were so filthy it only burned his eyes.

He wanted to try to warm the child and swung his heavy head toward the blankets folded in the corner of the room but didn't think they were enough. Then he turned to the bathroom. He needed hot water, but the shower might as well have been on the other side of town he was so shattered from exhaustion.

Then the child shivered more violently.

If the child were shivering, the child was still alive.

In the Navy, there were times when they would push them to exhaustion like this, which was often when his training would begin, but he was *not* eighteen. He couldn't even *spell* eighteen right now. He just didn't have any strength left to move himself another inch, much less another person, but if he could pique his adrenaline once more…

He screamed.

He had to dig deep—down past his rational self and into that animal nature that still scratched at the dirt by ancient fires. He hated that he wasn't the young man he used to be that could hoist bags of trash or multiple gallons of milk on a whim, but he hadn't been that man in an ancient age.

He repeatedly pounded his head against the back of his chair and screamed at himself to get up. Get UP! MOVE!

He rocked forward onto his feet, hoisted the adolescent up, and stumbled into the bathroom in a single move, turning just in time to land on his back instead of on the child.

The young waitress heard Marvin lumbering down the hall like he was carrying something heavy as she turned and dropped the small box, which broke in half and splayed its contents across the bedroom floor.

She fell to her knees and groped for whatever she could find, pulling sharp shapes of various pieces of jewelry into her pockets that she couldn't recognize in the darkness. Then she dropped to her stomach and rolled underneath the bed.

As she crawled beneath the bed, her eyes followed a small chrome object, rimmed in moonlight, rolling across the bedroom floor and stopping only a few feet from where she was hiding.

It was a bullet.

The single bullet Marvin had taken from the box at the pawnshop had fallen out of his pocket and bounced into his bedroom.

Marvin now lay on the bathroom floor as tears streamed down his cheeks and dripped onto the tile. Then he slowly inched himself on his back towards the shower until he felt his head come in contact with the edge of the shower pan. And as gently as he could, he rolled the small bundle off of himself and into the shower.

He had to have broken something somewhere with that move, but he didn't care. Everything hurt so much that nothing called out in particular. He propped himself up on his elbows and reached for the shower handle. His long, frail fingers turned the dial as the faucet high overhead spat cold water in his face, making him flinch. Then it slowly warmed into a gentle shower that began to brighten him down deep in his darkest places.

At the outer edge of his consciousness, he could hear a voice that sounded like his own, telling him to call someone, but whoever that was would have to wait because he couldn't get up.

Chapter Eleven

Savannah lay motionless beneath the bed, waiting for any sign of movement from the bathroom.

At first, she heard Marvin crying and talking to someone, but now she only heard the shower, steam rolling from the open bathroom door. It had been fifteen or twenty minutes. Was he dead? There was already a body lying in repose directly above her. Had whatever killed her, killed him too?

Savannah's elbows began to ache as she buried her face in her hands and considered her options: She could wait until he came to bed and sneak out after he fell asleep. Or, she could try to get past the open bathroom door without being noticed and hope he was just taking a long shower, which would be ideal because she'd be gone before he dried himself off.

She strained to hear any sound of movement, but there was none.

What if he was hurt? Would he die if she didn't get help? The thought made her mouth go dry. Could Marvin die because she was too afraid to move? And what about the woman lying above her? Police would show up if two people died in an apartment on the same night, wouldn't they? Would they suspect foul play? Dust for fingerprints?

Fingerprints.

Her prints were all over the apartment. Why hadn't she thought of that? She should have worn gloves! What a stupid mistake.

She looked across the floor at the scattered pieces of jewelry, their edges glinting in the moonlight. How many of those pieces had her fingerprints on them? She had never been arrested before. Would the police know they were her prints if she had never been arrested? Maybe they wouldn't, but they'd have them on file now, and that would be another thing that might come back to bite her one day like a viper in a tall thicket.

She hated the idea of something else hanging over her head, but it was too late. There was simply no way for her to go back through each of the rooms and try to wipe clean everything she had touched. She couldn't even remember everything she had touched, fumbling around in the dark.

This isn't my life. This isn't me, she told herself.

How did things keep getting worse? What terrible mess had she gotten herself into?

She slowly crawled out from underneath the bed, her attention anchored to the bullet in the doorway. Why was there a bullet in the doorway?

She peaked around the corner of the bathroom.

Marvin lay under the flow of hot water, leaning unconsciously over the pile of his jacket, completely soaked black with blood. There was blood everywhere. Blood circled the shower drain. Blood on the walls, the toilet seat, and the shower handle. Had he been shot? At least he was breathing.

Her eyes grew when she saw the gun lying on the shower

floor. Why did he have a gun? Had he shot someone?

She followed the trail of blood out of the bathroom and down the hall, careful not to touch any of the gore spread around the apartment. She couldn't tell if the blood was from Marvin or someone else.

It looked like someone had been stabbed to death in the armchair, which triggered panic. She had to go. She had to go now, but she couldn't just leave him. She wanted to get help but couldn't be here when help arrived. She wanted to ensure it wasn't his blood running down the drain and into the Boston sewers, but she didn't want any of that blood on her hands.

Savannah pulled at her left eyebrow, trying to decide how she would help Marvin without letting too much of the worsening situation stick to her.

The front door was now locked and streaked with blood.

She rubbed her forehead and went to the kitchen where she found a rusting steel door. She forced the heavy door open with her hand in her shirt, trying not to leave more prints, and just as she was about to disappear into the night, she saw the old rotary phone hanging on the wall next to the refrigerator.

She hesitated. If she called the police, she could leave before help arrived, but what would she tell them?

She thought for a moment.

She pulled up the bottom of her shirt and used it to lift the receiver, dial 9-1-1, and held the phone up to, without touching, her ear.

"911, what's your emergency?" came a woman's voice from the other end.

"Uh, my, uh, neighbor fell in the shower. I think he's hurt. Send an ambulance, quick."

"Slow down, ma'am. Where are you?"

She tried to remember the address but couldn't. "Can't you just trace the call or something?"

"You don't know your address?"

"He's not at my house. He's uh, he's next door," Savannah said.

"What's your address?"

"Just trace the call!"

"Okay? Can you tell me what happened?" the dispatcher asked.

"I heard a bang, and I think my neighbor fell. He's an old man, and I'm worried he fell in the shower or something."

"Did you see him fall?"

"No," Savannah replied.

"But you heard a bang?"

"Yeah! A loud bang. I'm worried he fell and hurt himself."

"Could it have come from outside or somewhere other than next door?" the dispatcher asked.

"No! It couldn't have! Come on! I heard a loud bang, and I think my neighbor fell. Are you sending an ambulance or not?" she snapped at the dispatcher.

"Please calm down, ma'am. I'm just trying to understand what is going on. I've already dispatched an officer and medical team to your location. They should be on the scene soon. Can you give me your name?"

But there was no reply. Savannah was already gone, the phone receiver swinging against the kitchen wall.

Chapter Twelve

A loud bang from the kitchen startled Marvin to consciousness.

He moved very slightly and felt his arm still draped over the body of the child who had uncurled themself beneath the pile of his jacket, the shower still warming them both.

How long have I been out? He reached for his head, but his right arm shrieked in pain. The pistol's hammer, now laying on the edge of the drain, jabbed into his elbow.

He slowly sat up next to the child. Then he set the pistol on the back of the toilet.

Now that some of the blood had rinsed away, Marvin could see the child's blonde hair. Their head lay on their arm like a pillow, and a small foot stuck out from underneath his jacket. The child's eye was almost swollen shut, and their lower lip was large and purple. It looked to Marvin like the child had been pretty severely beaten.

Marvin didn't know where to begin the clean-up. Both he and the child sat in a bloody flow of water with a trail of red streaking across the bathroom floor and out into the hall.

He carefully lifted his jacket.

He could now see the child was a young boy. Their tender,

ivory skin a Rorschach of milky white mixed with the red and green of deep bruising down their back and onto their right side. Not seeing any other wounds, he still didn't know where all the blood had come from.

Marvin still had to call the police, but there was blood everywhere. He had the child's blood on his clothes, on the gun he had just illegally acquired from a late-night pawn shop, and all over his home.

They're going to think I hurt the child, not helped him, he thought.

And then he remembered Margaret, still lying in bed. What had he gotten himself into?

He slowly stood and stepped out into the hall to assess the damage, his ears ringing and his vision blurring at the edges.

Splatters of diluted blood in the shapes of Marvin's footprints stained the hallway carpeting, and he would have to throw out his favorite armchair. He wasn't sure how to accomplish that, but he clearly couldn't salvage it. He followed the bloody trail to the front door, a messy red handprint on the doorknob. By sheer luck, had no one walked past his entry? The rain, now a cooling drizzle, had washed much of the blood off his portion of the sidewalk, but there were still red traces as far down the street as he could see in the moonlight diminishing behind scattered clouds.

He looked at his watch. It was nearly twelve-thirty now. If he got to work, he might have enough time to clean the sidewalk before daylight.

He went back to the bathroom, peeled off his wet and bloody clothes, dropped his shoes, now completely ruined, into the small waist bin, and returned to his bedroom in his underwear, his gaunt form and hunched shoulders shuddering uncontrollably from the cold. Large purple-black bruises were already beginning to grow across his leg, arm, and shoulders.

The bullet from his gun lay in the middle of the bedroom floor. He picked it up and set it on Margaret's nightstand, which was a scattered mess. He knew the location of every tiny item on her nightstand so well that he could feel where they belonged. Her perfume. Her box of tissue. Her small crystal dish of jewelry. A framed photo of her, Marvin, and Ellie at the zoo feeding an orange and green parrot. But now, everything was on the floor. In the middle of everything, had he knocked everything off the table last night? He couldn't remember.

The jewelry box she kept in the dresser lay in two pieces on the floor, and most of the jewelry was gone, but he couldn't remember why. He would return and find the jewelry later since he had more pressing issues, like putting on some dry clothes, cleaning up the bathroom, and drying off the naked and hurt child lying on his shower floor.

"Don't worry, Luv, you just rest now. I'll take care of everything. I'm not quite sure how at this particular moment, but I will. You'll see," Marvin told Margaret as he went to their shared walk-in closet, clicked on the light, and took out some dry clothes, which he pulled on with no small amount of difficulty as his arm argued with more burning pain.

Then he thought about the child. He didn't have anything for a small child to wear.

He stepped out of the closet and looked at Margaret. He did have something for a small child to wear.

"I don't think Ellie would mind if he borrowed something," he told her, nodding.

He returned to Margaret's side of the bed, picked up the photo of Margaret, Marvin, and Ellie at the zoo, and turned it over. A key was taped to the back.

When Marvin returned to the locked door in the hall, he paused, noticing fingerprints in the dust on the doorknob. He then used the corner of his shirt to wipe the knob clean and unlocked it.

The room was dark and stale, a path of light falling into the room from the hall.

He clicked on a small lamp with a pink floral shade beside a bed. A Scooby-Doo poster hung on the wall next to a painted picture of a bird. Pink and yellow curtains hung over a window now covered in black plastic. Three stuffed, threadbare animals lay waiting for someone who would never return.

Marvin opened the top drawer of a white dresser where colorful denim and corduroy dresses lay neatly folded. The second drawer held two yellow jumpers and a stack of white blouses, and in the third, long tube socks and a small pile of little girl's underwear. Two pairs of tiny shoes sat in a neat row half-tucked beneath the dresser.

Not finding anything suitable for a boy to wear, he clicked out the light, closed the door, and returned to his closet. One of his polo shirts and a pair of khaki shorts would be better than a little dress, so he carried one of each back to the bathroom.

The young boy now stood with arms crossed and slightly hunched over in the middle of the shower with his back to Marvin. The light of the moon fell in through the bathroom window ringing the child's frail and slender form in an outline of bluish-grey light. Most of the blood had by now washed off, though his blonde hair was still streaked with tinges of dark red.

"You're awake," Marvin said, not expecting the child to regain consciousness, much less stand there before him. The child startled and glanced over his shoulder at Marvin.

Marvin held up a hand to calm him. "I'm not going to hurt you." He slowly stepped into the bathroom and laid the clothes on the toilet seat. "I was just bringing you something dry to wear."

Barely as tall as Marvin's hip, all knees and elbows, the child just looked at him.

"What's your name?" Marvin asked, but the boy didn't respond. "Do you know where you are?"

Nothing.

"Of course you don't. How could you?" Then Marvin sat down on the toilet seat, moving the stack of dry clothes onto his lap. "Do you know your phone number? Or the name of your mother or father?" He spoke softly and paused to let the child process.

Marvin thought the child looked scared and confused, but he didn't know much about such things anymore.

"What about your address?" he asked, but the child just looked at him. "I found you lying in the street, and I brought you home so I could call someone, which I must admit I have not done yet."

The child glanced at the gun on the back of the toilet, then back at Marvin, and Marvin looked at the weapon, then back at the child.

"I'm sorry about that," Marvin stammered, picking the heavy pistol up and sliding it beneath a towel next to the sink. "That's not supposed to be here." He took a deep breath. Then he turned his attention to the wounds on the child's face and back.

"Do you remember what happened to you, son?" he asked, reaching toward the child, but the boy flinched. "Did someone do this to you?"

The boy looked away like he was trying to remember something, then back at Marvin. But he still didn't make a sound.

"No one's going to hurt you here son; I can promise you that. But we need to get you into some dry clothes, and I can't do that until you let me finish cleaning you up. Child, you have some nasty mess in your hair, and I need to look you over to see if you have any cuts or open wounds. Will you let me do that?"

The child thought for a moment, then gently nodded and took a half step towards him.

Marvin handed him a washcloth. "You can put this over your parts while I look you over, but I won't touch you. I just need to see where you're hurt."

He carefully laid the jacket aside and looked the child over. A swollen eye, fat lip, scratches, and road rash all down his right side, but nothing that would produce nearly the amount of blood that was now painted across Marvin's home. "How about down there?" He pointed to the washcloth. "Anything down there funny colors or bleeding?" The boy peeked behind the washcloth, looked back at Marvin, and shook his head.

"Do you remember anything about last night or what happened to you?"

The child didn't respond.

"My name is Marvin Johnson. I found you lying bloody in the street," Marvin said, lowering his forehead and holding out an open hand. "I brought you home so we could get you some help, but I ain't goin' to hurtcha. You have my word, which might not sound like much since I'm a stranger and all, but it's God's truth."

The child looked at Marvin's outstretched hand for a moment. Then he laid his hand on Marvin's. *First contact,* Marvin thought.

When Marvin was a small child, his father owned horses, and he remembered watching his father reaching out to a young new colt they had just bought, in much the same way. His father didn't rush it. He just waited with hand open until that young thing came near enough to sniff his fingertips. First contact. All movement would be slow and calm until that colt would learn to trust his father's every word.

"I have some clothes here for ya, but you're still quite a mess. Would you let me at least wash some of the mess out your hair?"

The child slowly nodded.

Marvin pointed to the white chair folded into the shower wall. "I'm just going to open this here, and you can sit down while I wash you up a bit. Is that alright with you?" The child stayed calm and did what Marvin asked while Marvin washed his hair with enough soap to get most of his body clean. Marvin then pulled down the shower head with its hose and gently rinsed the rest of the mess away. As he did so, he looked around the child's head for any cuts or wounds but didn't find any. Marvin was enamored by how fine the child's hair was, delicate as a newborn's, and so very platinum blonde that it was almost transparent.

The child did not pull away as Marvin looked more closely at the child's bruises without touching him.

"Who did this to you?"

Marvin asked, but the child didn't respond.

"These look incredibly painful. Are you in pain, child? I have some fairly strong pills I could probably crush up."

The boy thought about this, then shook his head.

"No pills or no pain."

No comment.

"Can you speak?"

Marvin watched the child's face register confusion and wonder at this question.

"You know what? It doesn't matter," Marvin told him. "Don't you worry about a thing right now. Let's just get you in some clothes, and we can take care of the rest in the morning."

Marvin turned off the shower, slowly dried the child, then helped him into the clothes that hung loosely on the child's shoulders and hips.

"I think I need to find you a belt," Marvin said while the child hoisted up the edges of the shorts with both hands.

"Are you hungry?"

The child's eyebrows raised at that.

"I'll take that as a yes," Marvin told him. "I can't guarantee I have anything you'll like," Marvin said as they walked out into the kitchen, and he began looking through the cupboards. "How 'bout some toast with peanut butter and honey?" He looked at the child sitting at the small kitchen table where he and Margaret ate their last meal.

The child's eyes raised again.

Ellie loved peanut butter and honey toast. It was their family's go-to breakfast every morning before school, but he hadn't eaten it in decades. He wasn't sure why they kept some on hand. Honey for tea, but peanut butter? One of those details they never bothered to erase from their life. He rolled the peanut butter jar over and checked the date. It was nearly two years old. He opened the lid. No mold. Does peanut butter go off? he wondered. Then he pulled two nearly burned pieces of toast out of his toaster, coated them in a thin layer of the rich, brown nut butter, and drizzled on enough honey that it spilled over the sides of the bread.

As he set the peanut butter-covered knife down into the sink, he saw something shine up at him from the floor. It was a small turtle pendant with a mother-of-pearl shell on a thin gold chain.

How odd. It wasn't Margaret's. Was it the boys? That didn't seem right. Then he turned it over. The word "Kuuipo" was engraved on the back. He didn't know what Kuuipo meant, so he slid it into his pocket and turned to see the phone hanging from the receiver on the wall, beep beeping like it had been off the hook for at least a few minutes. Had he already called the police? He thought for a moment but couldn't remember.

As the child waited, he scooped a finger-full of butter from the stick on the table, rubbed his fingers together, and smelled it. Then he tasted it and immediately scooped another finger-full from the yellow cube into his mouth. The child watched Marvin put the phone back on the receiver and set a plastic plate of toast down in front of him, along with a faded plastic cup of lukewarm water from the sink.

"We haven't had guests in a while," Marvin told him, sitting across the table from the child and watching the strange behavior. "I think you'll like this even more," he said, but the child just looked at the toast.

"Go on then," Marvin said. "I expect you're hungry."

The child picked up one of the pieces of toast, looked it over and touched the dripping honey with a finger, then tasted it. The golden, liquid sugar brightened his countenance.

Marvin watched the boy lick the edge of the toast and then the top. Then he smiled. He had forgotten the warmth a child brings into a room. *What will happen to this little life?* He wondered to himself, watching the child rake the toast over his tongue, leaving a tiny pile of honey-dripping peanut butter on the tip of his nose and smearing it around his cheeks. Then he looked back at the phone. *When did I call the police?* He just could not remember.

He turned to the blood in the hall, and his mind started racing with doubt and worry. How long until they arrived, and what would they possibly think of all the blood? And with his wife lying dead in their bedroom? Somehow he had become the villain in his own home. Their prying eyes, doubting everything he said. They'd probably think he was the one who had done something to hurt the child instead of helping him. "Where did you find him? Why did you take him home? What's the story with the gun?" they would ask.

The gun.

The shop owner said he would report the gun stolen. Stolen. He had stolen a gun, of all things. "Were you the one who stole the gun from the pawn shop on the night of the 18th?" they would ask. He didn't care if he had stolen a gun or not a few hours earlier, but now? Now everything had changed. Would they arrest him? Put him in prison? Had he already broken the law by not calling the police as soon as Margaret died? Would he ever see his home again? Would it ever be his home again, really be the home he knew? Without Margaret, how could it be?

And what would happen to the child? What if they found

his parents or whoever had done this to him and the boy was too scared to tell them the truth? Would the police just give him back to them? What if the boy had been kidnapped and they couldn't find his parents? The thought made Marvin shift in his chair. He had found the child naked. Had he been kidnapped and abused and somehow gotten away?

Marvin had watched a Newshour special on children who had been kidnapped and shipped across the country or overseas to be used in unspeakable ways. He gripped the table's edges, trying to process what level of trauma the boy might have survived to be left on the street, naked and bloody in the rain. What had this child endured that would cause him to stop talking?

How hard would the police try to find his parents? Around these parts at least, the police were nice enough when asking questions, but they sure didn't come when you called.

Maybe he would call the FBI. How does someone even call the FBI? The FBI would definitely find out about the gun. Perhaps he should contact the local police first, get them to come out and take Margaret away, then call the FBI. So many options. So much confusion.

And Margaret, still lying lifeless in his bed like she was asleep, but she wasn't. He wasn't far enough gone to be mistaken about that. He wasn't trying to keep her or anything. He just wanted to clean her up and get her ready for her final farewell when he decided to take the journey with her. Now this mess.

"You're not going to fill up much if all you do is lick the good stuff," he told the small boy who looked up at him over the edge of the second piece of toast. "I guess it don't matter much," Marvin said quietly.

He checked his watch—1:15. Exhaustion was pursuing him again.

The child took a big drink of water, leaving a peanut butter ring along the edge of the cup.

Marvin rose and went to the sink, moistened a paper towel, and handed it to the boy, who didn't take it.

"To clean yourself up," Marvin told him, but he just looked at him, so Marvin gently wiped down the boy's face and hands.

The child yawned.

"You and me both," Marvin said, throwing the moist towel and paper plate into the waste bin beneath the sink.

Marvin thought for a moment. There was only one place for the child to sleep since the child could not sleep in bed with Margaret, someplace that had been sacred and off-limits for most of Marvin's life.

Ellie was the last one to sleep in that bed.

"I think we need to get some rest before the craziness starts," he told the boy and placed his hand on his shoulder. The boy didn't wince or pull back this time. He just slowly lifted his head and looked at Marvin with tired eyes.

Marvin rechecked the front door, an old habit before bed. How long will it take me to clean all this up, he wondered again, glancing around the apartment at the windows to make sure they were all locked.

The backdoor stood ajar.

Why wasn't it locked? Margaret couldn't have opened it, and he never used it. Maybe the nurse? he thought, running his hand over his hair.

He sighed.

Nothing was adding up. Not yet. He was too tired. He had other things to worry about just now. He'd sort it all out tomorrow.

He relocked the door, walked to the bedroom to fetch the bullet, and returned to the bathroom for the pistol, which he took out from underneath the stack of white hand towels and clicked open the cylinder. He paused and thought for a moment about what he was doing. Margaret would never have stood for a gun in the house. But she wasn't here anymore, was she? And he couldn't very well let a gun or bullet just lie around, not with a child in the apartment.

He slid the hefty bullet into one of the chambers, clicked the round cylinder shut, and slid the gun back into his pocket.

Then he returned to the kitchen, where the boy was lying with his head resting on his arm on the kitchen table.

"I'd carry you if I could, but I got nothing left," he said, taking the boy's hand and leading him into Ellie's room, where he pulled back the covers.

The boy crawled into bed and rolled over.

Marvin started to leave the room, but the boy sat up and looked at him. "Okay, okay. But just for a few minutes," Marvin told him, sinking down into the plush rocking chair in the corner of the room like he used to do when Ellie had had a bad dream or a bit of a cough and couldn't otherwise sleep without him.

The child laid back down and watched Marvin through heavy eyes.

They looked at each other until Marvin felt exhaustion overtake him, and he fell asleep.

After some time, Marvin woke to sunlight spilling into the dark room from the hallway.

How long had he slept?

He cleared his throat and looked over at the child.

The yellow bed sheets were pulled back, and the child was gone.

Chapter Thirteen

avannah sat on a darkened bench across the park from Marvin's apartment, surveying the various pieces of jewelry she had managed to scoop into her pockets before diving beneath the bed: One earring, probably silver. A handful of rings, one of which had what she hoped was a decent-sized diamond surrounded by little rubies. A knotted bunch of thin gold chains. A watch.

It wasn't Marvin's watch, the one she had come to the apartment hoping to find, but it looked just like it, only smaller. It had a rectangular face with Roman numerals and a brown leather band.

She turned it over. Rolex was marked on the back, along with two words carefully etched in a delicate script: La Chaim.

She rubbed her thumb over the crown logo, weighing those words in her mind. This wasn't just a watch. It matched the one she had seen Marvin wearing, and it was engraved. She nervously scratched the side of her neck not liking the idea that it must have been an engagement gift or birthday present. She wouldn't be able to just pay this one back. This was something special.

She looked towards the apartment. "Ambulances are on

their way," the dispatcher had told her. She couldn't go back. Not now. Not tonight. She'd hold on to it for a bit and drop it in his mailbox tomorrow, no trouble. He'd never know. Until then, she'd have to see what she could get for the rest of the jewelry. She looked at the ring again. "Please be a diamond," she said.

As she walked, it slowly began to sink in that she had broken into the home of an elderly man intending to steal his watch and ended up robbing his dead wife instead. She had taken something irreplaceable and left him lying in a puddle of blood on the shower floor.

She went numb at the thought.

The world was twisting her thinking, and she didn't recognize herself anymore. Savannah was winning. The thought came to her for the first time that she might not actually survive this. She was doing everything she could to get rid of Savannah, but in the end, it may be Savannah who got rid of her. She remembered how hard it used to be to lift a single pack of Ramen noodles from the grocery store, and now she was breaking into homes. And where did she learn to pick a lock? She couldn't even remember anymore.

She knew the only place that would buy the ring this late at night, and in this part of town, was the 24-hour pawn, and she had done business there before.

SAVANNAH PUSHED the cracked button by the front door and heard a distant buzz through the store.

That dirty waif of a man, with his long, bony arms and dirty baseball cap was nowhere to be seen, so she buzzed again. Nothing. She leaned against the window with her hand over her eyes, trying to see through the glass' reflection. The store was empty, but the lights were on, and she never knew Johnny to be closed, so she went around back.

Johnny sat on an overturned orange Home Depot bucket in the alley behind the store. His slender and sinuous fingers pinched the white paper and glowing ember of a cigarette. His long thin arms resting on his long thin knees gave him the appearance of a spider-creature in human form waiting for its prey in the corner of a back alley.

As she approached, he squinted at her, cautious of who might be approaching him behind his store in the middle of the night, but when he recognized her, he stood up and flicked his cigarette at her. She stepped aside and let it pop into tiny fireworks as it hit the ground.

"What do you want?" he asked.

"I'm looking to sell," she replied.

"Not interested."

"It's easy stuff," she told him, wondering why he was acting more gruff than usual. "Just some family jewelry."

"Not. Interested." He turned and reached for a round, flat lock on the back door with black buttons that protruded out like pegs on a child's toy. Then he paused, looked at her, covered the pad with a hand, and clicked in the numbers until the lock popped and the door leaned open.

She grabbed his arm, but he jerked it away.

"The cops came by for the last family jewelry I bought from you!" He said, pressing a long dirty finger against her cheek and pushing her face away.

Anger and frustration plumed like a fire up her back, and she could feel her face turning red. She bit her lip and decided not to slap his nose bloody because she needed him.

She pulled the fist full of the jewelry out of her pocket and held it out to him. "Look, it's easy stuff. I just need a hundred and fifty bucks, and I won't come around anymore."

He couldn't help but glance at the yellow metal she held out to him.

He looked into the store, feigning disinterest.

The cops had come and she had caused him some trouble, but he had always been too fascinated by the glint and glitter of gold and diamonds to look away for long, ever since he sat on his father's knee learning how to use a jeweler's loop.

He sighed and looked back at her, then down at the jewelry, then grunted. "There isn't fifty bucks there," he said, wiping his nose on the back of his hand.

"What about this," she asked, lifting the ring out of the pile and holding it up to him.

His left eye twitched, and she knew he was more interested than he let on.

That's probably glass, he thought to himself, *but maybe not.* Now he was curious.

He tossed his head to the side, motioning her to come in, and she followed him into the store. While he never let anyone in the back of his store, he didn't want to transact this business under the watchful eye of his cameras, creating some semblance of plausible deniability. And besides, he quickly figured he could very nearly beat her to death if she tried anything funny at all.

The front of the store was clean and organized, with everything carefully labeled, but the back of the shop was like the back of a bowling alley, with peg-board walls holding metal hooks that speared through stacks of old invoices. Dusty and disused tools no one ever bought were piled in one corner, and a large grey safe stood from floor to ceiling that looked old like one she had seen in old west photos of banks. 1879 was printed in gold leaf on the front.

He motioned her to a chair on one side of a brown steel desk, not unlike the one Susan had been sitting at in her office at the Blue Bonnet, only this one didn't have diner receipts. Instead, it had a stack of black trays with rows of rings and jewelry sparkling underneath a lamp mounted to a scissor arm screwed into the desk.

He didn't take his eyes off of her as she sat down, and he reached into the top drawer of the desk and took out a smooth black, rectangular case the shape of a pencil box, only smaller.

He set a small empty black velvet tray on the desk and pulled the lamp closer. Then he motioned her to put everything on the tray as he unbuttoned the black case and took out a narrow grey meter with a digital display and a needle on the tip. He looked up at her with no small amount of incredulity as he removed a single black latex glove from the drawer and pulled it on with a sharp snap.

He poked through the various items, separating everything into two piles. In one pile were the chains and the ring, and in the other pile was everything else. Everything except the watch. She hadn't shown him that. Instead, she was fingering it in the front pocket of her hooded sweater while she watched him, still annoyed by his audacity to touch her face but also slightly intrigued by what he was doing…and hoping. Hoping it was all worth something. Hoping the ring was a diamond.

He flipped open a small beige magnifying glass, known as a jeweler's loop, about the size of a quarter, and held it so close to his eye that his thumb touched his cheek as he looked closely at the clasps on each of the chains. Each time looking up at her as he reached for the next item. Then he picked up the ring and used the loop to scan the inside of the band, around the underside of the crown, and each of the stones. He set the loop aside and looked at her again.

She tried reading his face, hoping for a glimpse or hint at what he might be thinking. Some little tell that might tip his hand in her direction and offer her some small opportunity for bargaining, something she had very little room for, which she knew she had broadcast to him when she grabbed his arm in the alley.

He pushed and held a red button on the grey device as its display glowed to life. He picked up the ring and pressed the tip of the needle onto the large center stone. After a few seconds, it beeped.

Every time he heard that beep, it spiked his adrenaline, and he shifted in his chair. Sure, he wanted to feed his kids, but that little beep was really why he was in the business of going through other people's junk and reselling it. Of course, he didn't see himself as a junk dealer at all. He saw himself as a treasure hunter. And that little enigmatic beep meant he had found treasure. Diamonds to be specific. But he couldn't make a profit if he paid what the jewelry was actually worth, and the subterfuge was part of the game.

However, the young woman had also heard the beep, and she saw him shift in his chair, which he had done in a moment of distraction. Now he was the one broadcasting his tells, giving her some breathing room to negotiate.

He licked his lips, pulled off his glove, and reached into a second drawer in the desk; this one held shut with a key. He took out a fifty-dollar bill and dropped it onto the desk in front of her.

"You've got to the kidding," she said with a chuckle.

"There's some junk gold here. That's all."

Junk gold. What an odd turn of phrase. She had never heard the two words used in the same sentence before.

"And the ring?" she replied.

He looked away, then back at her. "It's worth $30, maybe $40, and the chains another $30. That's all."

"Forty plus thirty is seventy, if I remember my numbers right, but I think your little machine just told you that that's a diamond. And I need at least one-fifty for a real diamond… plus fifty for the chains. And what about the rest of it?"

He snorted a laugh.

"You can take all of this junk and throw it in the trash for all I care," he said, pointing to the pile on the right. "And I have bags of these chains I can't even sell. I just mail it all off to Texas for scrap. Fifty is all I can do."

She reached across the desk and picked up the ring, but he snatched it out of her hand.

She just looked at him.

Now he was telegraphing his intentions loud and clear.

"A hundred for the ring and thirty for the chains," she replied.

He pursed his lips, and his eye twitched as he scratched at the corner of his desk.

In his early days, he had learned the trick of showing someone the cash. People have a hard time saying no to a stack of green dollar bills, even if the quantity is far lower than it should be.

"Seventy for the ring, you keep the chains, and I don't call the cops," he told her, sliding everything back across the desk except for the ring.

She took a deep breath.

She wanted to walk, but the seventy dollars lying in front of her wouldn't let her. It was enough to keep her fed for at least a month, but it wasn't enough to get her car running again; it wasn't enough to get her on the road and back to what she had set out to do.

She fingered the watch still in her pocket.

If she could clear two hundred bucks, she was pretty sure she could get Clifford fixed, have a decent meal and get back on the road. Maybe just maybe, the watch would let her do that. Only, it was real, and it mattered to someone. It wasn't like stealing a candy bar or some food from the diner. This mattered. This really mattered. This was a Savannah moment. A moment of change that would either let her get back to her life or damage it beyond repair. She thought that if she could get two hundred for the watch, it would help, but that tiny voice rooted deep down at the bottom of who she was told her that it wouldn't help her at all. It told her this might be what pushed her over the edge.

Suddenly Johnny shook his head and said, "You know what, never mind. I don't think this ring is worth another police visit."

This was just another negotiation tactic. He wanted the ring and was gambling on her wanting the cash more than she was willing to walk away.

"Wait," she said. "There's something else."

He raised an eyebrow. Something else? What something else?

She set the watch on the desk in front of him.

He swallowed hard and set the diamond tester aside.

He wasn't watching her anymore. He was now completely

distracted by this something else. This was something else indeed.

He picked it up, cleaned the face with a small cloth, and held it up underneath the light. He had seen a watch like this just a few hours ago; only this one was a lady's Rolex. It must have been a matching set.

Family jewelry, huh? He thought to himself, but all that was aside now, and he didn't want this one to walk out the front door as the last one had. A fast $4,000 or slow $5,000, he remembered telling himself when the first one had stepped into his little shop on the corner, but he hadn't been able to take his mind off that watch all night. He kicked himself for not offering more money once a little online research showed him that a Rolex just like this one, and without as nice of a band, had sold at auction at Christie's in New York two months earlier for $18,700. And that wasn't a pair. This pair had to be worth close enough to $50,000 that it was worth a try.

A pair like this was a unicorn. A pair like this was precisely the kind of treasure he was looking for.

The idea of selling the pair etched itself like an oubliette in his mind. He wasn't holding the pair, but if he could get this one, maybe the other would come walking back through his door one day.

He turned the watch over and read the back. "La Chaim," he whispered.

The girl's ears perked up.

"Do you know what these words mean?" he absently asked her, not taking his eyes off of the letters perfectly etched in a half circle around the top of the watch back. And without waiting for a response, he answered his own question. "La

Chaim is To Life in Yiddish," he told her.

Reading the words changed his mood, his demeanor, his entire attitude. He had gone from a hard-balling street hustler to someone who might, with a little soap, resemble something that looked like a human being.

Those words pulled him back in time to when he was a little boy sitting next to his pot-bellied father hunched over a workbench where those Yiddish words, also known as Hebrew, were etched in a plack on the wall above him. "Precision is the handiwork of Yahweh," he remembered his father saying, magnifying lenses over his eyes, a precision screwdriver in one hand, and a watch, or maybe a bracelet in the other.

The young woman was sure she could get at least two hundred for the watch now, but before she could start negotiating again, he slowly reached into the second drawer, pulled out a stack of hundred-dollar bills folded in half, and held together with a rubber band.

Her eyes grew.

He pulled the band back onto his wrist and counted off ten bills that he laid out, one by one, in front of her. Then he refolded the stack, put the band back onto the bills, and dropped the pile into the drawer.

"That's my best and final offer," he said, with his voice still lower and softer than it had been when he flicked the cigarette at her and laid his hands on her face.

She felt herself not breathing. A thousand dollars. Cash money. Right here in front of her. All she had to do was pick it up and walk away. So that's what she did. She folded the notes into the pocket of her hood and stood up.

"Pull the door shut behind ya' would ya'. Sometimes it sticks.

And if I ever see you again, I'm callin' the cops," he said, never taking his eyes off the watch.

Her walk back to Clifford was probably the loneliest she had ever felt. She felt manipulated by the world into doing things that made her hate herself—assaulted by Johnny putting his hands on her face. Tired—so tired she struggled to remember what street she had parked on. Hungry—she hadn't had time to eat any of the groceries she had bought earlier. And scared—always scared, never not scared.

She wasn't just someone trying to survive now; she had become a villain.

The guilt followed her down the street like an unseen monster with pointed ears and pock-marked skin, taunting her from the shadows and cursing her for her foolishness. It reminded her of how she had lied to herself, telling herself that she would one day pay back all the things she had stolen. It told her how ridiculous of an idea it was that she would ever get back to that life she knew before her mother left. She thought she should be crying, but she was just numb.

Even though she now had enough cash to get back on her feet, every single one of the bills she carried in her pocket felt filthy, like she was pregnant with some sort of hideous mutation of a Guilt baby.

Her guilt and deep sorrow for herself were momentarily dampened at the sight of Clifford still sitting under the broken street light across from the Blue Bonnet diner. She didn't bother looking through the diner windows to see who was on shift. She didn't care. She just took the key off the blue and white cotton thread around her wrist, jostled the passenger handle, and climbed into the back where she pushed off her shoes with her toes, set them in the corner, and flipped a tiny switch on a transparent square device the size of a matchbox. A string of white fairy lights flicked on and gently lit this private space she had made for herself. Her own little Holy of Holies. Photos of her and her mother were taped to the walls. She dropped onto the blanket and pillow and rolled onto her back.

When she had first moved into Clifford as a younger girl, she had been short enough to stretch her legs out when she slept, but now she had to sleep with her knees slightly bent.

She took the money out of her pocket and let it splay out on the floor next to her. Then she looked up at a photo of her mother, young and healthy, who smiled back down at her from the ceiling, and Savannah started to weep. Her mother wore a light blue dress on a beach somewhere, with the white foam of waves cresting at her feet. A small turtle pendant hung from her neck with a mother-of-pearl shell on a thin gold chain.

Savannah reached up and touched that same chain the way she did every night to comfort herself to sleep, only now, there was no chain around her neck. She fumbled nervously around her hair and the collar of her sweatshirt but couldn't find it. She sat up and franticly searched her blankets, her pillow, and underneath her backpack. Then she spun open the purple lock on her bag and dumped the contents onto the floor of the car, but it wasn't there. *The necklace has to be here somewhere!* She crawled up to the front seats searching around the floor with her hands, but the turtle pendant was nowhere to be found. She stumbled and fell out of the car onto the sidewalk and looked around beneath Clifford, desperate to find it. She pulled her hair back and rubbed her face with both hands while Guilt mocked her and mocked her, taunting her that this was only the beginning of her getting what she deserved.

She leaned her back against the car, slid to the ground, and sobbed so hard she dry-heaved onto the curb. After all, she had nothing in her stomach to throw up.

Chapter Fourteen

Unprocessed grief is like an unfinished sentence in the story of our life, always forcing us to question whether the person we love is really gone.

Marvin now existed between two realities: One where he would help Margaret out of bed to begin their morning ritual and another where he was alone. This left him in what felt like a waking dream. He knew she was dead, but his body didn't know she was dead. His quiet unspoken self wasn't ready to let her go, which his logical self knew would quickly become a problem, but he didn't know how to bring those two divergent realities into focus. Not yet.

Marvin sat in the plush chair in the corner of Ellie's bedroom, wondering where the small boy had gone.

He took a deep breath, rubbed his face with both hands, and stood to look for him. He had forgotten about the gun until the weight of it pulled at his pocket and reminded him of everything that had happened the night before.

The living room and kitchen were empty and quiet, and the front door was locked and bolted from the inside.

He walked down the hall to the bathroom and saw the blood, now dry on the tile floor and small carpets, but no child. Then he went into his and Margaret's bedroom.

There in the glow of morning light, the boy stood next to Margaret's body holding her hand with a look of gentle concern like he had known her personally.

"Don't! She's ..." Marvin began to say, but he couldn't finish, his throat closed and his mouth went dry.

The boy looked at Marvin and saw the sorrow on his face, then turned back to Margaret and laid his hand on her forehead. "She's just sleeping," the boy said with a tenderness that gave Marvin pause. These were the first words Marvin had heard the boy speak, and a sense of total calm filled the room. This child was a stranger in Marvin's home, but he didn't feel like a stranger at all. Something in the way the boy touched her comforted Marvin, like the tender caress of a father or long-time friend.

"I'm afraid she's dead," Marvin said, wiping a tear from his cheek with the back of his hand. And just like that, he said it: She's dead. Something about giving words to his pain somehow released it. It hadn't gone away, not entirely. It had just decreased in pressure enough that he straightened his back and, for the first time, could see past it, if only for the briefest of moments. His wife, best friend, lover, and reason for being was gone, and she was never coming back.

The boy turned to Marvin with sadness, but not for Margaret. "She's not gone forever. She's just sleeping," he said.

Tears streaked down Marvin's cheeks. "I wish it were true, but it just isn't." He took a deep breath. "She's dead, son."

The boy looked at Margaret again for another long moment, then left the bedroom.

Marvin stepped towards her and touched her hand. It was cold now and waxy. He really did need to call someone. He had kept telling himself that, but now he was finally beginning to accept it.

He stepped out into the hall and pulled the bedroom door closed behind him.

The child now sat in the plush chair in Ellie's room, legs pulled up to his chest, and Marvin stood in the doorway looking at him. What was he going to do with this child now? He'd tell the police about him. He didn't have a choice, but would they be able to help him? He hoped they would do the right thing, but the possibility of the child ending up back in the hands of whoever had done this to him was a horrible toothache of a thought he couldn't completely ignore. If he was going to call the police, he had work to do.

Marvin returned to the kitchen and found a small yellow bucket Margaret had kept for spot cleaning with a small red scrub brush. He filled it with a few splashes of whatever chemicals he could find underneath the sink and pulled on a pair of purple latex gloves. Marvin didn't know how to clean up blood, but he knew the water had to be cold. Why did he know that? He had no idea. Maybe Margaret had mentioned it to him once upon a lifetime.

He carried the bucket to the front door and looked outside. There was now no sign of blood down the sidewalk anymore. The rain must have offered him some measure of grace. So he turned to the entry, slowly got down on his hands and knees, and began scrubbing. Then Marvin lifted his head to see the boy stepping out of the kitchen with a dish brush. Marvin smiled, took off his gloves, and handed them to the child.

As the boy reached for the gloves, Marvin saw his hands again and slowly took the boy's hands in his own.

The child's hands lay small in Marvin's and looked so frail, so perfect, so unusual. The child had six beautiful fingers on each hand. *What a strange child*, Marvin thought to himself. He had heard of this before, but Marvin had never seen it for himself.

The child quietly watched as Marvin turned his hands over, examining them on both sides. Then Marvin gently brushed some hair away from the boy's eyebrow and lifted his chin. He couldn't be certain, but it looked like the child's puffy purple eye and swollen lip were already healing. Maybe the child's wounds weren't as bad as he remembered, or perhaps he hadn't seen them clearly enough in the evening light.

"I'm not sure these will fit you," Marvin said, picking up the gloves and handing them to the boy, who looked at them with curiosity and took one. At first, he slid a glove on backward, but Marvin corrected him with a soft smile and helped him. Each of the fingers bent in half, being too large for the boy's hand. This made the boy giggle as he fluttered his fingers up and down, causing the ends of the purple fingers to dance about like tiny worms. The gloves were so large that all the boy had to do was tuck his sixth finger into the side. Then he awkwardly picked up the dish brush, dipped it into the soapy water, and held it up to Marvin with a smile.

The boy's laugh comforted Marvin again.

As Marvin and the boy spent the next couple of hours cleaning, Marvin kept questioning where the boy had come from, who he was and what had happened to him, but every time he asked a question, the child simply ignored him, so Marvin decided not to push. Maybe the boy couldn't even remember. Marvin had heard how sometimes trauma could be so bad that the mind just completely blocks it out. So instead of talking, they quietly scrubbed the entry floor clean, rolled up the carpet runner in the hall into a black trash bag, and completely scrubbed down the bathroom until Marvin's hands ached from the cold water and his numb fingers.

As Marvin sat at the kitchen table resting, trying to figure out how they might get the living room chair out of the apartment and into the dumpster in the alley without everyone in the neighborhood seeing the bloody mess, there was suddenly a hard three knocks at the front door.

Marvin stood, peeled back the purple gloves, and draped them on the edge of the yellow bucket, now sitting in the kitchen sink.

He glanced around the apartment for the boy as he walked to the front door but didn't see him. Perhaps he had returned to Ellie's room to lie down.

Marvin opened the door a small distance to find a police officer and two EMTs standing on his front porch. Both of the EMTs carried large orange duffle bags over their shoulders.

"Good morning sir," the officer said. "We got a call that someone might be hurt at this residence. Do you mind if we come in?"

The blood-covered chair sat in his living room, and Marvin still had a loaded and illegally acquired pistol in his pocket. He swallowed and put on his best gentle grandfather smile. "Yes of course, just a moment," and he closed the door without giving the officer a chance to respond. He leaned against the inside of his front door.

What am I going to do NOW?!, he wondered to himself and quickly tried to find some way to move or hide the blood-stained chair sitting in the middle of his living room. And where was the boy?

He quickly went to the kitchen, poured the bucket of dark-red water down the drain, trying to carefully but quickly not spill anything onto the sides of the sink, and shoved the bucket and brushes into a pantry. He then went to his bedroom, took a folded sheet with a dark floral pattern out to the living room, and tucked it around the bloody chair, hoping it would look enough like a chair cover to pass suspicion. And all the while, Marvin kept peeking into each of the rooms, trying to find the boy, but he couldn't find him anywhere. "Child! Where did you go?" he whispered, leaning into Ellie's room, but there was no sign of him in there either.

He was worried the officer and EMTs would start to get suspicious if they waited any longer, so he gave up looking for the child and returned to the front door.

He paused to take a breath, put on his best smile, then opened the door. "Please come in."

The officer and EMTs looked at each other, stepped inside, and the officer scanned around the entry. "Is anyone in the apartment hurt?" a muscular young man asked, who was in his twenties and wore a blue cap with the letters EMT embroidered in red metallic thread.

Marvin sighed. "Yes. But there is no emergency. I came home last night and found my wife in front of the television. She had passed on while I was out having a bit of dinner."

The EMTs looked at each other. "And where is she?" he asked.

"Just this way," Marvin replied, leading them down the hall to where Margaret lay.

The officer stood in the hall outside the bedroom while both EMTs quickly knelt over her, the muscular one checking her pulse while the second one, a young woman with long brown hair, set her bag down and took out a clipboard.

"What time did you find her?" she asked.

"Oh, probably 'round 8, 8:30."

The officer took out his pad and flipped it open. "We didn't get a call until 10:23."

"And you were so quick to get here," Marvin retorted.

The officer pursed his lips, looking into the small room and back at Marvin.

"There was no indication from dispatch that anyone was in any sort of critical danger. If you had found her at around 8, why did you wait to call?"

Marvin found this odd. He didn't remember calling the police at all, but they were here, so he must have. But why would he have told them that someone was hurt and not dead? "Can I be honest with you, officer?"

The officer crossed his arms and leaned forward. "Of course."

"I can't remember," Marvin said.

Sensing Marvin's confusion, the officer asked: "Sir, are you alright?" Then he reached over and touched the side of Marvin's cheek. "He has blood here," he said into the bedroom, and the female EMT looked up from her clipboard and came over to Marvin.

"May I?" she asked.

But Marvin pulled away. "I think I just scratched myself moving her," he said, suddenly realizing that he still had some of the child's blood on him. "I really am fine."

The officer and female EMT looked at each other, and the officer nodded, so the EMT returned to Margaret. "Is there anything you can do for her?" the officer asked through the door.

The EMT shook his head. "She's been gone for at least a

few hours. Maybe more."

The officer paused, looked at Marvin, then back at the EMTs. "Do you see any sign of foul play?"

The male EMT stood and shook his head. "That's for the coroner to say for sure, but none that I can tell. It looks like she died in her sleep, possibly cardiac. No way to tell from where I'm standing."

The officer nodded and turned back to Marvin.

"Sir. I need to ask you some questions. Can we sit somewhere?"

Marvin could feel the heavy pistol cold against his leg and thought about the chair in the living room and the young boy missing somewhere in the apartment.

"Of course," Marvin replied and led the officer out to the small kitchen table. "Can I get you a cup of coffee or tea?" he asked, actually wanting to move the officer along but not wanting to look or sound like he wanted to move him along.

"No, thank you," the officer replied, sitting down at the table.

"Well, don't mind if I put the kettle on for myself," he said, then turned back to the officer and sat down.

"Why don't you tell me what happened last night, from the beginning," the officer asked as he flipped his notepad open and clicked his pen.

As Marvin rubbed his head, trying hard to remember anything about calling the police, he became transfixed on the officer's polished brass badge.

Chapter Fifteen

What had happened? Marvin wondered, as he sat in the dust of the old country road, waiting for the approaching car to either help him or finish him for good. He tightly held Moses' lifeless body close to his chest, not wanting to lay him on the road. His legs burned and his body shuddered from the growing cold as the sun slowly sat across the distant horizon behind him.

His mind raced, trying to understand what had happened. Had Moses waited for him as long as he could and drowned? Had the boys found him? Had they pelted his little body with rocks until they knocked him from the platform and left him for dead? Marvin didn't know. But somehow, and from somewhere, the tears that had already dried up began flowing again.

A green Chevy pickup pulled to a stop in front of Marvin, and some part of him wondered if it might be one of those boys, or maybe all three of them, or maybe a hundred of them, pouring out of the truck like a swarm of hornets coming to finish him off, but the man who quickly climbed out was someone Marvin recognized as working with his father.

Marvin couldn't remember much about what happened next except that he wouldn't let the man take Moses' body from him. Instead, the man wrapped them both in some wool blankets from the back of his truck, and rushed them to Marvin's home, where Marvin watched his mother and father come running out of the house as the truck drove down their country lane.

While Marvin could never remember what anyone said, he always remembered how that night would be the only time he would ever see his big bear of a father weep like a small child.

As the night stretched on, Marvin sat numb in his bed, watching his mother rock his brother's lifeless body and sing to him the lullabies he always needed to fall asleep.

They had tried to get Marvin to tell them what had happened, but he didn't have the strength to say a single word. Not even when his father threatened to whoop the skin off his backside if he didn't tell them what had happened, he just didn't have the strength to care. They could have choked him to death with their bare hands, and he wouldn't have cared a single lick. All the care he had in him died that night with his brother.

And just as his father was about to start to fulfill his threats, his mother pulled him off of Marvin, saying that she couldn't tolerate any more violence on a night like this. So, his father, slumped and humbled, wrapped Marvin in blankets and let him be.

Then there were three loud knocks on the cottage door.

Marvin looked out the window next to his bed, which had been slightly propped open to let in some of the night air, and saw two sheriffs standing on their porch.

From where they stood in the porch light, they could not

see Marvin watching them from the dark of his bedroom.

Then Marvin's father opened the front door. "Yes, sir." His father said, filling the doorway to the small home with his bulky size.

"We got a report that your boys were down by Mason's pond this afternoon. Is that right?"

Marvin's mother continued rocking his brother by the fire, moaning this deep wordless moan only a mother could make. First cursing God, then praying to Him, and finally dedicating Moses' tiny soul into the hands of her almighty savior. All the while, never letting him go. Even when his father tried to take the body from her, she just shrieked at him shaking violently until his fearful father stepped away and let her be. Now, as the two sheriffs stepped past his father without an invitation, she paid them no mind.

"What of it?" Marvin's father asked.

The older of the two sheriffs put his hand on the pistol that hung at his side. "The Johnson boys said your boys were swimming at Mason's pond, and you know they can't do that."

"Did they tell you they did this?" his father asked, holding open a hand to the dead child.

The younger of the two sheriffs took off his hat.

"So, your boys were down there," the older one asked again.

"Are you telling me that my boy is lying dead and cold in his mother's arms, and all you care about is whether they were swimmin'?"

The older sheriff clenched his jaw, then held a gloved finger up to Marvin's father.

"If they hadn't gone where they wasn't supposed to be, maybe this wouldna' happened. And you should watch your tongue boy, or there might be more accidents 'round here."

The towering farmer took a step forward, and the sheriff took a step back. The younger sheriff, quickly put one hand on his partner's shoulder and the other on his revolver. "I think he answered our question. Maybe we should leave them be," the younger man said. Then he put his hat back on and went outside.

The older sheriff glared at Marvin's father for another moment, looked at the small child still lying in his mother's arms who hadn't even opened her eyes to acknowledge the men when they came in but just kept lowly and slowly singing to her baby. Then the older sheriff left, and Marvin's father closed the door behind them.

Marvin turned and watched the two men on his porch, transfixed on their shining brass badges and low-hanging batons.

"I'll call on the Johnson boys in the morning and ask some questions," the younger of the two said.

The older man sucked a gob of snot out of his nose and spit the green lump onto the porch floor as he walked over to a quilt Marvin's mother had spent weeks sewing that now hung on the porch railing. "Don't bother," he said. "One less nuisance to worry about."

He then used the edge of the quilt to dig a piece of mud off of the heel of his boot before walking back to his truck.

Chapter Sixteen

The police officer repeated his question: "Does anyone else live here with you?"

A long stray thread hung from the right shoulder of his uniform that Marvin desperately wanted to reach up and pluck. Then he glanced at the backdoor and realized it was slightly ajar.

Marvin rubbed his hands together, trying to stop them from shaking and drank the last swallow of his tea.

The officer had been dotting him with questions for fifteen or twenty minutes, and the EMTs had since left with Margaret's lifeless shape beneath draping fabric on a gurney.

"Not anymore," Marvin replied.

"What about family? Do you have anyone you can call?" the officer asked.

Marvin shook his head.

The officer reached up and touched the spot of blood on Marvin's neck. "Are you sure this wasn't from you?"

"No. I'm fine," he replied, touching the spot and looking at his hand.

"I'm going to have a social worker call in on you. Just to see how you're doing," the officer said.

Marvin looked at a small clump of mud on the side of the officer's left shoe.

"We don't wear shoes in the house," Marvin quietly told him.

"Excuse me?"

Marvin looked up at him. "I said, guests who are polite, take their shoes off when they enter our home. And you've tracked mud into my kitchen."

The well-built man, in his fifties with a slight dusting of grey hair, looked down at the floor between his feet and saw a small brown smear on the green tile. Then he reached down, untied his polished black shoes and took them off. He then used a folded paper napkin from the table to carefully wipe up the mud. "I apologize, Mr. Johnson. I didn't mean any disrespect. I can't imagine your loss."

"No, I don't reckon you can."

"But it sounds like you're alone and could use some help." The officer paused. "Have you thought about a facility? Somewhere where you..."

Marvin interrupted him. "Now, you can stop right there. No one ever called on us to help us all these years I was feedin' and clothin' my invalid wife!"

The officer held up a hand. "Maybe someone should have."

"Get out," Marvin said, pointing a shaking finger past the officer to the front door.

The officer took a breath and rose. He picked up his shoes and carried them to the entry. "You can expect a call in a few days, and you can decide with them if you should stay here alone or find a better place," the officer said as he took a business card out of his buttoned shirt pocket and handed it to Marvin.

Marvin plucked it with contempt from the officer's fingers and closed the door behind him. Then he leaned against the small entry table and dropped the navy-blue card into a dish. The possibility of having to leave his home was too much. His chest tightened, and he wrung his hands together, trying to get them to stop shaking.

He returned to his bedroom where blankets and pillows lay scattered across the now empty bed and stood in the doorway of what felt like someone else's room. He remembered how Margaret used to kick one foot out from beneath the covers when she got too hot at night.

Why do I feel like this is only the beginning of all this craziness? He asked himself. Then he returned to the kitchen, where the back door stood slightly ajar. He had an idea of where the boy might have gone.

Marvin then took the small turtle pendant with the mother-of-pearl shell out of his pocket and considered where it might have come from.

He looked up at the phone. Then he turned and looked down the hall and into the bedroom where the broken jewelry box sat on the dresser.

Someone must have been in the apartment, but when? The officer had said that a young woman had called 9-1-1 around 10:23 last night; he was either at the pawnshop or had just gotten home. Had someone seen the trail of blood out front after all? She had said she lived next door. Maybe it was one of his neighbors, but when had she come inside his house?

He returned to the jewelry box and opened it. It was empty. He searched through the dresser's top drawer but didn't find what he was looking for, so he got down on his hands and knees and looked around on the floor beneath the furniture.

Where is Margaret's watch? he wondered.

He squeezed the turtle pendant in his fist with frustration, and his hands shook again. *Strangers in my home. This is what happens when I let strangers into my home,* he thought.

He sighed and looked down at the small piece of jewelry with its thin chain draping between his fingers and had an idea.

But first, the boy.

He set the pendant aside and filled the tin kettle sitting on his kitchen counter with water as his hands shook so violently that he splashed water onto the stove. He tried to steady himself as he took a thermos from the pantry and poured in two packets of Swiss Miss hot chocolate with marshmallows, sending a little puff of chocolate powder into the air. *Every child loves hot cocoa,* he told himself.

Then he paused for a moment and rubbed his hands together again, trying to calm the fear and frustration he felt rising inside him from all those strange people coming into his home.

Why had they torn her blouse like that? They could tell she was gone. And why did they have to move the furniture? He shuddered and leaned against the sink. A stress headache throbbed at the back of his head.

No one other than Margaret and him had crossed his threshold in more than a decade, and now three strangers, a small child, and perhaps someone else had invaded his privacy, moved his things, muddied his floor, and possibly stole his wife's jewelry.

Marvin leaned against the refrigerator as his vision shifted slightly, and his mouth went dry. He rubbed the back of his neck, trying to calm himself, but it wasn't working.

His breathing picked up, and his heart began to race. The sense of losing control, being violated—Margaret being violated clouded his mind. He was having a panic attack.

He sat at the kitchen table and put his head between his knees, trying to catch his breath. A bead of sweat rolled down his forehead, and he sat back and began counting. One. Two. Three. Breathe. One. Two. Three. Breathe. He rubbed the tips of his fingers together but couldn't feel them. Should he call someone? No. There had already been too many people in the house. He just needed to find his way through.

He opened a cabinet above the stove where a dozen little orange bottles sat with various white labels, but he couldn't read any of them. He picked up the first one as the room shifted around him, then the second. His shaking hand swept several off the shelf that bounced onto the floor and into the sink. He squeezed his eyes shut, trying to focus his vision, but the print was too small. *Why is the print SO small on these things?* He grabbed as many little bottles as he could and sat back down at the table where a pair of reading glasses lay that he often used for the morning newspaper.

Wearing the glasses, he finally found the bottle marked Clorazepate, pushed off the lid and dry swallowed two pink triangular pills. Then he started counting again. After what must have been more than ten minutes, the sight of the Swiss Miss hot chocolate packets torn open and lying on his counter came back into focus. His breathing had slowed, and he rose for a paper towel to wipe his forehead and face. He was sweating like he had just run a marathon.

He picked up the thermos and smelled the chocolate powder, which centered him. The sweet smell made him smile and brought him back to a cold Saturday afternoon in November when Margaret, Ellie, and he packed up some blankets and hot cocoa in the same thermos and walked out to the playground on the North corner of the park across the street. He and Margaret had been whispering about a certain someone's ninth birthday party while Ellie pushed a small tuft of snow off of the swing and launched herself forward like an airplane, with arms outstretched.

He wanted to stay in that memory, stay there with Margaret, so beautiful with the afternoon sunlight on her hair and the sound of Ellie's laughter dancing around the playground. An afternoon he had come back to so many times in his mind as his perfect day, a trick his therapist had taught him just after Ellie's death.

But then another thought wedged its way in. A thought he hadn't entertained in many years: *Maybe he was in the park that day. Maybe that was the day he first saw her*, that nameless he who would take their daughter away from them less than three weeks later.

Marvin shook his head and pushed the questions away; questions that had awoken him in pools of sweat countless times those first weeks and months; questions that nearly tore his and Margaret's marriage apart until...

The kettle whistled.

He poured steaming water onto the pile of chocolate powder, screwed the cap, and shook the long grey cylinder back and forth.

He then draped a green wool blanket over his arm and carried the thermos of cocoa up the metal fire steps, zig-zagging past the second and third floors to the roof, stopping halfway to take in heavy breaths that burned the back of his throat in the morning air. He couldn't remember the last time he had climbed these steps, and now he remembered why.

Ms. Phipps, his second-floor neighbor, often left out pots of lavender on the fire escape, their fragrance uplifting him in spring and early summer, but she had already taken them in for the season.

He unlocked a heavy metal gate at the top of the fire escape with a large rusting key, now many years unused, and thought that a healthy boy of seven or eight would probably be able to climb the gate if he wanted to. He wasn't certain the child would be up here, but there was nowhere else for him to go. He figured that either the child was on the roof or gone for good, and when he saw the back door standing slightly ajar, he decided this was as likely as not.

Ventilation piping twisted around one side of the roof and a wood-frame greenhouse stood on the other, with clear plastic panels protecting rows of old clay pots that now held nothing but dry and weeping vines of dead vegetables. Toward the front of the building, looking out over the park, were raised flower beds long dry and forgotten, and in the center of the flowerbeds sat an old cast iron bench with peeling red paint. This is where Marvin found the young boy leaning forward on his knees and looking out over the street below to the beautiful park turning golden in the autumn air. There was Frog Pond, where children kept cool in summer, a large gazebo in the center of the park, and of course, Tadpole Playground, where he, Margaret, and Ellie would often walk in the afternoons.

He took the wool blanket from his arm and draped it over the young boy's shoulders as he noticed a small bunch of purple-blue Mountain Cornflowers breaking through the dry soil of one of the flower beds with their fingerlike petals and silver-green leaves. These were Margaret's favorite flowers.

How odd they should be growing this time of year, he thought to himself as he sat down beside the boy with great effort.

Even though his knees burned and his lower back ached from the climb, the fresh air cleared his mind. This had once been Margaret's private sanctum from the busy city, now forgotten and lifeless except for this small bunch of spider-like flowers reaching for the morning light.

"I thought you might be up here," Marvin said quietly, hushed by the stillness of the morning. "I brought you a blanket to warm your shoulders and something sweet to warm you from the inside." And he poured a steaming stream of brown liquid into the thermos lid and handed it to the boy, who took the red plastic top that doubled as a drinking cup and smelled the hot beverage. His eyes closed, and he smiled at the sweet chocolaty smell.

"Every child loves hot cocoa," Marvin remarked, setting the cylinder down beside the leg of the bench. "What I don't know is how you knew about this place," Marvin said, watching the boy drink back the entire cup and handing the lid to Marvin, a liquid-brown half-moon cresting his lips.

"I'd like some more, please," the boy said, smiling at him.

"Oh, I bet you would." And Marvin reached back down and filled the cup a second time and a second time handed it back to the boy.

The boy started to drink but stopped. He looked at Marvin and reached the cup out to him. "You have this one."

"No, that's alright," he said, holding up a hand and gently pushing it back. "I prefer tea. Always have. And I've had my morning cup already. You go on and enjoy that now. It should help warm you up just fine."

The boy smiled again, holding the cup to his lips with both

hands and taking another drink.

Some of the young boy's mannerisms were so much like Ellie's that it made Marvin's heart just hurt being near him, and so much like someone else's who he hadn't thought about for a long, long time. Then he realized that the bruising around the boy's eye and lip was gone, and Marvin gently touched the back of the boy's neck, which had been so severely scratched just hours earlier. Now all Marvin could find was fresh, soft skin, pale as cream.

"The police just left. You should have gone with them," Marvin said.

The boy looked at him. "I want to stay with you."

Marvin chuckled. "You can't. I'm an old man and you're just a child. Besides, they won't just let you stay with me. Someone's going to come looking for you."

The boy pulled his legs up to his chest, and Marvin could see that this made the boy confused and uncomfortable.

"Did someone hurt you, son?" Marvin asked slowly, but the boy didn't answer.

"The police will take care of you. They have people who do this sort of thing. They can look after you, give you a place to stay, and even find your parents."

"I want to stay with you," the boy said in nearly a whine, pulling his legs tighter to his chest.

Marvin nodded in understanding. "What's your name, son?"

"Michael."

"Michael. Well, that's a start at least," Marvin sighed. "Do you live 'round here?"

Michael didn't answer.

Marvin sighed again and looked out across the park.

A homeless man and woman sat huddled together on a

bench, eating some form of breakfast out of a crumpled white wrapper.

"Well, I ain't goin' to kick you out on the street, but you can't stay here for long. Someone's going to come lookin' for you, and if they find out you were with me for very long, I figure they'll think I was trying to keep you against your will. And you know what they call that?"

The boy shook his head.

"They call that kidnapping. And kidnapping gets you put away for a long time. And I don't know if you noticed, but time ain't somethin' I got a lot of these days."

The boy leaned in to Marvin's shoulder.

"Why were you so sad last night," Michael asked.

Marvin took a deep breath. "I was sad because my wife died. Someone I love very much."

"But you're not alone. You have me. Besides, you'll see her again."

Marvin glanced at the boy. What a peculiar comment from such a small child, he thought to himself.

"I used to believe that, but I don't anymore. Now I figure, when we die, that's it. We're gone. Whatever it is that makes us who we are just falls asleep and never wakes up again, like candlelight snuffed out. I think maybe that's why I'm so sad—maybe why I've been so sad for so long. Because I can't quite understand how someone as unique and beautiful in all the world could just disappear, never to be seen again or heard again or kissed or loved again. They're just gone."

The boy sat up and looked at him. "But you're different than candlelight. Fire has no control; it just burns. It's a force, like the wind. You have a choice. You remember your wife even after she is gone. You love and laugh and cry. You know you exist. Or do you think that you just blinked into being from nowhere?"

Marvin thought about what the child was saying, then replied: "Animals laugh and cry. Elephants in Africa will mourn their dead."

The boy leaned against him again. "Animals can feel. But none of them have ever stopped to consider right and wrong. They're also driven by hunger and comfort and a need to survive. The lion does not stop to consider whether it should eat the zebra. "Should" is a question planted into the heart of men by God. It is His voice trying to gently guide you to a life of peace."

"This sure is some big thinking for someone your age," Marvin said, looking down at Michael. "Did your father teach you that?"

"Yes," Michael replied.

Then they sat together quietly for some time as the morning slowly warmed with the rising sun.

Marvin looked at the Mountain Cornflowers standing so full of color and full of life, amazed that they weren't as dead as everything else up here.

"Those used to be Margie's favorite. She said they always reminded her of her daddy's farm where she grew up. You plant them, they grow, and then they die. Now they're here, and she's gone. She planted this garden after my little girl died, just to give her hands somethin' to do," Marvin said, calmly and quietly, looking out over the park, remembering.

"She'd be up here every morning after the washing up, just planting and pruning and watering. I think it gave her something to focus on. She found a way to put her pain into this garden. Something I wish I could have done. Instead, I just got angry."

"Angry at who?" Michael asked.

Marvin grunted. "Everyone. Angry at myself for not being home when my little girl was taken from me. Angry at Margie for *being* home. Angry at the police for not finding…." His voice quivered, and he could feel anger and sorrow rising to the surface. "Not finding who killed my little girl right in front of my house. Angry at God for letting it happen."

"I'm sorry you felt so alone," Michael said mournfully.

"I dedicated my entire life to that old fairy tale, and I needed God then more than ever. I called out to Him. I begged him to give me my little girl back. But all I got was cold silence. That's when I *knew* for sure He couldn't be real. If I wouldn't have let that happen to my beautiful and perfect little girl, no way could a loving God let that happen." Marvin shook his head. "When I was a child, I thought as a child, I spoke as a child, I understood as a child, but when I became a man, I put away childish things."

"For now, we see things dimly as though through a faded glass, but then we will see things clearly," the child replied, finishing Marvin's verse from Corinthians. "You needed God not to exist so that you could go on living?"

Marvin didn't respond for a long while, rolling the question around in his mind like a piece of hard candy. "I guess I did."

Chapter Seventeen

Officer Peter Stevens strained under the cold aluminum bar as he focused on keeping his elbows square and breathed out as he pushed the bar up above him, lowered it down until it just touched his chest and pushed it up again. His arms shook as he exhaled and felt his eyes burn from sweat as he leaned the bar back slightly and into the weight rack above him. He sat up from his last set of bench presses and wiped his forehead with a towel. He looked at himself in the mirror on the wall across the gym and flexed. Tight rope-like muscle bulged beneath his skin and a webbing of veins rose. He let out a heavy sigh and picked up his phone. It was not quite 6 a.m. He still had a little more than three hours before the tow truck was supposed to arrive to impound the waitress's car, and he thought that being there to help her get her car back and let her off with a warning would be an excellent opportunity to talk to her again. Maybe she'd even feel a little ingratiated to him.

He clicked on his phone and looked at a photo of her he had taken from across the street at the diner. It was blurry, but it was the best he had of the dozen or so he had taken.

He rose from the black padded bench, took a white spray

bottle from a shelf next to a roll of paper towels, and carefully cleaned the bench, bar and weights even though he was the only one who ever used the equipment in this tiny private gym setup in his basement. Then he sprinted up the steps to the main floor of his townhome.

While he showered, he imagined what he might say to her. He'd show her the small tag that he knew she had stolen from someone, let her know that it was a class one misdemeanor that carried a fine of $5,000 and up to eighteen months in jail, but that he would, of course, be more than happy to let her off with a warning if she'd have coffee with him or even lunch. He could get in trouble for that "if." Was there a way he could imply the coffee without actually saying it? She probably wouldn't report him, but she had already turned him down, which made him scrub his fingernails faster as he thought about it. The water pouring over him was so hot it made his skin bright red, and steam filled the white-tiled bathroom until he could barely see his way to his towel.

"Maybe I could let you off with a warning *this* time." Yes. He liked that. He wasn't offering her a tit-for-tat trade, but she should get the message if she had any sense, though he thought women often didn't.

He cracked his bathroom door open to let the steam out, wiped the fog from off his mirror and took a twelve-inch metal ruler out of his medicine cabinet along with a razor and comb. He lined the items up very carefully, piece by piece, next to the sink in order of how he would use them.

Once he finished shaving and wiping the remaining foam from his face, he lifted the small black comb and began parting his blonde hair that he spent $150 having cut every two weeks on Thursday afternoons without fail.

He looked at himself in the mirror and remembered the first time his father taught him to comb his hair properly. It was the morning after his seventh birthday, and he, his mother, and his father were preparing for church when his father, Justice Marshal Stevens, a county judge, stepped into their bathroom.

"Go get the ruler from my desk," his father told him, and Peter complied. The ruler was exactly like the one that now lay on the sink basin waiting for its turn. It was a heavy steel engineer's ruler 1/16th inch thick with black etched markings and exacting corners and edges. It was the kind of tool, not used by common school boys, that his father had on the shelves of his study, along with tomes and volumes of Smyth County law and Virginia history.

His father laid the ruler on the edge of the sink. "Now, show me how you comb your hair."

Peter tried to repeat what he thought he had seen his mother do many times before. He wet the comb and pulled the hair across his head to the left, looking at himself in the mirror this way and that until he thought that he had done a pretty good job smoothing out the bumps and lining up the part on his right side. Then he looked up at his father, with his long greying handlebar mustache and perfectly square tie.

His father lifted the ruler, laid the cold, sharp edge across Peter's part, then furrowed his brow and said, "Hold out your hand."

Peter wasn't sure what that meant, so he held out his hand, and without notice, his father slapped the palm of Peter's hand with the steel ruler so hard it sent the small boy onto the wood-planked floor between the sink screaming.

His father calmly waited the length of two deep breaths,

then said, "stand up." Peter took a minute before he did, but he knew not to keep his father waiting for long, so he slowly pulled himself up on the edge of the sink, wiped his red face with the sleeve of his shirt, and looked back at himself and his father in the mirror. His father sat the ruler on the edge of the sink, picked up the comb, and raked it across Peter's head with such force that Peter thought his scalp would bleed, until his hair lay in a piled mess on his forehead.

"Again," his father said, showing no emotion, anger, or sorrow at his son crying in front of him, no joy—nothing.

Peter's hand shook. He tried to pick up the comb with his left hand, but he couldn't properly guide the comb in the mirror without his dominant hand. He was still a bit confused about how to navigate the mirror's reflection anyways, so he shifted the comb to his right hand, nearly frozen from pain and starting to turn purple. With incredible effort, he pulled his hair across his head and slowly straightened up the part on his right side. He squeezed his eyes shut and took a breath as his father lifted the ruler and held it up to the part.

"Hold out your hand."

Peter's stomach turned with terror. He didn't want to hold out his hand, but worse would he get if he didn't. He knew that his father refused to suffer what he called "rebellion" more than anything else, and he might think that Peter was being defiant if he didn't hold out his hand, even though the cold sting of the steel across his palm was still fresh and bright.

"I'm sorry, daddy. Let me try again," Peter asked through streaming tears.

"Hold. Out. Your. Hand." His father said with greater emphasis.

Peter's whole body shook as he held out the hand that he

couldn't open all the way, but he didn't have to wait long before the sharp slap from the ruler burst across his palm and up his arm, igniting blisters of cold fire from the steel and sending the child into the fetal position in the corner of the bathroom wailing.

He didn't even hear his father the first time he told Peter to stand again, he was crying so hard. It wasn't until he heard the deep gravel of his father's voice quote Proverbs 29: "Discipline your son, and he will make you proud. Now stand up."

Peter looked up at the man now standing over him and saw him differently than he had seen him before. His father, before now, had let his mother "do the correcting," which was always in compassion and love, and always with a why; why he had to eat properly or why he had to wash behind his ears. But from this day on, it would be his father who would "Raise up the child."

"If I have to ask you again, I'll use my belt. And if that don't work, I'll use somethin' else," his father calmly warned.

Peter wanted to throw up. But the sheer terror of the warning lifted him to his feet.

Once again, his father raked the comb across his head, from front to back, pulling the blond hair into a pile as tears dripped from Peter's chin into the sink, but he didn't cry out again.

"Again," his father said.

Peter couldn't hold the comb in his right hand, so he did most of the work with the left, but slowly—trying to let his right hand come back to life enough to be useful. Then he took the comb between the middle and index fingers of his right hand, not being able to close his hand now, and as carefully as he could muster, finished smoothing down the bumps and straightening the part. This time, before his father could pick up the ruler, Peter took it in his left hand and laid it across his part, slightly adjusting it with the comb between his right fingers. Then, with a shaking hand, he handed the ruler to his father and looked at him with terror.

His father's mustache, yellow at the edges from chewing tobacco, twitched as he laid the ruler across the part himself.

"Now you know how to comb your hair," he said, handing the ruler back to Peter. "Now go put this back where you found it."

And Peter did.

That lesson left scars on Peter's hand that always reminded him of the importance of doing things correctly, and he took the ruler in his left hand, laid it over his part, and combed his blonde hair down with his right. Then he put each of the items back in their exact place in his medicine cabinet and went to get dressed.

A few minutes later, Peter stood in the kitchen, now in his navy-blue uniform, weighing out exactly seven ounces of oats, one tablespoon of vanilla protein powder, six blueberries, and one-half tablespoon of brown sugar into the Ninja blending machine sitting on his counter and pressed the screen of his phone again. He still had more than two hours before he planned on meeting Savannah, so he flipped open his officer's notebook and looked up the information that the dispatcher had given him when he ran the waitress's plates:

"1975, orange Gremlin hatchback, registered in Boston to a Susan Wilkins, age 47. Registration: expired. Request to move: outstanding, 9:30 a.m."

He opened his laptop and typed "Susan Wilkins" into the search engine. Dozens of results, some with photos, populated his screen. He looked back at his notes, then added "Boston" to the search query, and a middle-aged woman with black hair appeared before him, standing next to a younger version of the waitress. He clicked the link, a WhitePages.com entry, where her name was listed with a last known address and phone number. According to the website, Susan's last known address was an apartment building only twenty minutes North of Wakefield on I-95. He'd have time to drop by.

He wanted to cross-check the address with his dispatcher, but he had learned some time ago to do some things through unofficial channels since official channels were carefully tracked and traced.

Chapter Eighteen

Savannah felt the pieces of her life being pulled away, one thread at a time, forcing her to cling to the few strands of normalcy that remained.

She finished folding her blankets and carefully counted out the ten one-hundred-dollar bills, hiding this much cash in several places in case someone broke into her car. She slid two beneath the front seat, folded one into the front pocket of her backpack, put two in her pillowcase, and slipped the rest into a small hidden pocket of paper folded and glued into the back of her journal. Then she blew into her hands, trying to warm them enough to write, and opened to the last journal entry. $5.27 was written in the margin next to two sentences: "I got fired for missing the bus, and I only have $5 left. Savannah's winning."

She scratched a line through the $5.27 and wrote $1,000 with a purple gel pen and paused to let all those zeros sink in for just a moment. That was a lot of money.

She smiled. Money gave her options. Money gave her hope. Then she did some quick calculations. She would have enough to get Clifford fixed, fill him with gas, have a decent breakfast—one of the hot ones with eggs and bacon—and get back on the road to find her mom. She even had enough to get a hotel room for a couple of nights on the road. And that meant a shower. Her smile grew. She hadn't showered in over two weeks, and she stank. She knew it. She tried to keep herself as clean as possible as often as possible, but there was just no substitute to letting a waterfall of lavender oatmeal body wash pull the street down into the drain in a swirl of beautifully fragrant suds. She might even turn on a little jazz saxophone. Maybe John Coltrane or Charlie Parker. Her mother loved Charlie Parker and would often listen to him whenever she was in a good mood. The thought of all of this warmed her deep down.

I might just be alright, she thought to herself.

"I came into a little bit of money," she wrote. "I had to do something that I wasn't proud of, but there's no going back now. Today: Get Clifford fixed, eat breakfast, find my necklace, and GET OUT OF TOWN." She underlined those words in large letters three times.

Then she read the words she had written last night: "Savannah's winning." *"Maybe not,"* she thought and scratched a line through those two heavy words, which felt like some sort of small victory.

She flipped shut the purple book, slid it beneath the front seat, clambered out of the car, and stretched. She was hungry—always hungry. Even though the diner was next door, she wanted something more, so she locked the car door and started walking towards a French cafe and patisserie two blocks down, a beautiful white restaurant full of people in suits and dresses carrying bags with names like Louis Vuitton and Coach pressed into their leather.

Places like this were usually so expensive she simply ignored them, but not today. Today she had a few dollars to spend, and she wanted to remember how the other half lived.

She flipped open her small grey phone, called Mike, and reassured him that she not only had the money he needed to fix Clifford but that she wanted to pay him back for the other times he had helped her.

"Who'd you kill?" he asked her through what sounded like a pre-coffee haze.

She laughed, rose onto her tiptoes, and spun on the balls of her feet like a ballet dancer. She felt so much lighter this morning, so much happier. "Ah, Mikey, no one's dead." But she remembered someone had died, which flattened her spirits a bit but not by much. "I just came into a few bucks is all, and you always took care of me. Besides, I'm leaving town, and I'd like to settle up."

"Leaving town huh? Where you goin'?"

"Hawaii, actually," she replied.

"Hawaii? You did come into some scratch."

"It's not what you think. I have family there," she replied.

"Hmm. I always took you for Mexican, but I guess I can see it."

She knew he didn't mean anything by that, so she ignored his comment.

"What time do you think you can get here? I want to get going as soon as possible," she asked him.

There was a long pause. "I'm booked across town until at least three."

"Mikey! Come on," she groaned. "They're going to tow my car. I have to move it."

There was silence.

"I know I've asked a lot, but if you can pull off one more

miracle for me, I'm gone. I'm completely gone, and you'll never have to hear from me again," she pleaded.

There was a labored sigh. "Look. I guess I can come to you first. I don't know what parts you'll need, but I should be able to get it to the shop. I'll have Franky get into it there so I can get to my crosstown. But so help me, you better be there waiting when I pull up. I'll only have fifteen, maybe twen'y minutes to get you movin'."

"Mikey, I could kiss you!"

"Yeah, yeah. Alright. Just be there."

She clicked the phone shut, took off her hooded sweatshirt, wearing a thin, white tube top beneath it, and stepped into the cafe.

Silk vines of white roses hung from the exposed rafters of the cafe between enormous black and white photographs of flowers, and a wall of jars rose to the ceiling filled to overflowing with every color of bakery confection she could imagine. Pink sprinkles. Silver buttons. Yellow and white bows. Purple wrappers. Twisted sugar lollipops. Four kinds of rice Krispy treats drizzled in chocolate and yogurt and stuffed with strawberries. She thought she might get a sugar rush just from the smell, it was so thick in the air.

Today was going to be a great day.

A feeling of warmth filled her as she stood in front of a large marble countertop piled with powdered and folded pastries with French names she couldn't pronounce. Maybe this was finally over. She had been trying for months to survive, and now with a little money in her pocket, she might finally be able to get rid of Savannah and erase her from her life once and for all.

Her uncle, on her mother's side, was a direct descendant of

King Kamehameha, which gave him ancestral rights to one of the only homes on the small Hawaiian island of Lanai, and she was hoping desperately that he might know something about where her mother might have gone. Before they moved into the motel, they had received postcards from him two or three times a year, always with the most amazing azure blue waters, and she was ready to reconnect with her Hawaiian roots. He had always told her that she should come to visit, and maybe she could stay with him for a few months. Maybe she could get a job. Maybe she could go back to school. She actually missed school. She was good at school.

She leaned back in a quiet corner booth near one of the large windows relishing the Croque Monsieur dripping down her finger, two chocolate croissants, and three hot beverages. A caramel latte, a vanilla latte, and a cappuccino dusted with mocha powder. She wiped her finger along the inside edge of the cup, scooping up the last drops of chocolatey white froth, and slowly savored every single thing about this place.

She had about an hour before she needed to meet Mike and tried to remember where she might have dropped her mother's necklace. She knew she had it at work yesterday but couldn't remember seeing it after. She had already checked her car, which meant it was either at the diner, the pawn shop or...

She squeezed her napkin. What if she had dropped it at Marvin's house? Was it lying under his dead wife's bed? She swallowed. If it was, she was afraid she'd never see it again.

She leaned over crumpled napkins and her empty cappuccino cup with her head in her hands. I'm such an idiot, she told herself. Then she took a deep breath. Maybe it's not. Maybe it's at the pawn shop or in the park somewhere. She'd have to double-check.

SAVANNAH HAD NEVER BEEN in the Blue Bonnet in the morning. The small diner looked entirely different in the day than it did at night, with all of its neon signs turned off and with sunlight shining through the windows highlighting many of the 1940's Art Deco features that were either hidden in the evening or she had simply missed in her frantic hustle through her shifts.

"Good morning," a young man said, in his twenties, with a single earring as he walked up to her, not recognizing her. "Just one?"

She shook her head. "I actually work here, uh...worked here—the graveyard. And I might have left something last night. Do you think I can just take a look at the lockers?"

He shrugged. "Sure, hun. Take your time. If you need me, just holler." And he walked off to check on his tables.

She dug through the jackets and random pile of detritus staff and customers had left behind over the years and clicked open her locker. But there was no necklace. She leaned on the glass of her manager's now dark office with a hand over her eyes, trying to see if she could spot the small chain and turtle pendant in the office anywhere. No luck.

She'd come back and ask Marty if she had to, but she hated that idea, and Susan had said she'd call the cops if she ever saw her again, but that must have been a joke, right? She hated the thought of waiting around the city for yet another day just to face her manager again. But she couldn't leave the necklace behind if there was any chance at all it was there.

"Any luck?" the waiter asked as she walked back out to the

main dining room.

She shook her head.

"What's your name, hun? I can keep my eyes open for it."

"Savannah."

He paused. "Savannah? You have some tips."

"Tips?" Nicer words hadn't been said to her in a long time. The diner may not have been a great place to work, but she missed the easy access to food and a little cash in her pocket at the end of every shift.

He came back and handed her a twenty-dollar bill tucked into a napkin.

"Thanks," she said.

She returned to Clifford and leaned against him, looking at the money and unfolding the note written in Marvin's rough hand.

"Don't let your life be smothered out before you even have a chance to live it. I may not fully understand whatever it is that you're going through, but I do know that the night is always darkest just before the dawn." – Martin

She smiled, seeing that he had intentionally signed the incorrect name she had accidentally called him the night before when she handed him his piece of birthday pie.

She looked at the twenty note. All he had had was a piece of pie and coffee, and he still tipped her twenty dollars.

Not having found her necklace in the diner, she searched Clifford again, but there was no necklace.

Savannah still had thirty minutes and wanted desperately to leave town as soon as Mike finished her car, so she took the opportunity to scour every inch of sidewalk between Clifford and Marvin's home, but when she came out of the covering of trees in the park, she saw a police cruiser sitting in front of his narrow apartment building. She stopped and stepped back behind the park gate.

This was terrible news.

She pulled a long strand of hair out from behind her ear and twisted it around her finger. Were they there for her? Had the old man called the police on her? Of course, he must have, she thought to herself, having no idea that they were simply very late responding to her call from the night before.

She scratched at her temple. She had wiped down the phone and some of what she had touched in the kitchen, but what if they found her prints in the bedroom?

She looked up and down the street but saw no ambulance. Had they made it in time to help Marvin? It was too late for the guy's wife, but what about him?

Then there, in the front window above the parked police cruiser, glinting in the morning sunlight, hung a thin gold chain and turtle pendant with a mother-of-pearl shell, and she gasped.

An immediate wave of both relief and anxiety rolled over her. The fantastic news was that she had found it. The horrible news was that Marvin had *also* found it. But why was it hanging in his window?

Stepping closer, she could see that it was her necklace alright, taped to the inside of the window.

This wasn't so bad. At least now she knew where it was. She would just have to come back and get it tonight. It would seem that the city would not let her go for one more night at least.

Then her phone chirped in her pocket. It was Mike.

She quickly crossed the park and flipped the phone open. "Hey, you're early! I'm on my way. I can be there in five minutes," she told him.

"Didn't you say your car was sitting by the diner on 46th and Jacobson?"

"Yeah?"

"Well, it's not here," he snapped back at her with frustration.

"It's not in the parking lot. It's on the street, next to the newspaper machine," she told him, a bit confused.

"Yeah. I'm standing here. And there is NO orange hatchback parked on either side of the road."

Then she started running.

Chapter Nineteen

Officer Peter pulled into the parking lot of the Sunny Shores Motel in his glistening black Ford Raptor pickup truck and flipped open his notebook. This was the correct address.

He leaned over to his glove compartment and took out his badge and a matte black Gloc-9 pistol in a holster molded to the gun. Then he clipped the gun and badge onto his belt and walked up to a door with peeling wood paneling and fading yellow letters that read: OFFICE.

The office had brown carpet that smelled like urine, and a small bell sat on the counter next to a note that read: Ring for Service!

Ding! He clicked the bell and rested his hand on his pistol.

A narrow-eyed man came out from the back, missing three front teeth. He had several long, single hairs growing out from his chin where a beard should be, and a cigarette hung loosely from his lips. He squinted at the young officer. "Can I help you?"

"Do you know anything about a Susanne Wilkins?" Peter asked.

The man glanced down at Peter's badge, then at his gun.

He sniffed and pulled a long drag from his cigarette before dropping it into a Coke can on the desk behind the counter piled with a dozen cigarettes worth of ash. Peter wasn't there on official business, but he knew it didn't really matter. The badge carried weight, and the gun carried weight. Whoever he was questioning could decide for themselves which of the two they were most influenced by.

"She still owes two months' rent," the man replied.

Peter pulled his long, narrow black notebook out of his back pocket and opened it. "How long ago did she move out?"

The man lifted a thick green book up from behind the counter and flipped it open to a page marked with a black paperclip. Then he dug something out of his ear that he wiped on his trousers as he looked over his notes.

"September. That's when we finally went in and cleared out their junk. But I hadn't seen anyone but that girl of hers 'round for at least a few weeks before that."

"A girl?"

"Yeah. Her daughter, Sam...somethin'."

"Sam...something?" Peter shook his head, waiting for more.

The man looked away for a moment, scratched his chin, and then replied: "Samantha, I think."

Peter wrote "Samantha Wilkins" down in his notes. Samantha wasn't the waitress' name. It was Savannah. Sister maybe?

"Did she leave a forwarding address or anything?" he asked.

The man lifted an eyebrow in annoyance. "You think she'd skip out on two months' rent and stop to leave an address?"

"Any idea if Susanne had more than one daughter?"

The man shrugged, "I don't know."

"What did this Samantha look like?" Peter asked.

"A real beauty. Long black hair, but I never saw her bringing any guys by or anything, which is what most of 'em do. A non-stop line of guys comin' and goin'. Not her. Always clean. Always polite." Then his wandering gaze came back to the officer. "She's not in some kinda trouble, is she?"

Peter ignored the question. "You said you saw her around for a few weeks longer than her mom?"

"Yeah, coming and going in that Orange car of hers."

"Do you know where she was going?"

"Noooo," the man replied, emphasizing annoyance at the idea that he was paying any attention to a teenage girl.

Peter clenched his jaw at that signal of annoyance and leaned forward across the desk. "Do you know anything about a Savannah?"

The man looked away, now intimidated, which empowered Peter. "No."

"I'd like to see where they were staying," Peter said.

"Do you have a warrant?"

Peter's eye twitched as he glared back at the man, then calmly smiled, pushed open the small swinging door built into the counter, and stepped back behind the counter to within inches of the man.

The man took a step back.

"I'm asking nicely," Peter said with a smile.

The man swallowed hard. "I'll get the key."

The motel room made Peter feel like he had to wash his hands just looking at the place, even though it was technically clean. There was a small kitchenette with fading yellow tile, a small bathroom, and a queen-sized bed, but there wasn't much else.

"How long were they here?" Peter asked, trying to imagine the waitress living in this tiny place with her mother, which was smaller than the gym in his basement.

"Six, maybe seven months," the man said, standing in the doorway.

Peter didn't turn to him when he enquired: "What did you do with their stuff?"

"Storage 'round back. I was about to toss it out."

"I'd like to see it," Peter replied.

The man was happy to oblige the opportunity to step away from the officer.

Now alone in the motel room, Peter went to the bathroom and clicked on the light. The sink had rust spots, and one of the lights over the mirror sputtered and died while he stood there in front of it. Then he turned and walked to the bed, where he ran his hand over one of the pillows and lay down on the covers, imagining the young waitress, with her long, smooth black hair sleeping next to him. After a moment, he stood back up and smoothed the front of his jeans.

"Here's their box," the man said, coming back into the room, a fresh cigarette hanging from the side of his mouth and a cardboard apple crate tucked against his hip. He also carried two trash bags with him that he sat down on the bed.

"Is this all of it?" Peter asked.

The man flicked his ash onto the carpet and replied with a wave at the box, "that's it."

There was some plastic Tupperware, a few random papers, photos, and a couple of glass angel figurines in the box. The trash bags only had clothing and a few towels.

"I'll have to take this with me," Peter told him.

"Who's going to settle their bill?"

Peter looked at him with indifference. "That's not my problem."

"What do I do with these bags?" the man asked.

"Toss them," Peter replied. Then he carried the box down to his pickup truck.

He checked his phone.

He needed to get to the diner if he was going to be there when she showed up.

He lifted one of the photos from the box of Savannah on a beach in a bikini. "Sam—15" was written on the back. *"Samantha,"* he thought to himself. Then he folded the photo and put it in his pocket.

Chapter Twenty

Officer Peter pulled onto 67th as a large flatbed truck—with Three Tony's Towing painted on the side—finished winching Savannah's orange hatchback onto its bed.

Peter parked partially on the sidewalk, quickly got out, and waved his badge at the driver, who set down a CB radio and rolled down his window.

"You need to release the car," Peter said.

"Excuse me?" the driver replied.

"There's been an extension on the request to move."

The driver lifted a thick steel clipboard. "Not according to this."

Peter nodded. "You can put the car back."

The driver shook his head. "No can do. I was told to pick the car up, and that's what I'm going to do. If there's a problem, you can take it up with the yard boss." Then he rolled up his window and drove away.

Peter looked around for any sign of Savannah, but there was none. He climbed back into his truck and hit the steering wheel. He had wanted to be there when the truck pulled up so that he could help her sort it out, but he was too late. He hit the steering wheel again, watching the truck turn the corner in his rearview mirror. He quickly weighed his options. Should he stay or follow the truck? Savannah might not come back all day—or ever, and if she did, what would he tell her? He couldn't help her anymore from here, so he followed the truck back to the yard.

A FAT, BALD MAN sat behind the desk at Three Tony's Towing, who only glanced up when Peter entered the office, badge shining from his belt.

"One of your trucks just brought in an orange Gremlin hatchback, and I need access to it," Peter said, standing, arms crossed, in front of the man's desk.

The man reached, without looking, to a metal shelf sitting on the corner of his desk and handed a form to Peter. "Fill this out. We need an hour to process the car, then the contents will be available for pickup, but the vehicle can't leave the lot until either a 14-22 is signed by your evidence department or the owner of the vehicle comes to pick it up." And he returned to pecking at his keyboard with both pointer fingers.

Peter looked at the form, then left the office, crumpling it into a ball and tossing it in a waste basket outside the office doors next to a vending machine and some well-worn benches.

On one of the benches now sat a slender woman with red hair and a little blonde girl bouncing a stuffed yellow monkey on her leg, who looked up and smiled as Peter stepped out of the office.

"Look, mommy, a policeman!" the little girl shouted.

Peter didn't really have time for this, but he was still wearing his badge, so he knelt in front of the girl. "What's his name?" Peter asked, pointing at the monkey.

The little girl held it up to him. "Mr. Wadsworth," she said.

"Mr. Wadsworth? Would Mr. Wadsworth like a sticker?" he asked.

The little girl nodded with a flourish and a big grin.

He took out his wallet, where he kept a few extra stickers for just such an occasion. "Well, look at that! I just so happen to have enough stickers for Mr. Wadsworth, you, and your lovely mommy, if she wants one," he said, glancing up with a flirty smile at the mother.

"Here, mommy! Take a sticker," the little girl said, handing one to her mother.

"What do you say to the nice and handsome policeman?" the mother asked, peeling the sticker off its back and plastering it to the front of her dress.

"Thank you," the little girl said.

"Oh, it's my pleasure," he said. Then he rose and went out to his truck.

As he sat back in his pickup, his thoughts returned to Savannah. What leverage did he have now? Where would she go? How was he going to find a way to talk to her? The diner maybe? Find out when she would be on shift next?

He picked up some of the photos in the box next to him and flipped through the images of two happy people: Savannah, a young girl sitting on the back of a horse with a black riding cap and knee-high boots. A photo of her and her mother laughing at a cafe, Savannah, with a small pile of hot chocolate foam on her chin. Another of Savannah, now in her early teens, standing on a podium with a gold trophy; a large banner on the wall behind her read: National Geographic Spelling Bee -

National Finals.

Then he lifted a small frame out of the pile. In it was a blue and pink image of Dumbo the flying elephant, with the words Mother and Daughter printed in pink at the top and a silly child's poem in the center.

He opened his notebook and wrote down some questions he wanted answered: Where is Susanne? Why was Savannah seen at the motel for weeks after her mother? Who is Samantha? He underlined this question three times and wrote: Probably an alias.

He clicked his phone to life and typed Savannah Wilkins into the internet browser. There were no results. Then he typed in Samantha Wilkins, and several dozen pages populated the search query list. He clicked a link to a social media profile and more photos of the waitress filled his screen, pictures of her with friends at school or the zoo. The last post, dated nearly a year ago, showed her excited to be nominated for a Junior Ambassadors of America grant.

Peter was beginning to realize two things: First, the waitress he had been paying attention to at the diner was younger than he thought she was. He had assumed she was in her twenties, maybe early twenties, but this profile suggested someone much younger. Second, Savannah and Samantha were one in the same person. He put a check next to that question in his notebook. However, things didn't add up. The girl behind the bar at the Blue Bonnet was always nervous and frazzled, but the girl in these photos looked happy and healthy. Same girl but two different lives. He scrolled back through her life and found no evidence of the shy and guarded young woman he met at the Blue Bonnet.

As a police officer, Peter knew that people often live

different lives. Like the teenage boy he helped the FBI arrest last year who ran a hacking scheme out of his bedroom. Or the mom of five he arrested for selling prescription pills to her yoga students. He had come to assume that everyone was someone else just beneath their veneer of propriety. But the girl in the photos on his screen didn't look like she had anything to hide. She actually looked happy. What happened?

A woman with SECURITY embroidered on the front of her navy-blue polo left the small booth by the front gate to the tow yard, and Peter climbed out of his truck. He approached the booth and glanced around. No cameras. He grunted with discontent at the lack of security and passed through the small booth and into the yard. He had watched where the flatbed truck had taken the orange hatchback when it came in, so it only took him a minute to find it parked in the yard between a taxi with no tires and a silver minivan with smashed-out windows.

He knew from the night before that the driver's door was wired shut, so he went around to the passenger side, glanced around for prying eyes, took out a small black utility knife that he flipped open, and quickly broke the rusting door lock. Then he slid into the passenger seat and shut the door behind him.

He stopped.

The car smelled like her, which made him smile.

It felt different now that he knew she must be a teenager, more dangerous and exciting.

He wanted to enjoy the visceral experience of being in her space, so he slowly slid his hands across the dash like he was caressing her arm.

Between the dash and front dials was a photo of her mother.

The seats were torn, with yellow foam pressing through threads that did their best to hold the seat cover together. Then he clicked open the glove box. There were some parking receipts, an orange fading Chilton Repair and Tune-up manual labeled American Motors 1975-82, and a vehicle registration, which had expired three months earlier.

He turned to the sheet hanging behind the seats and tore it down, little pins dropping and bouncing onto the vehicle floor.

Now he knew why she had taped black plastic over the back windows: she had been living out of the car.

A strand of Christmas lights hung from the roof, along with three or four more photos of Savannah—Samantha—and her mother. There was also a pile of blankets, a pillow, a sports bra, and a small black duffle bag sitting in one corner.

He unzipped the small black bag, and a more potent waft of her fragrance filled the car. Shea butter lotion. Nail clippers. A nearly empty bottle of black nail polish. He set the bag aside, picked up her blanket, and smelled it. The hairs on his arms stood on end. Then he noticed something purple down behind the driver's seat.

The purple-cloth-covered journal was frayed at the edges and held shut with an elastic band. The first page was dated nearly six months ago.

Peter heard the crunch of gravel and slid lower in the seat. A tall, slender man with overalls and a grey trucker's cap walked past Clifford looking for something but kept walking. Peter watched him in the rearview mirror until he was out of sight. Then Peter quickly sat up, dropped the journal into the black bag, and grabbed the rest of the photos from the back of the car along with the sports bra. It was time to go. As he climbed out, he quickly swept his hand underneath both of the front seats looking for anything else she might have hidden and found two folded one-hundred-dollar bills. Why was someone living out of a car hiding hundred-dollar bills beneath her seat?

He couldn't wait to get home and read her journal.

Chapter Twenty-One

Marvin buttoned the top button of a fresh shirt as he stood in the doorway of his walk-in closet, looking at the now empty bed where his wife's body lay for the better part of a day and where she had slept next to him for the better part of sixty-five years.

The emptiness of his loss was so vast it echoed. A thick, dull emptiness, unlike anything he had ever felt before. The room was empty. The apartment was empty. And he hadn't had much time to think about it since everything had happened, but he wondered how empty his life would now feel as well. He wasn't interested in just sitting around waiting to die. What if he fell and hurt himself? He could lie in the middle of his kitchen floor for two days before the nurse would get there, probably messing all over himself, crying out for help like an animal or small child. Or what if they came and forced him into a home where eventually he'd have to be fed oatmeal by a stranger? No, he wouldn't have any of that. But where would he do it? He knew how to do it so that the bullet would be quick and painless from what he had seen in his days in the Navy, but he also knew it would make an awful mess, and he didn't like the idea of leaving his home in disarray for anyone else to find.

Something about the bed where he and Margie spent a third of their life together, and plenty of happy times, had a certain romanticism to it, but he figured they'd never get the stains out of the carpet, and he wasn't sure how long it would take someone to find him. What about the bathroom? That shouldn't be too terribly difficult to clean. After all, he and Michael had done a decent job of it after the mess they had made the night before. Yes, that sounded like a good plan: In the bathroom, curtain closed, water running. He could call the police, tell them what he was going to do, hang up, pull the curtain and pull the trigger. All the mess would stay in the shower, and someone should be able to find him quickly enough to tidy it up in time for dinner. Done and done. He nodded and picked up the cold chrome pistol. Yes, this was a good idea.

The small boy walked into the bedroom just then, and Marvin quickly slid the revolver into his pants pocket. He was starting to get used to its weight and had learned to tighten his belt an extra notch to make sure the gun's heft didn't pull his pants down.

"Why are you carrying that gun?" Michael asked.

Marvin had forgotten how straightforward children's questions could be, but he didn't answer. Instead, he gently touched the boy's chin and looked at the side of his face. "You look like you've healed up nicely," he told him. "I'm not sure I've ever seen scrapes and bruises like yours heal quickly."

"Can I have a snack?" the boy asked.

"Well, sure. I guess. But I'm not sure what sort of snack you're interested in. I don't really have the kind of food I'd reckon a boy like yourself would like, and I can't feed you toast mornin', noon and night. But let's have a look."

Michael seemed interested in some oatmeal, so Marvin made him a bowl and scooped on what he realized afterward was probably too much brown sugar. Then Marvin explained how they would be going out for some groceries, some clothes that might fit the boy, and a stop at the park on the way, which Michael didn't argue with even though he still wasn't saying much.

Together they walked awkwardly down the sidewalk, Marvin slow and slightly bent forward. Michael so young and tender in a pair of shoes so large for him they clopped and nearly fell off, shorts that hung past his knees, and a polo that looked more like a dress on him than a shirt, but he didn't seem to mind. He just held the old man's hand, and together they made their way across the street and through the scattered sunlight breaking through the autumnal leaves in the park.

Marvin had always found the Commons especially beautiful in autumn. The crisp crunch and fusty fragrance of red-brown leaves blanketing the benches and grass like a royal mantel fit for the wealthiest of monarchs lying in stark contrast to the cold concrete and filth of the neighborhoods surrounding it. Ellie especially had always loved the leaves. Of course she loved running through them and throwing them like any child her age, but she especially loved their shapes and how much they looked like bright fire when she held them up to the sunlight. One of Marvin's favorite photographs was of her holding a leaf up to the sunlight as a red-tinged shadow lay across her cheek.

The sunlight warmed Marvin and cut through the sharp cold, lying low in the shadowy streets between the tall city buildings. He welcomed the warmth and having someone to walk with.

"Have you remembered anything about where you come from?" Marvin asked Michael as they walked.

Michael didn't answer.

"Or about your parents? It really would help if you could remember something because, like I told you before, you can't stay with me long. I'd rather not let the police take you, but I may not have much choice."

"But I don't want you to feel so alone," Michael finally responded, looking up at Marvin.

"It's not your job to worry about an old man like me. You're just a boy, and we need to get you back to where you belong."

"How do you know I don't belong here with you?" Michael asked.

"Because you've got to have your own family somewhere, and they'll be looking for you, child," Marvin's voice deep and rich.

As they passed two homeless men asleep on a bench, without realizing, Marvin pulled Michael closer to himself and slid his hand into his trouser pocket, where he could feel the comforting mass of the revolver. Michael, not appearing to be bothered by the men at all, asked: "Why do you sleep in a bed and they sleep outside? Why don't they sleep in a bed too?"

"Oh, because they probably don't have a bed to sleep in."

"But, why?"

"There's a lot of reasons why. Maybe they couldn't afford a home anymore, or maybe they are sick in the head and can't even live in a home if they had one."

"Sick in the head? How does someone get sick in the head?" Michael asked.

"It's not like the flu or anything you can catch, so don't worry. It's just that sometimes people are either born with their wires crossed, or they hurt themself in a way that they get their wires crossed."

Marvin could see that Michael had to think about this for a while, trying to imagine what it meant to get your wires crossed as they walked up to the entrance of Tadpole Playground, where a giant brass frog sat on an arch, welcoming children to come and play.

"You used to bring her here, didn't you? The girl who used to live in my room," Michael asked.

"I did," Marvin said painfully lowering himself onto the same bench he and Margaret used to sit on and watch Ellie run and giggle.

"What happened to her?" Michael asked.

At one time, Marvin could think of nothing else but what had happened to her, but the years had dulled that rusty knife.

"Oh, she died," Marvin said, watching several children play in a fountain squirting randomly up from three spouts in the ground, causing them to laugh and squeal.

"How?" Michael asked, sitting down on the bench next to Marvin.

Marvin didn't immediately respond, pained by the question and the memories they brought to the surface. "You don't want to hear about that. Go on and play. That's why we came."

"You felt alone then, didn't you?" Michael asked, watching a couple of children run back and forth in a game of tag underneath some of the tall green legs of the park equipment.

Marvin sat quietly, remembering those first days after Ellie's death. He had never told anyone how there were nights that he awoke so terrified and alone and angry he could very easily have murdered whomever it was that had taken his little girl from him. Nights when he woke to the sound of Ellie crying, just to find her room dark and empty. Nights when he would sit in her rocking chair, aching to hold her. Sleepless nights when he would walk the streets of Boston at two or three in the morning, only to find himself paralyzed at the sight of a homeless man asleep under a bus shelter, wondering if this could be the person who attacked his daughter and left her to die on the front steps of his home. But instead of giving words to this deep and personal grief that had unknowingly become so sacred to him, he and Michael sat together watching the children play.

For quite a while, they said nothing before Marvin noticed Michael paying especially close attention to a blonde girl with Down Syndrome trying to rock herself back and forth on the swings without much success.

She smiled and waved when one of the other children ran past her, but when they ignored her, she went back to trying to copy what she had seen other children do to make the swing move. But as much as she tried, it would not move for her. Without a word, Michael stood and walked over to her. She didn't notice him at first until he began talking to her, and then she tilted her head to one side as he asked: "What's your name?"

"Sarah," she said with a big smile and waved her hand back and forth.

"Hi, Sarah, I'm Michael. Can I push you?"

She gave him an energetic nod that made Michael smile larger than Marvin had ever seen him smile.

The two played together for the better part of an hour while they took turns pushing each other on the swing, chasing each other in their own game of tag, and hanging from the same monkey bars Ellie used to love. Never once did any of the other children acknowledge either Michael or the little girl's existence, which clearly didn't bother either of them. They were in a world entirely of their own making, and that was fine by them.

Marvin smiled at this, remembering how Ellie had also always been so open and happy to find a new friend. Children are remarkable like that, he thought to himself. They have no guile, no deceit, no hesitation to grab the hand of someone they have never met before and quickly become fast friends. On days when the park was tranquil, maybe in the colder first days of winter, she would be downhearted if she hadn't met someone new to play with.

Marvin thought how wonderful it would be if the same gentle simplicity returned to you late in life, even though it unfortunately did not.

He looked at the empty bench beside him and imagined Margie sitting there next to him, reaching over and taking his hand, smiling at him, then turning back with a look of total peace and contentment as she watched the children play. But the bench was empty now, which wasn't going to change. Truth be told, even though he meant what he said to Michael when he told him he couldn't stay with him for long, Marvin was grateful to have someone else in the house, if only for those first few days he was alone. Simply knowing there was another heartbeat in the house was the only reason he had not yet made the call, closed the curtain and pulled the trigger. And for now, he resolved himself to lean back on the bench and enjoy the growing warmth of the afternoon and the laughter of the children at play.

Chapter Twenty-Two

Peter sat at a glass table in his carefully pressed officer's uniform and looked at the small black duffle bag he had found in Savannah's car. It had bleached spots on one end, and the black strap had been replaced with a blue one that didn't quite match. Looped through the zipper pull was a small National Geographic keychain with a yellow dial lock holding the bag shut.

Peter looked at the lock carefully for a moment before going out to his garage for a pair of wire cutters and clipped the silver loop of the lock with little effort. Then he slowly unzipped the top of the bag.

These were her things, and now they were in his home. They had been precious to her, and now they were precious to him. He would take care of them for her until she was ready to have them back.

He leaned forward and took in the bag's fragrance, the smell of shampoo, hair, vanilla lotion, and some sort of sweet and fruity perfume like a young girl would wear. Inside the duffle was a smaller, black overnight satchel with deodorant, a half-used tube of toothpaste, and other toiletries, which he laid out item by item on the tabletop. A round hairbrush had tufts of Samantha's black hair that he gently pulled off and set on the table in what looked like a small bird's nest. He unfolded and rubbed the fabric of her clothing between his fingers and set aside a pair of pink studded earrings and a small cluster of clear rubber bands he imagined her using to hold her hair back. Then he found a small yellow tube of Burt's Bees ChapStick, coconut and pear.

He took off the lid and smeared some on the tip of his finger, imagining her applying it before going out in the morning or meeting friends. He rubbed the tips of his fingers together, looking at the creamy color and feeling the smooth texture, then held his fingers beneath his nose and smelled them. The pear smell made his mouth water. Then he put some on. From her lips to his. He liked that.

Every item in the bag brought them closer together, and he liked that too. He wanted her with him now, but he was willing to wait. He had learned well that it was safer to be patient.

He put the lid on the ChapStick and slid it into the left breast pocket of his uniform. This way, he could keep her close to him.

He set the empty bag onto the floor and slid the purple book into the center of the table, running his hand over the hard cover and feeling the textured cloth surface. He picked at one of the worn corners with his fingernail where she had colored the board underneath dark purple. There were sticky residues on the back in the shapes of stickers.

He slowly opened the cover to the first page, and her smiling face looked up at him from a small stack of photographs, a photo of her blowing a kiss at the camera. He picked it up, tore a piece of tape from a black dispenser sitting on his desk and taped the photograph to the wall in front of him, trying to extract details about her life from what he could see in the photos.

None of these images, or the ones in the social media feed he now had bookmarked on his phone, looked like someone who would end up living out of a car. Had someone hurt her? Had she gotten caught up in drugs? Maybe he could help her find a way out. Maybe he could protect her. Maybe he could even give her a place to stay.

He looked at the image again and touched her lips, then began reading the first page of the journal, covered in looping purple letters.

"Mom's been gone for a week now. I don't know what I'm going to do. I got $30 for her bracelet and a couple of rings, but that's almost gone. That creepy property manager who keeps looking at me came by asking for the rent. I told him we'd have it tomorrow, but I don't think he believed me. It's $650! Where am I going to come up with $650!?! Mom's never been gone this long, and when I try her cell, it says it's disconnected. I'm starting to get scared. I don't think he will let me stay here much longer, but if I leave, how will she find me when she comes back? Mom, where are you?"

Peter clenched his jaw at the thought of someone else looking at Samantha.

"Mom's been gone for eleven days, and I'm starting to worry she isn't coming back. She's never not come back, but she's also never been gone for more than a couple of days. Where are you!? I went by Three Taps, but they said they hadn't seen her in months. I even called Chris, but he said he hadn't seen her and then hung up on me. She wouldn't just leave me. Something's keeping her, but what? Did she get arrested?

They'd have to give her a call, right? Wouldn't she call me if she got arrested? The manager just came pounding on the door, at 10:30 at night! I think he was drunk. He said that if I didn't have $1,000 by tomorrow morning, he was calling the cops. Rent is supposed to be $650, so I don't know what he was going on about, but I have to leave tonight. I don't know what I'm going to do."

Peter gently touched the paper where her tears had dimpled the page.

He wrote "Three Taps" and "possibly arrested" in his notebook and scanned over his notes again, then circled "What happened to Susanne Wilkins?" Maybe if he could find her, he could get closer to Samantha.

He flipped to the back of the journal to see if she had found any recent information since that first entry when he noticed a bulge at the back of the book. He turned it over, ran his finger along the inside edge where the back cover met the last page, and felt a slight separation in the binding. He flipped open his utility knife and carefully slit the edge of the paper where he found a stack of one-hundred-dollar bills.

"Bingo," he said to himself.

He laid out the notes in a row and counted five of them. $500 wasn't solid ground for probable cause, but maybe it was close enough. Car parked illegally; ran the plates; false registration tag; the presence of a stack of cash. He nodded. That should be enough to excuse a criminal history check. But he'd have to run it on duty. It would constitute a class six felony if he didn't have cause.

He looked at his watch. Forty-five minutes. He could wait forty-five minutes, so he kept reading.

"WHERE ARE WE?" MICHAEL ASKED, HIS FACE BLUE from the neon light of the Blue Bonnet Diner.

"Someplace with delicious pancakes. At least, I reckon they're delicious. I've seen plenty of people ordering them. Do you like pancakes?" Marvin asked as he and Michael stepped into the small dining room.

Michael thought about that, then shrugged his shoulders.

"Child, how do you not know if you like pancakes?"

"I don't know," Michael said, stepping in front of the fading red jukebox and putting a hand on either side as he leaned forward to look at the row of old records the jukebox still played.

"Hey, Marvin!" Marty said with a smile from behind the front counter, where a young man with a skateboard typed away on a laptop. "You want your usual booth?" she asked.

"That'd be fine," he replied, taking off his cap and jacket.

"Well, it's open for ya'. How you doin' tonight?" She asked, following him to the booth.

"Ohhh, everything's doing just fine."

"And Margaret?"

Marvin looked at Michael, who sat across the table but didn't say anything. Then Marvin sighed. "Margie left us last night."

Marty touched the cross hanging around her neck, one of several necklaces she wore. "Oh, no! Honey, I'm so sorry. How'd it happen?"

Mavin shook his head. "I came home last night after leaving here and found her sitting in front of the tv. She was just gone. The EMT said it looked like her heart gave out. Nothin' more to it."

"Marvin. I'm so sorry," Marty replied, touching his shoulder.

CHAPTER TWENTY-TWO

"Dinner's on the house tonight and…."

Marvin held up a hand. "That ain't necessary."

But she shook her head. "No question, Marvin. No question at all. No question. And if there's anything else at all I can do—anything at all. You tell me darlin', okay? Anything you want is on the house, no question at all."

"Well, that's kind of you."

"You want some coffee? Some pie? We have some fresh apple right out the oven. And what about dinner? Have you eaten? I could have Frank put together a plate of pot roast with mashed potatoes and gravy if you like."

Marvin nodded. "I must admit I am a bit hungrier that I thought I was afore I walked in, and that pot roast does sound nice."

Marty nodded. "You want coffee?"

He nodded. "And I'd also like a double stack of your nicest pancakes and a chocolate milk."

"Pancakes and chocolate milk?" she asked, a bit confused.

"If you don't mind."

"Alright darlin', one pot roast dinner, a plate of pancakes, a coffee, and chocolate milk. You gonna have room for pie?"

Marvin smiled. "Oh, let's see how we do with that." And with that, Marty was back behind the counter, tapping away at the order screen with her long red fingernails.

"You're going to love pancakes," Marvin told Michael, unfolding a napkin and laying it across his lap. Then he looked up to see Michael watching him and lifted the napkin. "It's polite to take that napkin there and lay it across your lap like so," and he repeated the movement for the boy.

"Why?" Michael asked.

"Oh, so you don't drip on those new trousers I bought for

you."

Michael slowly unfolded his napkin and laid it across his lap the way Marvin had shown him.

"You asked me a question earlier today that I didn't answer for you that reminded me of something I had forgotten all about until today," Mavin said, carefully straightening his silverware.

"What question?" Michael asked.

"If I felt alone after Ellie died," Marvin replied. Then he watched Marty serve the young man with the skateboard though he wasn't looking at her as much as letting his gaze wander in her general direction while his mind took him entirely elsewhere.

"I did feel alone after Ellie died. Which is strange because Margie was right there with me goin' through the same things I was goin' through, but I guess our pain became like a brick wall between us, keepin' us from one another. So yes, I felt alone. Never felt so alone. Not before nor since. Not until now, anyway. But that alone was so much harder then."

"Why?" Michael asked, concern coloring his young voice.

Marvin didn't even hear Michael's question. "I was also angry. Angry at so many things, but mostly angry at God for leaving me alone when I needed Him most." A tear streamed down his cheek and he reached for his napkin to catch it. "Angry that He wasn't there for my precious little girl when she needed him the most—needed me the most. God wasn't there."

He paused, unsure if he wanted to share with this small boy what he remembered next.

"I was so angry I did something stupid," he finally said.

"Alright darlin', one pot roast dinner and one plate of

pancakes," Marty said, setting the two plates down on the table, and Marvin quickly wiped his face again with the edge of his napkin. "And I'll be right back with those drinks and some syrup."

Marvin just nodded.

The sight of the thick brown gravy spilling over the edge of the fluffy white potatoes was lost on Marvin as he remembered the night he carried a gun, not unlike the one he had in his pocket now, down a darkened street more than fifty years earlier.

"I wanted to hurt someone; I wanted someone to hurt me," he quietly told Michael, lowering his head in shame. Details and flecks of that night, previously lost to history, came back to Marvin as vividly as if he were there at that very moment.

"I bought a gun, a Colt Officer's Model, .38 special for seventy-nine dollars and twenty-five cents." He grunted. "Funny, how I remember that isn't it? Seventy-nine dollars and one single quarter." He shook his head.

"I told myself I bought it to protect Margie in case someone came back, but truth was I bought it because it made me feel like I could do something. I needed to do something. But Margie wouldn't have it in the house, so we started fighting over it. Of course, we weren't really fighting about the gun—I know that now. But it gave us something safe to fight about, if you see what I'm sayin'. How were we supposed to fight about our little girl being murdered? Neither of us could have done anything about that, but we were both so angry. So we fought about the gun. And boy, did we fight about that stupid thing.

"It turned into this burning hot coal of emotion neither of us could take our hand from even though it threatened to consume our home, our lives, our marriage.

"And to make matters worse, I had started on the whiskey again. Oh, I hate the taste of the stuff, but that's exactly why I always went to it. I figured if I drank something I hated that much, it would be easy enough to stop when I wanted to, which is crazy foolish. What happens is you get used to the awful taste and start seeing it as a medicine to keep you from screaming filthy things at your wife in a rage and throwing glass bottles against a wall.

"So, one night, she finally told me that I could just get out if I didn't get rid of the gun. Looking back on it now, I don't blame her at all. I wouldn't want a hurt and angry man full of whiskey with a gun in my house either, but at the time, I only saw it as her keeping me from protecting my family, trying to control me, trying to tell me what to do.

"So, I left."

He paused, numb from the waves of guilt now rising to replace his renewed remembrance of anger from that night.

He looked at the boy—so young and innocent, so fare and naive—and decided there really wasn't any reason not to tell him the whole truth.

"I left looking for someone to hurt. I loaded the gun, put it in my pants pocket, and went looking for someone to hurt. I was hurt, and I wanted to cause some hurt. Someone had taken something from me, and I wanted to take something from someone else."

Marvin turned away from the boy and looked out the diner window at a young couple hailing a cab.

"The first people I found that night was a young couple, probably out on some date."

Marvin's breath stuttered, and he gripped the table as guilt rose in him.

"I walked up behind them while they stood on the corner waiting for the light to change. I squeezed the handle of that Colt and …."

His voice caught, and he took another deep breath, his lips curling around his teeth. "And I imagined shooting them both in the back of the head, right there in the street." He covered his face with his hand, ashamed of what he was admitting. "But I froze. By grace alone, the light turned and they walked on while I stood there watching them.

"I don't know how long or how far I walked on after that, but before long, I found myself in a bar where everyone spoke in a thick Italian accent. I remember all the eyes on me while I sat down at the bar, all the ladies in their dresses and the guys in their silver suits, while I probably looked like I had just rolled out of bed. I don't remember everything about that night, but I sure remember how I kept thinking I didn't belong there, which is exactly what I wanted.

"I wanted to be somewhere I didn't belong, just to see what would happen. I still wanted to hurt someone. I wanted someone to hurt me, just so I knew I was still alive. And I had a pretty good idea that trouble would find me soon enough in that bar. I might have to push a little, but I wouldn't have to push much.

"The bartender told me at first that he wasn't going to serve me until I put a stack of money on the table large enough to catch his attention, and he poured me a single malt and told me to drink it and get out. But I did not. Instead, I sat there with that golden glass of liquid foolishness and glared at anyone I could make eye contact with until a pot-bellied Italian with hair slicked back and a solid gold ring on his little finger caught me looking the direction of his lady. And that did it. He whispered something to his waiter and pointed at me with his fat little sausage finger. Then two men in suits with no ties came out from the back of the restaurant, picked me up by either arm, and carried me out through a side door where they threw me into the street.

"We said some things to each other that I won't repeat to a small child, but needless to say, they weren't nice, when one of them punched me in the stomach so hard I nearly wretched. They were the trouble I was lookin' for, and here I was gettin' two for the price of one."

Marvin quietly blew his nose into a paper napkin he found folded beneath his silverware and looked at the boy who hadn't touched his food.

"So, I pulled my gun."

He shifted his fork and knife around the table again, still unable to touch his food.

"At least I tried to. But the hammer—the small metal piece at the back—caught inside my pocket, and I couldn't get it loose!" Marvin chuckled. "I pulled as hard as I could, but I couldn't get it out of my pocket. Can you believe that?

"One of the men started laughing at me and pointing when suddenly there was a crack so loud it echoed down the alley and made my ears ring. I fell backward. And apparently, they knew what they had heard because they quickly disappeared back into the club, while I just sat there wondering what had just happened.

"Well, what had happened was I had shot myself in the foot! Except I didn't feel anything. I figured I was in shock and patted myself down, trying to see if I was bleeding anywhere. Then I pulled off my shoe and saw where the bullet had gone through the top and bottom of my shoe; only problem was it did not hit my foot!" Marvin's eyebrows rose, and he leaned forward over the table, emphasizing what he was saying to Michael. "I had shot. Myself. In the foot. And somehow missed my foot! That don't happen. That just don't happen.

"Well, that scared me halfway to hell and back, so I picked myself up out the street and went home.

"On my way, I dropped the gun in one trashcan and the bullets in another, all except for the spent casing. I took that home with me and showed Margie the empty casing and the hole in my shoe where the bullet had gone through. Then I took off my sock, and we both looked over my foot as close as you could imagine. And can you believe that even the sock had two holes in it? But there wasn't so much as a scratch on my foot. Now, how is that possible? That can't be possible," Marvin said, sitting back in the booth.

"Margie, of course, immediately started praising God for His miracle. But I wasn't convinced. I thought maybe the bullet had somehow hit my shoe and ricocheted back up at the bottom, the whiskey still clouding my mind.

"But, whether it was God protecting me or not, it was enough to knock us both out of our stupor because the next day we decided to go together to Ellie's grave and say goodbye. Goodbye to her; goodbye to our anger.

"We both wrote out what we were feeling on pages of note paper. All the pain and anger we felt at each other and God and the world, we put there on those pages, and then we lit them on fire in a little bowl and watched our angry words slowly turn to ash and go up in smoke before God like incense in the tabernacle. That's how Margie put it anyway.

"She told me how selfish I had been, which was true, of course. And I told her how hurt and angry I was at her for not knowing that our baby girl was dying on our front door while she was no more than fifty feet away, upstairs foldin' the laundry.

"I also told Ellie that I loved her, and I was so sorry I couldn't be there for her, sorry she had died alone. I set that bullet casing on top of her headstone, and we went home.

"Margie and I decided that day to celebrate Ellie's life together—all of life together—instead of getting caught in her death like some quagmire. And that day became our life anniversary.

"One year later, Margie went out and bought us these watches," Marvin said, running his hand over the face of his and smiling. "They weren't us at all. We never would spend money on anything extravagant like this, we were always so frugal, but she said that was the point. So each year, we did something on our life anniversary completely frivolous, something completely unnecessary—maybe completely necessary—but for the sheer joy of it, and always remembering how happy our little girl was when she was alive and how grateful we were to have had the time with her that we had."

He unstrapped his watch, turned it over, and held it up for Michael to see the tiny marks etched on the back. "It says, La Chaim, which means to life. To joy. To Ellie." And he rubbed the back with his thumb.

Marvin's stomach tossed and turned from hunger and the froth of emotions that his memories had stirred up, so he ate every bite of his pot roast and enjoyed some apple pie without saying anything else to Michael. Then He thanked Marty for her kindness and said goodnight.

After he left, as she cleared the table, Marty wondered at the plate of pancakes and glass of chocolate milk that had gone

CHAPTER TWENTY-TWO

untouched.

Chapter Twenty-Three

As soon as Peter came on duty, he called in a background check on Susanne Wilkins, which came up with a driving-under-the-influence conviction, two counts of possession of narcotics below .5 ounces, and a last known address of 115 Mill St., Belmont, Massachusetts. McLean Psychiatric Hospital.

He had heard about this place as a child. His father had sent more than one person there after moving his family from Virginia to Boston, where his father sat on the Suffolk County Superior Court bench. McLean was the hospital Sylvia Plath had written about in The Bell Jar and where Jazz musician Ray Charles had gone, off and on, after he had been caught with heroin. Peter saw it as a home for the rejects of society that might have been euthanized at an earlier time in history.

Peter pulled into the driveway in his blue and white police SUV, crossed the browning grass beneath an elm still trying to hold onto the last few leaves of the season, and walked into the red brick building that was Proctor House at McLean Hospital.

"Can I help you, officer?" a young woman asked. She wore a nurse uniform and had shoulder-length blonde hair pulled back in a French braid and pink nail polish.

"I'm here to look in on a patient," he said.

"Can I have you sign in, please," she said, pointing to a clipboard on the counter. "And what's your name?"

"Officer Peter Stevens."

The young nurse smiled at him. "Are you here for Emily Stevens?"

Peter froze at the question in confusion. "No, a Susanne Wilkins."

"Oh, I'm sorry. I thought you were here to see Emily."

Peter shook his head. "You must be mistaken."

Emily Stevens was the name of Peter's mother, but she had left Peter and his father when he was twelve, and Peter had never heard from her again.

"Are you any relation to Judge Marshal Stevens?" the nurse asked.

Cold pain slowly crawled down Peter's back. "Yes?"

She quickly tapped her keyboard and looked closely at her computer monitor. Then she turned to Peter with a look of concern. "No mistake. Judge Stevens had her committed in 2008, sighting her as a danger to herself and her family."

Peter set the pen down, trying to process what exactly he was hearing, then turned and quickly left the hospital.

Back in his cruiser, he gripped the steering wheel with both hands and leaned forward, remembering clearly the morning his father had told him over breakfast that his mother had left and wouldn't be returning.

"What do you mean she's gone? Where did she go?" Peter asked, having turned twelve only a week earlier.

His father didn't look up over his morning paper. "She has decided that this isn't the life for her any longer and has left.

There's nothing else to it." Then his father looked up at him. "You're not going to blubber like a little girl who's lost her dolly, are you?"

Peter's face burned then as it did now, but at the time, he refused to let his father see him show any of the deep pain and sorrow that would, to some degree, never leave him. Now, sitting in the parking lot of the red brick building that towered over him with a look of cold detachment like his father had thirteen years earlier, his tears broke free, if only for an instant, and he quickly wiped his eyes with the sleeve of his shirt, feeling both dirty and guilty.

He swallowed deep, took a breath, and straightened the sides of his shirt. Then he looked at himself in the mirror and wiped his face again. His eyes were red and puffy. "Stop it, you pansy," he told himself, then slapped himself in the face. "If it is mom, and you don't know that it is, then he had a good reason to get her the help she needed." Yes. This had to be it. She was never able to take care of herself. The Judge had given them a home and offered them guidance, direction, and stability. He had given them all a life they could be proud of, a life in which they could hold their head high—a life of respect.

"If people don't respect you, you're nothing. You're worse than nothing," Peter remembered his father telling him many times. "You may not like me, but you will respect me," he would say after some long and painful lesson Peter needed to learn on his way to becoming a "real man."

Peter squeezed and twisted the steering wheel and clenched his jaw. Then he sat up and scolded himself in his father's voice again for being such a pansy, for crying like a little girl.

Then he tapped the computer screen to life, bolted next to his seat in his police cruiser, and got to work.

It probably isn't her anyways, he told himself.

Chapter Twenty-Four

Hope is one of the hardest things to find on the street. Life is reduced to scavenging for the cast-off fragments of civilization, and those who live there struggle with any vision of their future. You begin to fade. The part of you that can problem solve fades. The strength to defend yourself and do what is right fades. Your identity fades. The passion and vibrancy of your humanity fades until all that remains is a shadow of someone once unique and beautiful. You become invisible.

Samantha was fading into shadow. She had fought desperately to hold onto fragments of her hope and her identity, but fear was giving way to despair. She had gone from hope that morning, with a little cash in her pocket and a strategy for getting out of the city, to losing everything when her car was impounded, including most of the money she had received for the watch.

Now, all she could focus on was that necklace—her mother's necklace—hanging in Marvin's window, taunting her to come and get it; everything else for her was numb.

She had been waiting among the trees in the Commons, across from Marvin's apartment, for most of the day. Now the park was dark and the night was cold. She dug her hands into the pockets of her hooded shirt wishing she had thought to pull on a pair of jeans before she had gone out for breakfast that morning—hating herself for not just staying with the car until Mike came, scolding herself for being that stupid.

The street was empty. Even the house two doors down had clicked off their music and turned out their lights more than an hour ago.

She could wait all night, but Marvin wasn't going to be any more asleep than he probably was now, so she crossed the street, this time going around the building to the back-door. She quickly jumped the wooden fence, found the steel backdoor unlocked, then quietly slipped into the kitchen.

"Where's my wife's watch?" a voice cracked through the dark room, a voice that was aged but strong and angry. Marvin sat at the small kitchen table, pointing the chrome pistol at Samantha.

She froze. Of course, the unlocked kitchen door was too easy. Then she said the only thing that came to mind: "I don't know what you're talking about."

Marvin narrowed his gaze at her. "I'm going to ask you one more time," he said, slowly and belaboredly pushing the hammer of the pistol back to its cocked position with the meat of his left hand.

Samantha shielded her face with her hands. "I don't have it!"

"You're lying."

"I'm not," she quickly shook her head. "I just came for my necklace."

"Where's my wife's watch?" he snapped at her.

"I don't know anything about a watch!"

"All you people are the same—rotting my neighborhood to its core. Good people live here, trying to raise families here! And all you people do is take and steal and consume anything you can find, like rats in the sewers."

"Now wait just a minute…."

He slowly lifted the gun a few inches higher from the table. "You think you have the right to come into MY home and take whatever you want for your drugs and filth? You think you have the right to steal from my wife, my DEAD wife?" The thought of this made him even more angry, and he poked the gun at her, punctuating his anger. "This is my HOME," he said, pounding his chest. "This is my neighborhood." He hit his chest again. "And it is dying. Because of you!"

"Please put the gun down," she said.

"No, I will not put the gun down until you give me my wife's watch back!"

She looked around, but there was nowhere for her to run.

"Wait just a minute," he said, standing up and clicking on the kitchen light.

Samantha pulled back at the brightness and shielded her eyes.

"You're that waitress I seen down at the Blue Bonnet. What are you doin' here?" he asked her.

She ran her hands through her hair and couldn't see beyond the barrel of the silver pistol still bearing down on her. "Please. Stop pointing the gun at me, and I'll tell you."

Marvin could see the look of sheer terror on her face. So he took a deep breath and sat back down. "Are you going to run?" he asked.

"No," she replied.

He squinted at her, trying to decide if he could believe her, figuring that if she got away this time, he would never see her or his wife's watch again.

"I can't run. I can't leave without that necklace. Please put the gun down," she said.

"So you admit that that is your necklace?"

She sighed. "Yes." She had to tell him something to get him to stop pointing the revolver at her, and she knew that a mix of the truth was often good enough. But she had to think quickly.

"What's your name?" Marvin asked.

"Savannah."

"Savannah what?"

"Savannah Wilkins," she said.

It looked to him like she was starting to the truth, so he set the gun on the table but didn't take his hand from it.

She took a deep breath and put her hands down.

"Why is your necklace in my house?" he asked.

"I followed you home. From the Blue Bonnet," she said.

"Why? And don't you lie to me," he said, pointing the gun at her again.

She shielded herself with her hands again and turned away from it. "I won't. I won't. Please don't do that."

He set the gun back on the table. "Then you better start talking."

"I followed you home because I thought you needed help."

"With what?" he asked, eyebrows furrowing in deep piles on his forehead.

She was good at crying her way out of trouble, and the razor blade of stress that the presence of a gun elicited in her meant tears were quick to turn on. "I just got fired from the diner, and I really need a little cash to help me get out of town. I thought…I thought…" she didn't wipe the tears away as they trickled down her cheeks, wanting to make a good show of things. "I don't know exactly. I thought maybe I could help you clean your house or something. And I knocked on the front door," she lied, "but you weren't home. So I tried the handle, and it was unlocked."

"Unlocked?" Marvin tried to remember if he had locked the door that night. He always locked the front door, but maybe he had left it open in the haze of grief. It wasn't impossible. "So you just let yourself in?"

She let loose the tears now. "I'm so sorry. I shouldn't have! The door was open, so I stepped inside and hollered, thinking maybe you were just watching some television or something. I should have stopped there, but I was hoping you might have some chores or something." Then she slowly looked up at him, remembering that maybe she had a little leverage with her next comment, but she had to play it very carefully.

She wiped her face with her sleeve. "Then I saw that woman. That dead woman. In your bedroom. And I guess I got so scared that I knocked over a table. And a box, maybe? Then I ran."

Yes, this was working. She could see his face slowly softening from anger to confusion. She could work with confusion.

"It wasn't until I got home that I realized I had lost my necklace somewhere," she was running out of tears, so she covered her face with her hand and sniffed a couple of more times to highlight just how important that necklace was to her. "That's my mother's necklace," she looked up at him. "My dead mother's necklace. And I just have to get it back."

Marvin didn't know what to do with this. This was not at

all as clean-cut of a situation as he had imagined while sitting in his dark kitchen for the last two hours, waiting for whoever belonged to the necklace to come crawling back through his door, maybe some young street addict hyped up on drugs or a teenager with something to prove to their friends, but not this. This was something entirely different.

He ran a hand over his hair, trying to process what he was hearing. "Were you the one who called the police?" he asked.

She had forgotten about that and nodded.

"Why would someone trying to rob me then call the police?" he asked, rhetorically more than anything.

"Because I wasn't trying to rob you!"

"And you called the police because you saw my dead wife in bed?"

Yes, that sounded good to her, so she nodded again.

Savannah watched his grip slowly loosen on the pistol though he did not take his hand from it while he tried to piece everything together in his mind. Fragmented memories of the night and shards of recollection of what he had seen in the room while he was cleaning up earlier that day. He couldn't deny that what she was telling him sounded reasonably plausible. Plausible enough that the gun now felt a bit heavy-handed. Maybe she had come by looking to help him. After all, someone had called the police, and the police said the call came from inside the apartment. Why would someone try to help him who was also trying to rob him?

"What I don't understand, if what you say is true, is: Where's my wife's watch?"

"I don't know," she replied, shaking her head. "Maybe it fell when I knocked over the jewelry box. Did you look on the floor or under the bed?"

"I looked everywhere!"

She tried harder. "Maybe it fell into a drawer or behind something. I lost a ring once and looked all day for it until I found it that night in the cuff of my jeans."

"The cuff of your jeans?" He shook his head. The absurdity of the thought and the situation made him feel foolish. What if it had simply fallen somewhere, and he just hadn't found it yet? And who was he to think he would get any answers at the end of a barrel, some cowboy?

"Alright, Miss Savannah Wilkins. I'm a let you go. But the next time you want to help someone, you might start by knocking on their front door and WAIT until they let you in."

Her anxiety began to lift. Her little drama had worked. No one ever suspects a young girl.

"Can I have my necklace back?"

He shook his head. "No."

"No?"

"No. What you say might be true, but it might not be true too. And I'm still missing my wife's watch."

"But..."

He lowered his gaze at her and slowly lifted the pistol again, this time letting it hang loosely in his hand instead of pointing it at her directly. "I think it's time you be going," he told her.

"I can't leave without that necklace," she said.

"Oh, I think you can unless you want me to call the police and let them sort it out. But, I tell you what: I will look harder for that watch. You come back in a few days, and if I've found it, the necklace is yours. If not, maybe you can find it for me, wherever it went."

Samantha decided that had to be good enough. As much as she absolutely did not want to leave without her mother's necklace, she was more than ready to be away from that gun.

"And this time, maybe you use the front door," he told her, it not being lost on him that she had come in through his backdoor but still unable to reconcile all of the details of what she was telling him with what little he could remember of the night.

Once she was outside and safely far enough away from the apartment to let her guard down, she collapsed on the sidewalk and started bawling.

The stress of having a gun pointed at her and losing her car and losing her mother's necklace and having her white-knuckled grip on her sanity ripped away from her made her cry until she threw up for the second night in a row. As a child, she had never realized the world could be so cruel and so cold—so unrelenting.

She had never felt so vulnerable, not even when her mother left.

She had to find a way to get off the sidewalk, but she could not. Her strength had faded to weakness—her confidence to insecurity. She was a broken vessel poured out on the ground like a sweet wine turned to vinegar.

She lay sprawled out on the cold concrete and resolved to let the darkness consume her. Whatever it was that stood against her could have it all. She had no fight left in her. Then through her despair, she heard some distant music and slowly sat up. A bar on the corner was just letting out for the night. Maybe she could find someone to take her home—give her a warm place to sleep and a meal, even if it meant she would have to trade favors.

This was an entirely new way of thinking for her, an altogether new low. She had never even considered trading her body for food or safety, but what choice did she have now? Maybe it didn't matter what happened to her anymore. Perhaps she was just a dead woman walking; a statistic waiting to happen; another nameless, homeless person lost to the street not even worth mentioning on the evening news. Maybe she was just another cliche.

She pulled herself up and began walking towards the music.

Chapter Twenty-Five

Samantha pulled open the frosted-green-glass bar door to a flood of light and the sound of a country jukebox playing. She wiped her eyes and went inside.

"Excuse me," she said, but the tall and slender bartender with a black Metallica t-shirt continued pouring drinks for other patrons. After a minute, she said again: "Excuse me," and held up a hand. But there was no response. "Excuse me!" she hollered over the music and slapped the bar, but no one, not even the bartender, paid her any attention until a muscular man with hair as long and straight black as hers, wearing a thick leather bracelet, stepped out from the back. "Can I help you?"

"Bacardi," she yelled over the music.

"Got some ID?" he yelled back.

She scoffed at him. "Yeah. Here," and she reached into her front pocket and pulled out her middle finger.

He only raised an eyebrow.

"Just give me a Bacardi, will ya?" She set one of the few twenties on the bar she had left from breakfast. She had never drank before. Bacardi was what her mother's boyfriend always leaned on before he disappeared from their life.

"Sorry. No can do, kiddo. No ID, no drink."

"Common. Do I look like I'm from the FDA or whoever?"

He ignored her comment. "What are you doing in here anyways? You're not one of the regulars."

"Maybe I should be," she told him, then noticed a thick tribal tattoo wrapping around his left arm just above his elbow. "Are you Hawaiian?"

" 'ae. I am kama'aina."

She smirked. "I haven't heard that in a long time. So was my mother."

"Your mother, but not you?"

"I'm not anything," she replied, half under her breath. "Can't you just cut a fellow islander a break?"

His eyes narrowed. "You know what? I think I can, this time." And he went into the back.

She watched around the bar for a few minutes, but at no time did anyone pay her any attention.

When he returned, he sat in front of her a large dish piled with rice, a hamburger patty, and a fried egg covered in brown gravy. Then he poured her a glass of cold water.

She was dumbfounded. "Is this loco moco?"

He smirked.

"How do you have loco moco?" she asked.

"It's a special tonight, on the house, for fellow kama'aina."

The fragrance of the beef and gravy made her mouth water.

"What's your name?" the bartender asked, handing her a fork. "In Hawaii, my name is Mikala, but around here they call me Michael."

"Savannah," she said, taking a bite.

"Funny. You don't look like a Savannah to me."

"Oh yeah, who do I look like to you?" she asked, wiping a

pearl of gravy from her lip.

"You strike me more as a Samantha," he told her, and she looked up at him but didn't say anything.

As she ate, it was as though the bar, music, and other patrons had disappeared. She was back home. Somehow, in this little bar in the middle of Boston, she had found someone who had made her favorite comfort food, strikingly just the way her mother used to make it for her growing up. It warmed her and made her sleepy.

When she finished, she looked up and realized she hadn't noticed where the bartender had gone. Only the slender man with the Metallica shirt poured another shot down the table from her.

"Tell him I said thank you!" she hollered, but the man paid her no attention.

Now that her stomach was full, she desperately needed to find somewhere to sleep. Then she had an idea. She rose from the barstool and made her way out of the crowded restaurant and into the night.

Her small four-by-eight storage unit and her cell phone were the only two regular payments she fought to keep up with, and now she stood in front of a dark Self Storage looking around for a camera, swaying from exhaustion. She knew there was a small camera over the front register, but she didn't see any around the property. There was a six-foot rod iron fence, but a previous visit had revealed that the shifting Boston hillside was slowly separating the bars from their column support, so she went around the back of the building, looking for a way in. Once she found what she was looking for, it only took a slight pulling to open the broken fence far enough to squeeze through.

In movies, storage units, and junk yards, both have dogs patrolling, but there was nothing like that here. It was simply lanes of grey and red units with rolling steel doors, each held shut with a thick round padlock.

She found her unit, rolled the heavy, cold steel door open, and closed it behind her. She was certain no one would be around for at least several hours.

The concrete and steel room was as dark as a tomb, so she flipped her phone open and tried to navigate by its small, glowing light. Some people might feel claustrophobic in such a small dark space, but to Samantha, tight spaces had always been cozy and comforting, and there was no one here to bother her. Here, for the next few hours at least, she was safe. She had lowered herself to sleeping in a storage unit, but she didn't care. When you are trying to survive, literally fighting to survive for just a few more hours, you will hide away in whatever hole you can find. Maybe Marvin was right. Perhaps she had become a rat—a street rat.

That was not the worst name the taunting voice in her mind had called her that night, a voice once comforting and encouraging, like the voice of her mother that had twisted into something entirely different. The voice had mocked her, swore at her, called her filthy names no one should ever hear. But, for now, somehow, that voice was silent.

She had seen other units as catastrophic piles of detritus others couldn't bring themselves to part with, but this was not so in Samantha's unit. This small concrete room was the last tiny private space she had in all the world, a meticulous museum of her former life. She had spent a few dollars at one point buying plastic shelves with drawers where she organized and hid away the more essential pieces of the life she once shared with her mother—items either too important, too valuable, or too large to keep in her car.

She was now so tired she could barely stand.

Some of the clothes her mother had left behind were in one drawer, and some of her own clothes were in another. She took out a warm pair of pajama bottoms and pulled them on over her shorts. Then she found some wool socks and slipped a warmer shirt on underneath her sweater.

She also had laid out knick-knacks from home: A ribbon from the national spelling bee, a small carved bear, a folder covered in colorful stickers full of art she had created for her mother. And next to these sat a plain-white teddy bear with matted fur from when she was a toddler.

She took the bear down and smelled it. It smelled like home. It smelled like her mother from the years they had shared a bed as their life shrank from a townhouse to a one-bedroom apartment and finally a motel room. And that smell pulled her out of the abysmal hell her life had somehow become back to the warmth and happiness of her childhood. She had buried that perfect place down so deep inside that nothing could touch it—a balm to her soul.

She slid one of the shelves forward far enough to unroll a large blanket her grandmother had quilted for her as a small girl, wrapped herself in the blanket, and laid down on the concrete floor.

She would eventually have to open her eyes again to the reality of this life, but not tonight. Tonight she would bury her nose in her teddy and fall back into her happy place.

And there, for the first time in many months, she rested peacefully.

PETER WIPED HIS FACE and the back of his neck with a towel as he sat down at the glass desk where Samantha's life, in the form of her journal, lay open in front of him. He had just finished showering after another weight-lifting session and vigorously shook a protein shake in a clear blue shaker before taking a long drink of the thick vanilla-flavored liquid and started reading again.

"I can't keep Clifford at the motel any longer. Not with that creep watching everything I do, but I'm going to try to stay as close as possible for as long as possible. Mom has to come by sometime. I've run out of people to call who she used to know. I even tried Kalon, who was excited to hear from me. He hadn't heard from mom, but he did say he would love it if I came and visited him in Hawaii. Mom never told me why she stopped talking to her brother, and I never questioned it, but Hawaii sounds nice. Apparently, I have a little cousin there I never knew about. I did something today that I wasn't proud of. I'm trying to keep minutes on my phone if mom calls, but I haven't had any other money since Tuesday. As I left the grocery store, I saw one of the young guys, probably my age, tossing out some day-old stuff. So, I waited until he went back inside and grabbed two loaves of bread and some apples out of the trash. It's not stealing if they threw it away, right? I've never eaten out of the garbage before, but it wasn't so bad. The bread was in bags, and I wiped down the apples with a towelette. I've never tasted anything so amazing, but I think it was because I was so hungry. How long is mom going to be gone? What if I have to leave? How is she going to find me? I have to keep my phone no matter what. And I'll stay close to the motel. She has to come by sooner or later, right? Oh mommy, please come back."

"That creep threatened to dump all our stuff on the sidewalk today, so I got a storage unit at Self Storage on Harrison and Traveler and took what I could. I got the first month for a dollar if I paid for two more. If mom's not back before then, I'm not sure how I'm going to keep paying for it. I was also at a cafe today when some guy handed me a folded paper and left. It said: I've been watching you. You have a pretty smile. You should call me. Then it had his phone number. The guy looked like he was sixty-five! I'm not sure what that even means by "call me." Why would he want me to call him? I just threw it away."

Peter noticed that Savannah had started writing a dollar amount in the top corner of each entry, which he presumed was how much money she had on her at the time, and most of the time, it was little to nothing. It almost felt like a daily score. Some days she was winning, and most days she was losing.

"I was on the bus today, going to the library to use the internet, and some guy grabbed my thigh! I mean, just straight up grabbed my thigh! What was he thinking? What gave him the right to put his hands on me? I pushed his hand away and moved to the front of the bus closer to the driver when I heard him call me a filthy name. I hadn't ever heard anyone call anyone that before. I'm not going to write it here, but it started with a C. When I got to the library, they said I needed a library card to use the internet and asked me my name. I don't know why, but I just told them my name was Savannah. They just wrote Savannah on the card and handed it to me. It feels weird seeing someone else's name on something I own. Savannah. At least it sounds like Samantha."

Peter opened his notepad and flipped to where he had

underlined the question: "Who is Samantha Wilkins?" and wrote down "Self Storage, Harrison and Traveler."

He looked up at his favorite photo of the ones he had taped to the wall, the one of her in her bathing suit on the beach, and said: "Hello, Samantha Wilkins. It's nice to finally meet you." Then he looked back over his notes. The name "McLean Psychiatric Hospital" anchored his attention. He looked at those few simple words for a long minute before rising from the glass desk, rinsing his shaker cup in the sink, and returning to his personal gym in the basement. This was like a temple to self where mirrors hung on every wall along with posters of athletes and male models flexing and straining.

"Are you here for Emily Stevens?" he remembered the nurse asking him from behind the hospital desk as he clicked on a sleek black and silver treadmill that began to whirr to life under his feet.

"There must be some mistake," he remembered telling her.

"No mistake. No mistake at all."

In his mind, she was as frozen and lifeless as a mannequin. "No mistake. No mistake at all." He clicked up the speed on the treadmill and started jogging.

"Are you any relation to the great and honorable Judge Marshal Stevens? The all-powerful, all-knowing, and never wrong in anything he does, perfectly honorable Judge Marshal Stevens?"

"Yes," he said, shrinking like a little boy to the gaze of a looming executioner.

"Oh, then there is no mistake at all. You are definitely the son of that worthless woman!" The mannequin said unblinking, jerking her head back and forth with every word as though her neck was a hinge and her head was on a string.

Peter clicked up the green plus button in front of him as the speed went from five to six to eight. Eight-point five. Nine. Now he was sprinting as he pushed the plus again and again.

"No mistake. No mistake at all. She was a danger to herself and her family," the mannequin's squeaking, crackling voice said, growing to a cacophonous scream in his mind as he sprinted as hard as he could.

"You belong here too, you know," the voice told him. "You broken pansy. Who are you to think you could ever be even a fraction of the man your father was? Why try? No one respects you. And you know that if no one respects you, you aren't even a man. You're less than a man."

He could feel the burning in his legs that he knew was the lactic acid buildup in his muscles, which would start to turn into nausea, but he kept running without slowing his pace, sweat streaming down his forehead and arms.

Then the voice started laughing, and the laughter turned from the nurse's voice into his father's, which was worse than his fears of failure. Worse than being called those names.

Not even the "correction" beatings his father handed out with the ruler, belt or some of the bamboo rods his mother used to use in the garden were as bad as the sound of his father laughing at him. He had never actually heard his father laugh; however, the voice of his father laughing now smarted to the core of where he was still that little boy yearning for his father's approval and hoping his mother would one day return home and once again become the focus of his father's brutal affection.

He hit the red stop button, dropped to his knees, and rolled off the slowing treadmill onto the gym floor, but the laughing did not stop. Instead, it became the laughter of a young waitress with black hair in a diner from two nights ago. Now she was the one laughing at him. Now she was the one taunting him relentlessly. Now she was the one telling him that he was less than a man.

He sat up on his knees, pulled at his hair with both hands, and screamed. Then he slowly pulled himself back together and looked at himself in the mirror. His shirtless torso was bulging with cords of muscle, and his face was bright red.

As he sat there looking at himself in the mirror, calmly burning with the memory of Samantha laughing at him in the diner, his feelings of lust and hunger to pick her up and hold and kiss that teenage girl began to turn into something else entirely.

Chapter Twenty-Six

T here was a knock. It was faint and distant, but it was there.

At first, Marvin wasn't sure if he was dreaming or awake, but slowly his attention began to focus on a knocking coming down the hall from the front door.

The cool blue of morning light enshrouded his bedroom in stillness as he reached for Margie but only found empty cold sheets and remembered that she was dead and he was alone.

Then there was another knock, this time slightly louder and more hurried.

He reached for his watch, sitting on the nightstand next to his bed, and squinted to read the time in the faint morning light. It was barely 7:45 in the a.m.

He sat up and accidentally stepped on Michael, who rolled over but didn't wake. Michael had pulled some blankets and a pillow into Marvin's room in the middle of the night and was now asleep on the floor next to him. Maybe Michael was alone too. But at least they were alone together.

Marvin rolled to the other side of the bed, went to the closet for his robe, and quietly walked out to the front door as another, louder knock caused him to whisper loudly: "I'm coming, I'm coming! Hold your horses, for sweet baby Jesus' sake. I'm coming."

Who in heaven's name could be pounding on my door at this ungodly hour? he thought to himself in frustration for being roused out of some of the better sleep he had had since Margie left him. He unbolted the three locks securing his front door and opened it far enough to peak out.

Savannah stood on his front step with her back toward him, shoulders raised, trying to guard herself against the sharp cold morning air.

"Child, what are you doing here?" he asked, taken back by the sudden rush of cold hitting his face. As she turned to him, he could see that she was in a terribly bad way. Her eyes were puffy and red from crying. Her hooded sweatshirt had a large tear down the right side, was caked with gravel, and her feet were bare. He could even see her footprints in the frost on his front steps where she had walked up and danced around in circles waiting for him to answer the door.

As soon as she saw him, she leaned against his door post and started crying.

He glanced past her down the street and then opened the door. "What happened to you?" he asked with wide and concerned eyes, motioning her to come in.

As she stepped inside, he closed and locked the door behind her, then went to the living room where Margaret kept a small basket of blankets and brought two out to the entry, handing one to Samantha and draping the other over her shoulders.

Then he noticed small dabs of blood in the footprints she left in the entryway.

"Come in here and sit down," he told her, holding the blanket over her shoulders.

Samantha followed Marvin into the kitchen, where he had pointed the gun at her the night before, and sat at the small kitchen table in Margaret's chair.

Without thinking, Marvin put the kettle on to boil, pulled down some packets of tea and sugar, and dropped two slices of granary bread into the toaster oven. Even if she didn't want anything, he might need some strength to have this conversation.

"I'm sorry," she began, her voice weak and wavering. "I walked around for probably an hour trying to think of somewhere else to go, but I don't have anywhere."

Marvin poured steaming aromatic oolong tea into a purple mug and sat it down in front of her, a sense of dread began to rise in him. "Did someone hurt you?" he asked.

She started crying; however, there was no manipulation this time. "It's so cold out. I went into a Dunkin Doughnuts to get a cup of coffee. I didn't even order at first. I just stood there looking at the menu, trying to warm up. But the lady told me I had to order or get out, so I ordered."

Marvin handed her a tissue, and she wiped her eyes and covered her face with her hand. She felt ashamed and didn't want to tell him what happened next.

"I should have stayed in the coffee shop, but the lady was so rude that I got my coffee and left. I didn't realize that two guys were following me until a couple of blocks away.

"I acted like I was going into a mall, but the door was locked. Everything was still closed. When they saw me look at them, they ran up to me. I tried throwing my coffee at them, but it missed, and they just laughed like it was a game."

Marvin sat down at the table next to her.

"One grabbed me by my shirt, and the other jerked my hair.

Then they pulled me into the parking garage next to the mall." Her voice low and stuttering through rolling sobs. "His hands smelled like oil. The one with his hand on my mouth, his hands smelled like oil.

She covered her face with her hand, unable to look at Marvin.

Marvin froze in fear for Samantha. He wanted her to stop but knew she needed someone to listen. His breath started racing, and his chest tightened like someone was sitting on it. He could feel a panic attack coming on. Anger, fear, sorrow, and a flailing range of emotions rose as his eyes began to burn for this child sitting next to him. He wanted to touch her hand but knew not to. He wanted to pick her up and hold her, but his instincts told him not to touch her in any way. This girl, this child, had just been attacked, and for some reason, she was sitting at his table, not at the police station. She was vulnerable in every way, and even his slightest touch could trigger any range of responses. And what about her clothes? She was still wearing the evidence, and he didn't even know how bad it was yet.

He rose and walked to his sink, his hands shaking, poured a glass of water for himself, and took the little bottle of pills from the cupboard, this time pouring four out into the palm of his hand instead of one. He stood with his back towards her, trying to hide his trembling hands, and looked out his kitchen window as she continued.

"I tried to fight. I pulled one of my hands free and slapped one of them, but he seemed to enjoy that. All I could do was beg God to help me. Over and over. I just kept begging and pleading with God to help me somehow. Send someone to hear me or hear them or something. I didn't know what; I just kept begging." Her voice grew sharp with surprise. "Then the car next to us beeped!

"When it did, they got quiet and told me if I made a sound, they'd choke me to death and pinched my nose shut. We could hear footsteps approaching, and one of them said, 'let's get out of here.' Then they ran.

"I don't know why, but I didn't make a sound. I just rolled onto my side, trying not to get run over by the car as it backed out and drove away. They saved my life, whoever they were, and they didn't even see me."

Marvin swallowed down two of the pills with big gulps of water, then turned and handed the other two, along with the remaining water, to Samantha. "Take these, child. They'll help calm your nerves," he told her.

She looked up at him, shaking her head in astonishment. "I begged God to send someone to help, and the car beeped. Then they got in and drove away, just like that." Quieter tears flowed now. "What if no one came? What if the car hadn't beeped when it did?"

Marvin could imagine full well what would have happened if no one had come. He had already lived through what happens when no one comes.

All he could say was: "I'm so sorry."

He sat with her for a while, letting her release everything she was feeling about what had happened. She took the pills and slowly drank the tea, holding it like a small child in both hands, then she ate both pieces of bread he had toasted, completely dry.

It wasn't until probably ten minutes of silence had passed that he finally asked her: "When was the last time you ate anything?"

She was quiet for a moment. "Last night, I went to a bar after I left here."

"Oh, child," he said, squeezing his eyes shut, feeling the weight of responsibility for what had happened to her. But she shook her head.

"No, it's not like that. The bartender was kind to me. He wouldn't sell me anything to drink and gave me some food." The memory of it slowly abating her tears. "Something that reminded me of home."

"And before that?" he asked.

"A little breakfast yesterday."

"I'd have guessed longer by the looks of you," he said, rising to the refrigerator. "Do you like eggs?"

She sniffed and nodded.

"How about bacon?"

She nodded again.

"It's a good thing I went to the store yesterday because I just so happen to have some fresh eggs and bacon even though doctor Murphy won't let me touch 'em. Due to my heart."

He didn't say anything else to her, and she didn't say anything else to him for the duration of the sizzle and pop of three scrambled eggs with cheese and four strips of bacon cooking on the stove, the weight of her story filling more of the space than there was room for in his small apartment. He was grateful to have something to do—something to focus on—for the few minutes it took for the pills to kick in for both of them.

When the food finished cooking, he sat down again next to her and asked: "Have you called the police?"

She shook her head.

"You need to call the police."

"NO!" She said, violently shaking her head. "Please don't. I know someone who was raped, and she said that talking to the police and the medical exam afterward was worse than when it happened. She had fallen asleep at a party, and some guy did something to her while she was passed out."

Marvin slowly looked away and rubbed his forehead. What was this world coming to, he wondered to himself. Is no one safe anymore? Is there no sanity at all anymore?

Then he sighed, realizing that his next question would begin to shift the weight of responsibility for her situation onto him. "Child, do you have anywhere to stay?"

She didn't answer but instead used the fourth piece of toast he had made for her, this time rich with butter, to soak up the last of the cheesy eggs.

She had forgotten how rich and comforting the smell of eggs and bacon are, like a thick wooly blanket for the senses.

Her silence didn't fool Marvin. He knew what no response meant.

"I have a room for you if you want it." And as he said it, the knowledge of how long that room had sat empty filled his mind. And now, two new residents had occupied it in as many days.

She quickly wiped her face with her sleeve and pushed the plate away.

"I shouldn't have come here. I have to go," she told him, the shame of what she had done to him quickly returning.

"You have to go?" Marvin asked, now confused by her response. "Go where? I don't think you have anywhere *to* go."

"I shouldn't have come here," she repeated. "This isn't your problem," and she ran to the front door.

Marvin calmly stood and followed her.

She managed to unlock the first two locks, but the third had a tendency to stick, and she pulled and pulled on it in frustration, trying to get the door open.

"I know you've been hurt, but that wasn't me. I ain't goin' to hurt cha," he calmly said and undid the third lock. She flung the door open and took off running.

Just then, Michael walked out of the bedroom wrapped in a blanket. "I'm hungry," he told Marvin, rubbing his eyes. Marvin looked one more time out the door for Samantha, but she was gone.

"Do you like eggs?" he asked and relocked the door.

PETER LOOKED AT HIS WATCH. It was 8:02 a.m. They were late. He couldn't stand it when businesses were late opening for the day. It felt like they were just wasting his time.

A skinny black boy in his early twenties, with a raiders cap, opened the glass front door to the office of the Self Storage on Harrison and Traveler. Peter stood up from where he was leaning on the hood of his pickup and walked into the small office where orange packing straps hung from the wall and stacks of boxes crowded the desk.

"Can I help you, officer?" the young man asked, walking back behind the counter and clicking the computer to life.

"I'm looking for the location of a unit belonging to a Samantha Wilkins."

The young man clicked away at the keys. "No Samantha Wilkins in our system."

"How about Savannah Wilkins."

He clicked the keys again, then looked up at Peter from the monitor. "Do you have a warrant?"

Peter hated that question. He always saw it as a challenge to his authority and an affront to the badge. If an officer of the law asked you for something, the only good answer was: Yes, Sir! So he leaned over the counter far enough to get uncomfortably close to the kid who sat at the desk just trying to do his job.

Then Peter sniffed.

"Is that pot I smell on you?" Peter asked.

The boy looked confused. "I don't do drugs. My momma would kill me."

Peter sniffed again.

"Yep. I *thought* I smelled pot. I bet if I had a look in your car, I would find something, wouldn't I? Now, either you can tell me where my *sister's* storage unit is, and I can help her with her business, or I can get into yours. Which would you prefer?"

This deflated the young man, who glared at Peter and bit his lip. Then he slowly stood, unlocked a metal box hanging on the back wall, and brought back a key that he laid on the counter in front of Peter. "317."

Peter smiled and took the key. "That's a good boy," he said as he left the building.

Samantha's unit was small and tidy. There were more photographs and linens and keepsakes on shelves that lined the walls. It was clear to him that this space was important to her.

He stepped in and gently touched the shelves.

Mementos of a happy and healthy child sat before him, but when he saw these things, it wasn't the fascination with her or attraction to her that he had felt reading her journal or going through her bag. Instead, the tightly twisting frustration of her rejection and her laughing at him stung the back of his neck. Then he stopped and knelt next to the ruffled and partially folded quilt she had wrapped herself in the night before. He gripped it in both hands and lifted it to his nose.

It smelled like her but dirty.

He rose at the disgust and swallowed hard.

The thought came to him: Everything in here was filthy. He wiped his hands on the legs of his dark blue Levis and decided he would need a bath after this.

He went to one of the drawers and slowly opened it, removing a long dress that fell and hung in front of him, which had clearly been her mother

's. It reminded him of his own mother's dresses—silk and yellow or cotton and grey. None of them expensive or fancy, but they were a delicate addition to the otherwise hard home his father commanded. Every one of them would go to the bin the day she left, except one—a dainty white spring thing with tiny blue flowers that Peter would keep in his room. One time, when his father wasn't home, Peter even tried it on. But, when his father found it nearly three weeks later, he would dole out one of the harsher "lessons" Peter would ever receive from him.

Peter dropped the dress onto the concrete floor and dug down deeper into the drawer, pulling the contents out onto the ground. Finding nothing of interest, he moved on to the next, then the next, until he came upon a folded pile of underwear, which revulsed him, and he slammed the drawer shut.

He went to his truck and returned with a stack of boxes and

swept all of Samantha's kick-knacks and memories into them with coldness. Her life belonged to him now, and she would have to come to him to get it.

HAVING LEFT MARVIN'S APARTMENT, Samantha carefully pulled apart the bars at the back of the Self Storage units, trying to avoid any sign of breaking in. She usually didn't care if they saw her coming and going since she kept up with her monthly payments, but she didn't want them to know that she had begun sleeping in her unit. If they saw her going in, they had to see her going out. She couldn't risk losing this last connection to her mother and her former life.

She felt dirty and worthless from the attack, like it had somehow been her fault, which was ridiculous, but she couldn't kill the feeling.

Her home was gone. Her car was gone. Her journal and sense of any security were gone. Now the privacy of her own body had been violated, but at least she could crawl back into her dark little rat hole, snuggle up with her bear and try to sleep away her life.

At least she had someplace safe to sleep, and that's all she wanted right now. She ached to disappear.

She stopped at the rolling steel door and stared at the lock. It was open.

Had she left it open? That wasn't like her at all. She always counted off four times to turn the key. Turn the dials or zip, unzip and re-zip her bag four times. Four was safe. Four was right. So why was it unlocked?

She looked up and down the lane of units. There was no sign of anyone else. But there, along the edge of the units, was one of her socks. She picked it up.

Why was her sock lying in the street?

She slowly removed the loosely hanging lock and rolled open the door.

Her unit was empty.

Chapter Twenty-Seven

Marvin and Michael walked quietly together towards Tadpole Park, leaves drifting slowly to the ground around them and the grass crisping in the chill autumn air. Marvin could feel that snow was probably on its way in the next few days. The morning paper didn't mention any, but Marvin had spent long enough in Boston to know how snow felt.

With a heavy heart, he couldn't help but continue to think about that young girl who had shown up in his life so suddenly. He wasn't sure whether she had stolen from him or not, but she didn't deserve what had happened to her. No one did. It gave him all the more reason to carry the weighty revolver around whenever he left the house. His sense of not being safe around the city anymore was accompanied by the hopeless feeling that no one would do anything about it.

He wondered about her past. Where had she come from? Could he have said anything differently—done anything differently—to help her feel safe? That look on her face before she fled his home made *him* feel like one of the monsters that had attacked her. And where had she gone? He was pretty sure she didn't have anywhere to stay, not anywhere safe anyways, but why did he think that? She hadn't responded when he asked. Had he misread her cues, had she misread his intentions? Oh no! Had she thought he wanted something from her? The horror of that possibility caused him to need to rest, so he stopped and sat on the nearest bench, and Michael sat with him.

"Are you okay, Marvin?" Michael asked, clearly concerned for his friend.

Marvin nodded. "I'm just old. And I'm tired. When you get to be my age, you get tired doin' just about anything." Marvin shook his head, remembering how healthy he used to be and how much energy he used to have. "Half the time I have to sit down halfway through buying groceries," he said, chortling at the thought.

"You look sad today," the boy said with a tender look of concern.

Marvin put his hand on the boy's back, appreciating the care in the observation. "I met a young woman recently. And someone hurt her. I guess I'm sad for her."

"At dinner last night, you said that you were angry at God for not being there for Ellie," Michael said, lifting his legs and tucking them underneath him. "Do you think God also left this girl alone?"

Marvin thought about that for a minute while he watched a young couple help their little girl toddle across the sidewalk in a pair of white shoes with little pink sequined stars glinting in the morning sunlight.

"No, because you can't be ignored by someone who doesn't exist."

"You used to believe in God."

Marvin grunted. "I also used to believe in Santa Clause and

the Easter Bunny. But when you grow up, you stop believing in fairy tales."

"Is that what you think? God is a fairy tale?"

"People are afraid of the unknown, and there is nothing more unknown than what happens after we die, so yes. I believe that someone somewhere maybe had a child who was dying, and to make that child—and probably themself—feel better, they told that child that after they died, everything would be just fine, pain would be over, and we would all see each other again in some big happy place in the sky. But I no longer find this intellectually honest."

Michael sat quietly, and Marvin felt that some of his comments might have been a little much for such a small child.

"I can see now why you're so lonely," Michael finally replied.

"Did your father teach you about God?" Marvin asked, wondering where all of these questions were coming from in such a small mind.

Michael smiled and nodded.

"Do you remember anything else about your father? Or mother? Maybe where you come from?" Marvin wondered if maybe things were starting to come back to Michael. But Michael just looked at him. "You can tell me, son. I won't let anyone hurt you."

"I believe you," Michael replied, hugging Marvin's arm and leaning against him. "But maybe I came so you wouldn't feel so alone."

"What do you mean, came? I found you on the side of the street."

"Are you sure you weren't supposed to find me there that night? Are you sure you aren't just seeing what you want to see?"

"What are you talking about?" Marvin asked, pulling away from the boy to better look at him.

"I know why you carry that gun," Michael replied with a calm and knowing look, like a father who had caught Marvin stealing candy.

The pointedness of the comment startled Marvin, who sat looking at the boy with no response. The boy had seen him with the gun, and the presence of a gun is no small thing for anyone to ignore, child or not. But what did he mean by *why*? Marvin himself wasn't entirely sure of the why. He simply *felt* like he needed it—*felt* like it somehow made him safer.

"You're scared," Michael added.

Yes, of course. That *was* the why. He hadn't thought of it this way before, but now, as Michael gave words to this twisted root of emotion suffocating his heart, Marvin recognized as clearly as the tinkling of a bell in his mind that Michael was right.

"But you don't have to be afraid," Michael said.

Marvin sat back and shook his head. So what if this child had realized something before Marvin had? That was no extraordinary feat at Marvin's age, but who did this child think he was telling Marvin what he should and should not feel?

"There's plenty to be afraid of. You're just too young to know better," Marvin said.

"Not if you can see past what's happening. Life continues. That girl was terrified, but someone came."

How did he know that? Had Michael overheard them talking in the kitchen?

"She wasn't alone in that garage, Marvin. And you are not

alone either. You have never been."

Michael stood up and hugged Marvin, who didn't really want to be touched at the moment; his emotions ranged from confusion to frustration, but he didn't push the boy away.

"And what I'm going to say next will be hard to hear."

"Oh?"

Then Michael held Marvin's head in his hands like he was the father and Marvin the child.

"It wasn't your fault."

Marvin pulled away. "What are you talkin' about?" The southern accent he had shed so many decades ago started to thicken as he became angrier. "Not my fault? What's not my fault?"

"Ellie's death wasn't your fault, Marvin. I know it haunts you, but it wasn't your fault. And it wasn't Margaret's."

Marvin stood up. "Now that's enough. That's enough, you hear? You don't know anything about that. That was long before your time. You don't know nothing about that."

"It haunts you like Moses' death haunted you for so long. Moses' death wasn't your fault either," Michael said.

Those words cut even deeper than what Michael said about Ellie, and Marvin was stunned at what he was hearing—stunned to hear the name of his baby brother after three-quarters of a lifetime—and from this child.

"How do you know that name?" Marvin asked, his voice barely a whisper.

Michael didn't respond.

"How do you know that name!" Marvin yelled.

He looked up to see the couple pull their daughter closer. Then he turned to find others in the park watching with concern. Marvin had been misunderstood before and wasn't about to get into it here, with all these strangers watching, so he turned and left for home, caring little about whether Michael followed him or not.

How did Michael know anything about Ellie, or Margaret or Moses for that matter? No way did Marvin have to listen to this nonsense—and from some child. He didn't need some little boy telling him, a grown man, how to feel. So what if he carried a gun? The city was dangerous. What happened to Savannah had made that clear, and he was too old to let anyone push him around. And if that meant he carried around a little help, that was his business, not Michael's. If anything, Michael should be grateful for everything Marvin was doing for him: Picking him up off the street, cleaning him up, and giving him something to wear, something to eat, somewhere to sleep. He had let that child into his home. He had protected him. And this child had the nerve to tell Marvin his business? No. No, that would not do. It was time for this child to go.

Bright pain flared in Marvin's right knee from a work accident years earlier, causing him to slow his pace, and as he approached his stoop, Samantha looked up at him from where she sat on his front step.

"You again?" Marvin asked, pulling his keys from his pocket and unbolting each lock.

She didn't respond.

"Well, come on in then," he said, motioning her into the house. Then he turned back to the park, but there was no sign of Michael anywhere.

"I'm sorry for what happened to you, but I can't help you if you don't let me," he said, dropping his keys in a small dish on his entry table. Then he paused, looked at her, picked them up again, and put them back in his pocket.

"I don't have anywhere else to go," she replied, ashamed of him not feeling comfortable enough to leave his keys lying around even though she couldn't blame him after everything she had done.

"Mmm hmmm. You said that."

He pushed off his shoes, hung his jacket and cap on their hooks, and sat in the entryway chair.

She knew it was time to be honest with Marvin. No more games, no more lies. He didn't deserve how she had treated him. He had never hurt or disrespected her. She had broken into *his* home; she had stolen *his* things. Not the other way around. If anyone deserved to be untrusting, it was him. But she needed him. She needed him more than she had ever needed anyone else in her life. Everything she had was gone. She couldn't put on clean clothes; she had no more clothes. She couldn't buy food; she had no more money. She couldn't even wash her hands; she didn't have a sink or a bar of soap to her name. She was sure she would not last the night if he cast her out.

"Please help me. I won't run this time," Samantha said.

Marvin sat there in his entry, arms draped over the armrests of the chair, exhausted from his walk and his frustration at Michael, not sure what to think or feel about this slender waif of a miserable creature standing before him.

"I can't."

"What do you mean, you *can't*?"

Nothing left to lose, she told herself. "You were right about what you said before. I have nowhere else to go. I think I ran because I didn't want anyone to know that I've been sleeping out of the back of my car for eight months."

Marvin's attitude, frustration, and resolve melted away at

the idea of this girl living out of a car.

Then she began to cry. This time it was genuine sorrow, nothing forced or for show. Instead, what came out was sorrow for the loss of her mother, something she hadn't let herself admit, at least not fully, until now. Sorrow for the loss of her former life, her real life. Sorrow for all of the horrible decisions she had made. Sorrow for all of the people she had hurt. Sorrow for everything she had stolen and all the lies she had told herself and had begun to believe about herself. It was time to let go of Savannah. As much as she hated Savannah, Savannah had protected her.

The tears that flowed now were honest tears coming from a place of brokenness, restoration, and healing. So she decided to tell Marvin everything.

Chapter Twenty-Eight

2017

The sizzle pop of popcorn punctuated the quiet evening, and its warm, buttery smell filled the house as Samantha, twelve years old, pulled a blanket over herself on the couch. She and her mother were just about to watch The Hunger Games: Mockingjay Part 2 on DVD as her mother filled a large bowl with the popcorn and dusted it with sour cream and chive popcorn salt.

"I feel like it's been so long since I saw the last one that I can't remember where we left off," her mother hollered from the kitchen.

"Come on, mom! Don't you remember? Gale had just saved Peeta, but when he reunited with Katniss, he choked her."

"That's right! Do you think Peeta's being mind controlled by President Snow?"

"Well, we'll find out as soon as I can push play!"

"Okay, okay," Susanne said, sitting on the couch next to Samantha and handing her the bowl of popcorn.

As the opening credits began to roll, there was a loud crash outside. Susanne rose to the front door and looked out the window. "Oh, dear god," she said under her breath. "Sam. Go upstairs."

Samantha paused the movie. "What is it?"

"Go!" her mother barked and went outside.

From her bedroom window, Samantha watched her mother pull her boyfriend, Phil, out of the grey Toyota pickup he drove, with a taped front headlight. The truck had missed the driveway and was half leaning over their front flowerbed with their white mailbox strewn across the yard in shattered pieces. He fell from the truck backward onto the grass, a large bottle of Bacardi in his left hand.

Mr. Jackson stood in his doorway across the street with one hand holding his night robe closed, and Susanne was shooing him back into his house, trying to stop him from calling the police and reassure him everything would be alright. Then she helped Phil slowly pick himself up from the grass and stumble inside with one arm over her shoulder.

From underneath her covers, Samantha listened to them scream at each other for the next hour, their voices often punctuated with loud bangs or the crashing of glass, until all she could hear was the muffled sound of her mother crying as she stumbled up the stairs, just outside Samantha's room, and close her bedroom door.

Sometime later that night, Samantha awoke to the creak of her bedroom door. Through her dreary haze and the darkness of the room, she thought it was her mother until the dirty Bacardi-stained smell of Phil's lips pressed against the side of her mouth and she startled and pushed him away.

"Come on. I said I was sorry," he whispered and pulled her closer, but she screamed for him to get off her and scrambled to the opposite side of the bed.

Phil groped at her covers and fell to the floor, then stood

just as her mother ran into the bedroom, swinging a large mirror with both hands that exploded across his face. He fell backward and pulled Samantha's dresser down on himself, as shards of mirror lay on the carpet reflecting the two women fleeing, hand in hand, into the night.

"And that was the last time we ever saw him. Mom never let me go back to the townhouse after that. She just returned once to get some of our stuff and moved us into the motel," Samantha said, her legs pulled up to her chest as she and Marvin sat at his small kitchen table.

"He seemed cool and all at first, taking her to fancy restaurants and buying her stuff. When he started hitting her, I tried to get her to leave, but I think some part of her actually loved him and wanted to help him.

"After that, she wasn't the same. I tried to help, take her out, get her mind off him, but for weeks it seemed like she didn't even want to get out of bed. Then she lost her job at the hospital, and we couldn't pay rent.

"I think that snapped her out of it because things got better for a while. But then she started coming home late or not at all.

"I think she was trying to protect me because she never brought anyone by the room, but I started to suspect she had another boyfriend.

"But she always came back! Until one day, she didn't.

Samantha took a deep breath and curled a long strand of black hair around a finger while she stared at the floor.

"I tried to stay as close to the motel as long as I could, but the manager threatened to call the police if he didn't get his rent. I didn't know what to do! I tried to explain, but he didn't care.

"I found one of her credit cards and was able to buy some gas and groceries with it for a couple of weeks, but then it stopped working."

Except for the twisting of her hair, it seemed to Marvin like she was in some sort of catatonic state.

"I started eating out of the trash and washing in bathrooms in grocery stores or malls. Then I started stealing. I tried to find work, but no one wanted to hire someone underage. So, I lied about my age, which was easier than I thought it would be. Restaurants especially didn't ask for an ID. They just handed me an apron."

She looked up at him.

"The night I came here, I had been fired. And I didn't come here looking to help you."

She took a deep breath.

Marvin just sat with a look of concern and compassion on his face, listening.

"I broke in looking for something to turn into cash. I was there when you came home, hiding under your bed. You were talking to someone, so I hid until it was quiet for a while, then decided to grab what I could and get out. I found your wife's watch. I also took some rings and other stuff. A bracelet, I think."

Marvin felt sorrow for this young woman as he tried to process everything she was telling him. "Were you the one who called the police?"

She nodded.

"Why would you call the police in the process of robbing me?"

Those words stung. But that's what she had done. She had robbed this man and his wife, and here she was sitting in his kitchen, asking for help.

"You're right," she replied. "I shouldn't have come. I've already hurt you enough. I'm so sorry."

He held up a hand. "Now, you said you wouldn't run again."

She had promised that. So, she just sat, waiting for Marvin to pronounce judgment.

"You didn't answer my question. Why would you call the police if there was a chance you could get caught?" he asked again.

"I found you in the bathroom, and I was afraid you might be dead. I couldn't leave you alone, even if it *did* mean I might go to prison."

Marvin leaned back in his chair. He had been wrong about her. She wasn't just some hoodlum. She was a young girl, scared and trying to survive, and he knew well that people do crazy things when trying to survive.

"Why did you come back?" he asked.

"My car is gone. I think the police probably took it. I had gotten a ticket to move it and tried, but it wouldn't start. That's what I needed the money for, actually. I was trying to fix my car, but now it's gone, so it doesn't matter. "

"But that was two days ago," Marvin said.

She wiped away a heavy tear rolling down her cheek and sighed. "Without my car, I didn't have anywhere to sleep, so I've been sleeping in my storage unit."

Wow, Marvin thought to himself. Just wow.

"But that's gone too. Everything I have in the world is in this bag," she told him, holding up her backpack.

"What happened to the stuff in your unit?"

She shook her head. "I don't know. I had been trying to keep up on the payments, but maybe I lapsed."

Marvin leaned forward and rubbed his face. Today he was feeling every bit his age.

Samantha was now exhausted. She hadn't told anyone else her story. She had always hidden it, protected it, pretended that her life was fiction, and would return to her real life any day.

Margaret would have been even more heartbroken than Marvin at Samantha's story, and he knew that she would have wanted him to do everything he could to help this girl, even though she had broken into their home and robbed them. That wouldn't have mattered to her. So that's what he was going to do.

Without saying a word, he reached into his pocket, removed the small key to Ellie's bedroom door, and handed it to Samantha.

Then he rose and went to his room to rest.

Chapter Twenty-Nine

The silver-grey bark of the bare cottonwood trees scattered around the grounds of McLean Psychiatric Hospital reached for freckles of afternoon light, and edges of frost retreated from the corners of the windows of Peter's police cruiser while he sat with a mug of coffee and Savannah's journal waiting for the 1 p.m. visiting hour to arrive.

He opened the book to her next entry, dated three months ago, with $7.58 written in the margin.

"I'm pretty sure the security guard at the library is following me. Every thirty minutes, he comes walking through whatever room I'm in. It doesn't matter which one. I don't know why he cares what I'm doing. I'm allowed to be there. I'm not hurting anyone. It's a public library! I also saw the bus driver watching me the last time I rode, so I've started to take extra precautions. I move my car every other night and never walk the same way back to where it's parked. I think I've found four spots I can park now, and I'll just need to keep rotating them until mom comes back. I had another spot behind the library, but I didn't trust that creepy security guard. It's also been a while since I've given anyone my name. I've even written a back story about where Savannah comes from, in case anyone asks. Savannah is from Detroit. Her father is in prison, and her mother died when she was a baby, so she had to grow up on the streets with a local gang. Savannah's not afraid to do whatever it takes to survive. Mom's been gone more than six months now, and I'm not sure how long I can stay in the city. I've mapped out a couple of places mom might have gone, places she talked about from before I was born. I think if I get maybe six-hundred bucks together, I can go out on the road and visit some of those places. I'm starting to wonder if she's dead. What if she is dead? How would I find her? Talk to the morgue? If she were dead, they probably would have buried her already. God, please don't let her be dead. I don't know what I would do if she were dead. I don't know how to do any of this on my own. Maybe Savannah was raised by a gang, but I wasn't."

The next entry in the journal was dated two days later, with $.37 in the margin.

"I got into a fight with a Freddy's Hot Chicken manager today. I had to pee and tried going into two different places to ask if I could use the restroom, but everyone kept telling me no, the restrooms are for paying customers only. I finally went into the chicken place and tried to go back to the bathroom, but the door was locked, so I went to the counter and asked for the code. The woman at the register said it was for paying customers only. I told her I was with some people I pointed to, but she said she didn't see me come in with them. I told her I had just been outside parking the car when they ordered, but she didn't believe me and wouldn't give me the code. I really had to pee, so I might have raised my voice a little. But then she called the manager over. The manager told me to leave. I said I'd leave if they just let me use the toilet, but the manager wouldn't give me the code! He told me the same stupid thing everyone else keeps saying, only for paying customers! What am I supposed to do if I don't have the money to be a paying customer?! I can't afford a $10 sandwich just to use the toilet! So, out of frustration, I pushed over a stack of cups. I shouldn't have, and I said I was sorry, but he told me to get out, or he would call the cops. So I left. Then I did something Samantha would never think of, but Savannah thought they deserved: I went behind the restaurant and peed in front of their back door. I got some on my shoes, which was gross, but they deserved it. What's so wrong with letting someone use the restroom? Doesn't everyone have to go to the bathroom? Where do all these people go who can't go at home or at work?! So yeah, that happened."

Peter's watch beeped one o'clock. He flipped the purple book shut, slid it underneath his cruiser's front seat, and went inside.

An old wooden staircase with hand-carved and twisted railings rose in front of him as he took directions from the nurse at the nurse's station to room 217. The second floor was well-lit and well decorated with a comfortable and calming motif of flowers and small woodland animals. As Peter walked past a large bird cage at the top of the stairs, several colorful canaries chirped at him. This was the ward for self-admitted patients who were free to leave whenever they and their doctor felt they were ready.

The door to 217 was standing open, and Peter could hear some John Coltrane playing on a radio inside the room. A silver nameplate on the door read: Susanne Wilkins.

Peter knocked gently, and a woman in her mid-fifties came

to the door much shorter than he, with olive skin.

"Yes? Can I help you?" she asked, looking at his uniform and holding the top of her blouse shut with a hand, a protective gesture that he often saw in women who were not acting aggressively or violent.

"My name is Officer Peter Stevens, and I'm here to ask you some questions about your daughter."

"Samantha? Is she alright?"

"Can I come in?"

"Yes, of course," and she stepped aside, letting him into the small room with white walls and wire mesh on the windows. "I'm sorry that I don't have much room, but you're welcome to sit there if you like," she said, pointing to a small corner table with some chairs. She clicked off Coltrane.

"Thank you, ma'am," he said, taking the pad and a pen from his shirt pocket.

"Is Samantha in some kind of trouble?" Susanne asked.

Peter thought about that question for a moment. "I have reason to believe someone is following her."

"Following her?"

"Do you know where she's staying?"

"We had a room at The Sunny Shores Motel," she said.

"I've checked there, but she was evicted back in June."

Susan looked worried. "Evicted?" Then she smiled. "Well, my Sam's smart. She's probably staying with some friends from school."

"Friends from school?"

"Yes. She was always popular, with her clubs and gymnastics."

"Do you know which friends she might be staying with?" Peter asked.

Susan thought for a moment, rubbed her hands together, then looked at Peter but didn't answer.

"Do you know the names of any of her friends, ma'am?"

Susan shook her head and laughed off the question. "She had so many. Who can keep track?"

Peter scratched out the word "friends" on his notepad. It was common in cases of neglect for the parent or guardian to be so focused on their own problems that they wouldn't know who their children were with or what their children were doing.

"I was sick for a while," Susanne continued. "Sam tried to help, but it was getting pretty bad, so I decided to come here rather than make her have to clean up after me." Peter could see some regret in Susanne's face at this comment. "But, I'm much better now," she said, perking up. "I've thought about checking on her a few times. They give us day passes, but I don't want to bother her." Then she stood up, retrieved a photo of her and Samantha sitting on the small table next to her bed, and handed it to Peter. "That's her," she said with a proud smile. "That's my little girl.

"I am doing much better. I'm just not sure I'm ready to leave yet. Not yet. It's so lovely here.

"I've made a life for myself here, you know. I'm just not sure I'm ready to go out. The nurses are nice, and I've even made some friends." She smiled. "We play Bridge on Friday nights, and I've even started attending chapel on Sundays. Can you believe that? Me in church? Well, the good Lord has helped me find rest for my weary soul, and I'd hate to think that seeing me again would hurt Sam.

"Besides, she's probably doing well in school and doesn't need to worry about her mother. She's probably dating some handsome football player or something. You're quite handsome yourself," and she started to reach towards Peter but caught herself and slowly pulled her hand back.

Peter was touched by Susanne's kindness and warmth when talking about Samantha, her voice reminding him of the warmth he had felt as a child when his mother would soothe him or tell him a bedtime story.

They say that inmates on death row call out for their mothers in their final hours, not their fathers. There's just something in the tenderness and compassion of a mother's heart that even the coldest criminals can't resist, and Peter felt that from this woman whom he had never met before. Confident that he wouldn't learn anything useful from her, he decided not to push with any more questions.

As he rose and thanked her for her time, she stopped him.

"Look out for her, would you? You look like a nice young man."

"You have a good day, ma'am," was all that Peter replied, then he left.

As he walked down the hall, past the chirping songbirds, and down the wooden, winding staircase, a song came to mind: El Shaddai. A Christian song his mother used to sing to him on nights when he couldn't sleep. She would wrap him in a soft, thick blanket printed with little sheep that often lay folded on the back of their couch and sing the gentle melody to him until he dozed off.

He hadn't thought about that song in years, and remembering those words brought him back to a sense of comfort, love, and security that he had not felt since he was a small boy.

Rather than leaving the building, he turned and approached the nurse's station.

An older Latino woman looked up at him. "Yes?"

"Can I have the room number for Emily Stevens?"

The nurse didn't even need to check her computer. "Emily is in the South wing. Just go out those doors, take a left, and it's on your left at the end of the drive."

He followed her directions down a brick path to a harsher-looking, whitewashed building with peeling paint and steel grates on the windows. He could not just walk into this building but had to wait at the locked front door.

"Can I help you?" a voice crackled over an intercom built into the brick.

"I'm here to see Emily Stevens."

There was a pause, then a buzz, and the door popped open a couple of inches.

Just inside, instead of a nurse's station with an open window and a waiting area that looked like an expensive doctor's office, an orderly in a white outfit sat behind thick scratched plexiglass in a narrow hallway with a second locked door at the other end. Peter immediately felt like this was closer to that of the county jail than a hospital.

"Name?"

"Peter Stevens. *Officer* Peter Stevens."

The orderly looked at his badge, wrote down his name and badge number, and slid a sign-in sheet chained to a pen through a metal box that let the orderly pass items back and forth to whoever was in the hall through the glass without coming in contact with that person.

"You can't take any of that with you," the orderly said, pointing to Peter's gun.

Peter lifted his arm and looked down at the equipment on his belt.

"You can either check it with me or leave it in your car, but you can't take any of that in."

Peter didn't like surrendering his gun to anyone for any reason, so he locked his belt in his cruiser and returned to the hospital. The orderly immediately buzzed him in through both doors.

"Emily's on the third floor," the voice squawked down the narrow hall.

The elevator was old and narrow and felt more like a utility closet ready to fall down a dank hole in the ground than anything patients, or doctors would use today. It even had the old steel grate that you had to pull back and forth across the door to ascend and descend between floors.

As Peter's elevator approached the third floor, he could hear screaming.

The elevator stopped, the outside door opened, and Peter struggled to get the steel grate to extend far enough to let him through.

Patients sat in wheelchairs in the hall near another plexiglass window where a heavy latino woman looked up at him. A slender man in his seventies with large bruises on his arms violently jerked his head this way and that as he walked up to Peter, who instinctively reached for his no-longer-present gun.

"Do you got a smoke?" the man asked, his eyes rolling up and around and never looking directly at Peter.

"Floyd, you leave him alone. He ain't got nothin' for you," the woman said through the window. And Floyd tapped the side of his temple with his finger and walked away.

"Can I help you?" the nurse asked.

"I'm here to see Emily Stevens."

"Emily? She hasn't had visitors in—well—ever, I don't think." Then she stood up, pulled on a large loop of keys connected to her belt by a retractable cord, and unlocked the office door. "Andy, I'm going to take this man to see Emily." The orderly sitting at a table towards the back of the small white office looked up from his game of solitaire and nodded. Then went back to stacking a jack on top of a red queen of hearts.

"We just finished lunch, which means she's either doing one of her puzzles in the common area or went back to her room to nap."

"She likes puzzles?" Peter asked, and the nurse nodded. She then led Peter through another locked door into a large open area where probably a dozen people of varying ages, genders, and ethnicities participated in various activities. Two men were sitting at a table where one laid down what looked to Peter like a poker hand while the other sat slightly away from him, staring out the window. A few watched My Little Pony on an old television set with a steel grate over it, and a slender woman with short, curly brown hair trimmed unevenly sat unmoving at a piano with closed keys.

Just then, a woman almost three times Peter's weight barked at him and growled from where she sat with a drawing and some scattered crayons on the table in front of her.

Peter took a step back, and the woman started laughing.

The nurse looked at him. "A bit jumpy for a cop, aren't you?"

Peter straightened his posture but didn't respond.

"It looks like Emily went back to her room. It's this way," the nurse said, unlocking a second door on the other side of the common area and leading Peter down another hall.

He could see into the small rooms, some with doors open

and some with doors shut. Through one door, he saw a man lying on a bed and reading A Movable Feast by Hemmingway. In yet another room, someone pressed their nose against the glass, watching Peter and the nurse walk past.

"Emily, you have a visitor," the heavy nurse said, lightly knocking on an open door towards the end of the hall. The light from a grated South-facing window was warm and let light spill into Emily's small room, where she sat at a table and mirror, brushing her hair with a pearlescent pink hairbrush.

"Imma wait for you down there," the nurse said, pointing to a chair back towards the common area. "Emily, you need anything?"

Emily turned, eyes large, set down the brush, and shook her head.

"Holler if you need anything," the nurse told Peter and walked away.

Peter didn't enter the room. Not immediately. Instead, he stood there looking at his mother, a woman he thought had left him and his father nearly ten years ago.

He had to some degree or another, come to terms with that years ago, or so he had thought. But now, here she was all this time, just twenty minutes down the road from where he lived.

This was the woman who had taught him the pledge of allegiance when he was eight and how to use the lid of a pan to make the perfect over-easy eggs. It was her voice that sang him to sleep and her perfume that lingered in his memories long after she had left.

"Hello," she said to him, her voice soft like she was speaking to a child.

He didn't respond. He just took a step forward.

Then she smiled. "It's you."

The recognition sparkled across his uneasy emotions.

"It's me."

"You came to visit. I didn't think I would ever see you again," she told him.

Peter took a deep breath.

He wasn't sure what he would find as he passed through the narrow halls of this old institution, but here she was; his mother. But she was also a stranger. Her thick mahogany hair had thinned and gone grey in the fifteen years since he had last seen her. She had also lost a lot of weight, and liver spots now freckled her arms in several places. But she was still beautiful. He could see reflections of that younger woman he remembered in her smile and how she touched the side of her hair.

A sense of tenderness and compassion began to rise in him, not unlike what he had felt toward Susanne just fifteen minutes earlier. Only this time, it was more profound and much more personal. This *wasn't* some stranger. This was his mother. The woman who had loved and nurtured and protected him from his father's violence for as long as she could. And how much had she gone through? He didn't know. As violent as his father could be towards him, he wasn't entirely sure just how bad the "lessons" were towards her—though he had an idea. Maybe he *had* been missing something—missing her—ever since she had left. Only, she hadn't left, had she? His father had put her in this place.

Peter looked around her tiny room, trying to understand something about what her life had been like these past fifteen years.

His father had put her here, but why? Why would he do such a thing? She looked healthy to him. She looked normal.

And why wouldn't she? She was his mother, after all, and Peter was healthy. He was more than healthy. He was strong. He was capable. He was the model of strength and masculinity, but maybe somewhere underneath all of that, he was still just a little boy who needed his mother.

He swallowed back tears. "To be honest, I wasn't sure you would remember me," he told her.

"How could I ever forget you, Marshal." Then she turned towards the mirror, realizing her mistake, and turned back to him. "Uh, your honor." And without thinking, she touched the side of her face.

At the mention of Peter's father, his heart sank.

She stood and touched her hair. "Please, please. Come in. I've been keeping the place just like you like it." And she moved her brush and a comb so that they lined up on her desk with a makeup compact and small bottle of perfume, all plastic. "I know the bed is a bit untidy, but I can fix that," she gave a nervous laugh and quickly began pulling up the sheets and top cover the way Peter's father had taught him. "No need for a lesson today. I'll get it right. You'll see," she said. And as she finished, she stood and smiled.

Just then, Peter saw that she was missing teeth on the left side of her mouth and immediately remembered how she had lost them.

Peter must not have been much older than ten the day he came into the kitchen for a snack, where his mother was finishing some dishes.

"What's this?" his father asked, pointing to two dishtowels hanging unevenly from the cabinet doors underneath the sink. But before she could respond, Peter watched his father punch his mother so hard she dropped to the floor, where she coughed up blood and spit out those two teeth.

"Our god is a god of order," his father said, kneeling over her and lifting her head out of the bloody spittle. "And you better remember that." Then he dropped her head back onto the cold floor. "Now clean this up before dinner." His father calmly stood, washed his hands in the sink, dried them on the dishtowels, straightened the towels, and returned to his study while Peter's mother lay there crying.

And now, on that autumn afternoon in McLean Hospital, what Peter saw sitting before him was not the hurt and abused woman who had given him life so much as a reflection of the inadequacies and imperfections he had spent his entire life trying to hide. In the eyes of his father, Peter had never been enough, but Peter spent every day trying to prove his father wrong. He was usually able to hide his insecurities beneath his carefully manicured veneer of perfect teeth and carefully presented mannerisms, but when he looked at his mother, all he saw were all of things about himself and his past that he could neither change nor accept. And if his mother *was* in a mental hospital, then there was a chance—even a small shadow of a chance—that he might be anything less than perfect, and he worked too hard to accept any of that.

Rather than compassion, seeing her filled him with anger and disgust. What a mistake to think that he might find his mother here instead of some woman with her name.

Before saying another word to her, Peter shook his head and left.

As the nurse rose and unlocked the first door back into the main room, Peter asked her: "What's wrong with her?"

"Schizophrenia. Today's a good day. Somedays she sleeps all day, and others, she'll wake up in the middle of the night screaming that her husband is in the room trying to kill her. If any of us try to calm her down, she thinks we're her husband, and things get violent. A few years ago, she stabbed one of my orderlies with the leg she broke off her chair." The nurse looked at him, pushing the button on the elevator. "Now everything in her room is bolted down.

But more than anything, she gets so angry. Angry at nothin'. If we forget to put two spoonfuls of brown sugar in her oatmeal, she'll throw the bowl at the wall and scream things that I ain't never heard before. Thankfully today's a good day."

He tried to process what he was hearing. "Is it genetic?" Peter asked.

The nurse raised her eyebrows, then turned and walked away.

He stood there waiting for the old elevator.

Coming here was a mistake, he thought to himself. Someone had the wrong information. They must have—a possibility that piqued his frustration. There was nothing wrong with his mother. She wasn't crazy. She was better than that. *He* was better than that.

Back at his cruiser, he put his equipment belt back on, then stopped and looked up at the old white building.

His mother left when he was twelve, and he would never see her again. He didn't know who that was upstairs locked up in that crazy house, but it wasn't his mother.

Chapter Thirty

arvin crossed the rooftop carrying two cups of hot chocolate, hoping to find Michael, his way of saying he was sorry for raising his voice earlier in the park.

He stopped to see vines of Margaret's tomatoes sagging under the weight of dozens of the plumpest and reddest tomatoes Marvin had ever seen. They were so ripe that tiny beads of juice were forming around their fuzzy green tops where the fruit connected to the vine. And it wasn't just tomatoes. All of Margaret's vegetables were coming back to life, filling the greenhouse with their vibrant colors. Red tomatoes and peppers. Yellow squash. Green tomatillos with their papery leaves. Purple cauliflowers and white eggplants with bulbs barely starting to ripen into their shining violet. Her flower boxes were also spilling over with rich colors. Dozens of shades of indigo Cornflowers, pink Anemones, violet Irises, and fiery Tulips. Marvin found it strange that everything had come back so quickly and so late in the season. He had never known tomatoes to ripen in late October. Then he saw Michael kneeling over the end of one of the corner flower boxes, pulling up some creeping vine and dropping them into a waste basket, his hands covered in dark soil.

"Doing some gardening, now are ya?" Marvin asked as he sat on the old bench and rested both cups of the chocolatey liquid on his legs.

Michael didn't answer.

Marvin tried to catch his breath from the climb. "Look, I'm sorry. There was no reason for an old man to raise his voice to a child like I did. You did nothin' wrong. And maybe you did something right," he added, looking out over the park. "All you were doin' was telling it like you seen it."

Michael stood and wiped his dirty hands on his trousers.

"Only, there's one thing I'd like to know," Marvin added.

"What?" Michael asked, sitting down next to Marvin and drinking his hot cocoa.

"Where did you hear that name, Moses? Did you read it somewhere in the house?"

Michael shook his head.

"Then *where* did you hear it? I need you to tell me now. You won't get in trouble. I won't be mad, but I need the truth."

"You want the truth?" Michael asked.

Marvin nodded.

"I was there."

"Where?"

Michael lifted the ceramic mug high to get the last drops of chocolate, then looked at Marvin. "I was there that day that you carried Moses through the magnolia trees to the swimming pond."

Marvin laughed. He had tried for the last few hours to figure out how Michael could have learned about his little brother, but at no time did he ever imagine this boy would claim that he was there.

"There is no way. No way you could have been there. You're crazy."

"I was there when Peter Mitchel, the sheriff's son, hit you in the back of the head with a rock, knocking you unconscious. Moses saw it happen and cried out for you, which is how they found him. If he had stayed quiet, he would have survived. You always thought it was your fault, but it wasn't. Those three demon-possessed little monsters were fueled by the hate they learned at home. Moses cried out for you and started swimming towards you."

Marvin stopped laughing now, and Michael looked at him with a look of knowing and profound sorrow.

"I was there when Johnny, Peter's older brother, walked out into the water and held Moses under until his beautiful little arms and legs stopped kicking. The other two didn't even try to stop him. They just watched. And I wept for him. And for you. I wept bitterly for you both as you found him and tried to wake him.

"It wasn't his time. He had a full, rich life ahead of him. A life cut short by hate.

"I stood there by the water's edge, and I saw you struggle to climb that hill with your brother's tiny broken little body on your back, refusing to stop—refusing to let him go."

Marvin tried to swallow, but he couldn't move. He simply could not move.

"But you found the strength, Marvin. And you carried your brother's body all the way home. You thought you were alone, but you were not. You never are.

"In empty bedrooms and lonely park benches. In covered garages or little orange hatchback cars parked behind diners. None of you are ever alone. I see you."

Then Michael opened his hand and held a spent bullet casing out to Marvin.

Mavin looked at it with ice-cold shock and reverential fear.

Then Michael smiled. "And I saw you dance for her that night," he said, lifting the brass casing with a single dimple in the back and looking at it closely.

"Dance. For Margaret?" Marvin asked, his broken voice barely a whisper, feeling fully like he had taken a heavy dose of one of the drugs he had sampled back in the seventies.

"The night I came to take her home," Michael said. "And I was there when Ellie died. She was not alone either."

Marvin tried to stand, but his legs gave out, and he stumbled forward off the bench onto his hands and knees, tears dripping from his nose. As he shuddered, he could not help but watch them pool on the ground beneath him. Then barely picked himself up and walked to the edge of the roof, where he leaned forward and tried to calm himself. His heart was starting to race, and he was having trouble breathing. He could feel a panic attack coming on, and he could already tell that this one would be bad.

"The not knowing was the hardest part for you, wasn't it, Marvin?" the calm voice said, rising from the bench. "Not knowing if she suffered. She did not. Not knowing why God would let her die alone on the sidewalk in front of your house. He did not. She was never alone."

Then Michael's tone softened, his pace slowed, and his voice lowered. "His name was Thomas. The son of two teachers. He served two tours in Vietnam where he lost control of reality before coming back to the United States. Thomas tried several times to get clean, but the drugs helped him sleep at night. The day Ellie died, Thomas had gone three sleepless days since his last fix. He hadn't intended to hurt her. He asked her if she had some change, but the poor girl got scared and started screaming, which startled him. He panicked and covered her mouth. He just wanted her to stop crying, but by the time he realized she *had* stopped, she hadn't been struggling for a while, and it was too late. So he ran.

"Three days later, he threw himself off a building on 47th, his guilt and torment becoming unbearable. The night terrors of images of the people he had killed in the war had become images of Ellie, and he couldn't take it any longer."

Marvin turned back to Michael, his hands now shaking so uncontrollably that he was sure he was having a heart attack. "Why are you doing this to me?" He asked, tears streaming down his face. "Are you trying to hurt me? Are you trying to…"

Then, from somewhere deep in himself, Marvin heard a voice like the sound of rushing waters: "Because you asked me to tell you the truth." And Michael reached out and took Marvin's hands. Marvin started to pull away, but as he did, a wave of euphoria swept over him, and he closed his eyes and breathed deeply. When he opened them again, his hands were no longer shaking, his heart was no longer racing, and his breath was steady, as if for the very first time.

"Who are you?" Marvin asked, the question slipping out of him as though he were more breathing it out than asking.

Michael smiled. "I'm your friend."

Marvin pulled away and pushed past Michael. He could not accept what was happening. This couldn't be real. He must be dreaming. There was just no way this little boy could know everything he was claiming to know. Did he get into a journal or photo album somewhere? Letters? Maybe a newspaper article stuffed in a drawer in Ellie's room that Marvin had forgotten about. Marvin didn't know, but he couldn't stand here. He went downstairs, pushed open his back gate, and started walking.

PETER STRUCK TWO LONG, WOODEN MATCHES and held them beneath crumpled pieces of paper in his fireplace, gently blowing on the rising flames.

"I'm glad you could make it. I've been looking forward to this for a while," he said, standing and walking to the kitchen. There he struck another match and lit two long-stem candles.

"What part of Boston are you from? Hawaii? I've never been, but I hear it's gorgeous." He smiled. "I'd love it if you took me some time."

Peter carried the candles to the dining room table and set them on either side of a large bouquet of red roses and baby's breath. Then he returned to the kitchen and began piling scoops of creamy white rice into a large wooden serving bowl he carried to the table. White linens and polished silverware sat next to wine goblets and cut crystal water glasses.

"We're having risotto. It was my mother's recipe," he said.

"You love risotto?" He smiled. "Great! It's one of those old recipes I make on cold nights. It has just enough cream cheese to give it a bit of depth without adding pounds to the waistline. Not like you need to worry about that. If you pardon my being forward, you have a fantastic figure.

"Can I start you off with a glass of wine? I know you're a bit young, but I won't tell anyone if you won't.

"Are you sure? Well, I might have just half of a glass myself. Can I get you anything else?

"Cranberry juice it is then."

He returned to the kitchen, filled another one of the cut crystal glasses with cranberry juice, and poured himself over half a glass of wine, carrying the bottle back to the table.

"Oh, you're very kind. Please let me do that." He filled a bowl with three large scoops of the steaming Parmesan Risotto, carefully wiped away a few stray grains of rice that fell from the rim, and set the bowl on the table in front of his guest. "I hope you enjoy it."

Then he served himself and sat down.

"Really? I had wanted to for a while," he said, taking a large drink of his chilled white wine. "Oh, I don't know. Nervous, I guess. You know how it is. Boy meets girl. Boy is too nervous to ask girl out. Boy finally gets up the nerve to ask girl out. They live happily ever after."

Peter smiled. "Well, I know we're not there *yet*, but a boy can hope. Besides, I don't know if you even like my Risotto. But before you taste it, I'd like to make a toast." He lifted his wine glass. "Here's to you! A young woman who's overcome so much hurt and hardship to be here with me tonight. But hopefully, that is all about to change. Together, you and me, we can overcome anything. Your life is going to be different now. I'm here now, and I will protect you—I can take care of you. So, to Samantha!"

Only, there was no one else in the room with him.

Across the carefully prepared candlelight dinner sat an empty chair where Peter had draped one of Samantha's spring dresses with little yellow flowers and a pair of dress flats.

Then he tossed back the rest of his glass and poured himself another.

"I understand. I'm glad you feel you can trust me." He

nodded. "There's so much I want to tell you too, but there will be time for all that."

He laid the napkin across his lap, used his knife to scoop a small pile of the risotto onto the back of his downturned fork like they do in England, and took a bite. Then he smiled and leaned back in his chair. "Perfect. Absolutely perfect," he congratulated himself. He set down his knife, pulled Samantha's journal towards his plate, opened it to the next entry, and began reading.

"I got a job today at the Blue Bonnet. A real dive, but I could really use the tips, so it's not all bad. There's so much grease on the backline that I don't have to walk. I can just slide back and forth while I take orders, and after only two days, my car just reeks of French fries and coffee. I will have to get a grocery bag to keep my shoes in so I don't get grease everywhere. Personal note: buy another pair of non-work shoes. So far, I've only worked the night shift with a waitress named Marty, but everyone calls her momma. Her ridiculously long nails are half the length of her fingers. I don't know how she types or keeps them out of everyone's food. Maybe she doesn't. A big plus is that I haven't been hungry the two days I've had shifts. I get a half-price meal during my lunch, and Marty doesn't seem to mind that I snack off and on. She said that it's not her business as long as Susan doesn't catch me, our manager. Most of the customers are cool too, but there is this cop that sits in my section for like two hours every night, just drinking coffee."

Peter sat down his dinner fork and shifted in his chair, realizing she had written about him in her journal. Then he looked up at the gown draped on the empty chair across the table from him. "I see you were thinking about me, even then." And he began reading again.

"He thinks I don't notice, but he watches me the entire time I'm there. The first night I thought he was going to arrest me, but then he started flirting. He's cute and all, but he's old enough to be my uncle. This is the last thing I need right now."

Peter read that line again: "he's old enough to be my uncle."

He quickly did the math. Samantha was almost eighteen. He was twenty-nine. Barely eleven years. He didn't see it as that big of a difference.

"I see you thought I was too old for you, huh?" he asked the empty chair. "But that's before you knew me."

That quiet thought dampened the burning he was starting to feel in the back of his neck. Then he read the next entry, where $7.42 was written in the margin.

"I got fired! That stupid Susan fired me. I almost screamed at her! Who does she think she is? It's just a stupid grease pit anyways. I got some groceries and washed up across town, but I missed the bus and was late, so she fired me. I was only late by like five or ten minutes. Maybe I had been late a few other times already, but I couldn't help it. The bus driver just took off without

me, and I had to walk like ten blocks. What am I going to do now? And on top of it, I got a ticket to move my car, which I keep trying to do but it won't start. Mike said he would fix it, but he needs like $100. How am I supposed to get that kind of cash without a job? I made $15 before Susan got rid of me, mostly from that cop creeping on me. He gave me his number tonight, and I couldn't help but start laughing. I didn't mean to, but really? Does he really think I'd go out with him? He's a cop. And he's like twice my age. And I'm pretty sure he takes a bath in that dollar store cologne he's wearing. It nearly burned my eyes the last time I walked past him."

Peter slowly tore a page out of Samantha's journal as he read that again.

"He's a cop. And he's like twice my age. And I'm pretty sure he takes a bath in that dollar store cologne he's wearing. It nearly burned my eyes the last time I walked past him."

Aqua di Gio by Giorgio Armani was *not* some cheap dollar store cologne. It was seventy-five dollars a bottle, and he did *not* bathe in it. He threw the balled-up paper across the room.

"I couldn't help it but start laughing," he read again; the word "laughing" was underlined.

Anger bloomed in his mind, and he pulled back a long drink directly from the wine bottle. Then he calmly rose from his chair and threw the bottle across the room and into the fireplace as hard as he could, just missing the fire and hitting the corner of the white brick, causing the wine to explode in a spray of yellow-clear liquid and glass. Then he screamed.

He could still hear her laughing at him in the diner, in front of everyone.

He tore a handful of pages out of her journal and threw them into the fire. The loops of purple ink glowed as the pages reduced to embers. Then he tore the book in half and threw the rest of it into the fire.

"Who do you think you are?" he said, turning and pointing at the dress draped over the chair. "Who do you think you are!" He screamed until his face turned red, pouring the heat of his anger into the volume of his voice.

There was something so satisfying about watching the purple cloth of her journal break away from its binding and curl back from the heat of the fire.

He went to his office, swept his desk full of her personal

items into a box, along with the photos he had taped to his wall, and carried them out to his living room, where he threw her things, one by one, onto the hot embers.

His body trembled, and his hands shook as he stood there savoring this form of permanently destroying her past—her identity.

MARVIN HAD LEFT THE HOUSE WITHOUT HIS JACKET, and the cold Boston evening stung his throat as he walked, but he barely noticed.

Words he had refused to speak anchored to emotions he had refused to feel were now breaking through a steel barrier of resolve that he had built to protect Margie, but she was gone now, and he had little care left. He had lived a good life; he had been a good person; he had been faithful to Margie to the very end; he had paid his dues. But what had he gotten from all of his hard work? Nothing.

And here he was once again, playing the good Samaritan for this child who was telling him his business—asking him about God. God? Where was God in all of this? Where was God when Moses died? Where was God when Ellie died? Where was that absentee landlord while everyone he loved had suffered?

Margie had never left him alone about God. "God still loves you. God hasn't forgotten you. God, please get ahold of Marvin's heart," she would pray at the dinner table while he was sitting right there next to her.

"Where were you?!" He cried out to no one in particular as he walked down the darkening streets of Boston. "You promised You'd never leave us—never forsake us! Where were you? You failed me. You are a liar!" Marvin shouted, pointing his finger out in front of him. "I believed You. I believed Your lies. And You never showed up. If you were real, you would be nothing but an absentee landlord. You'd be a liar, and that's how I know I'm just talking to myself. Well, I am done. I'm finished."

Marvin sat down on some cold stone steps and began to feel the weight of what he was about to say next. Some part of him *had* always believed in God; he had at least hoped in God. But God never had shown up, and there was nothing left to hold onto.

"I dreamt the dream of You. I wept for you." Tears filled his eyes. "I loved You so much, but you never came." Tears streamed down his chin and fell to the ground between his legs. "You were never a religion to me. You were real to me. But you never came. I waited, and You never came. I needed You. But You never showed up."

Marvin took the cold heavy pistol from his pocket and ran his thumb along the sharp ridge along the back of the gun. Then he clicked the chamber open to see where the single shell rested and clicked it shut again.

"I would have given you everything. I *did* give you everything." He swallowed, then whispered: "But when I needed You, a word, a touch, anything…You were silent. That's how much You loved me: You loved me enough to do nothing; You loved me enough to say nothing. You loved me enough to watch my family die."

With difficulty, he pulled back the narrow hammer with its coarse thumb grip.

"I'm so tired—tired of pretending. I'm sorry I couldn't be more. More for Margaret. More for Ellie. More for You. I'm sorry."

He pressed the cold tip of the barrel into the roof of his mouth and took one last deep breath.

Chapter Thirty-One

Marvin pressed the tip of the barrel into the roof of his mouth and took one last deep breath when suddenly he heard, through the otherwise quiet night, a voice deep and melodic singing:

"When peace like a river attendeth my way / When sorrows like sea billows roll / Whatever my lot, Thou hast taught me to say / It is well, it is well with my soul."

The words echoed inside of him. It was the song they had sung at Moses' funeral in the tiny one-room white-washed church back in Alabama.

Marvin slowly took the pistol out of his mouth and looked around.

The music echoed off the tall walls of the concrete and glass buildings in such a way that he couldn't tell where it was coming from.

He rose, walked to the corner, and saw the open door of a church down a narrow side lane, light spilling out onto the grey street.

As he approached, he could see through the open doors a bear of a man with a thick curly beard standing in front of a choir who supported his rich voice as he sang:

"It is well (it is well) / With my soul (with my soul) / It is well, it is well with my soul."

Marvin slid the still-cocked pistol back into his pocket, approached the church, and sat down in one of the empty pews towards the back. Then he watched the man finish his song and wipe sweat from his forehead. It was clear to Marvin that the choir was having practice as members laughed and discussed strategies to hit some of the higher notes in the song. Marvin welcomed the warmth of the building and the soft cushion of the pew. Then a more slender man stepped up to the microphone, and the piano began to play: I Surrender All.

The words broke Marvin's heart, and there in that empty pew, Marvin wept.

STILL PARTIALLY ASLEEP, Samantha felt soft blankets against her cheeks. She stretched her legs and realized there was room to stretch her legs. The clean, soft blankets smelled so wonderful that she didn't want to rise.

While the weight of her sleep continued to hold her in darkness, she was beginning to smell the rich dusty aroma of the room. She felt the complete release and freedom that came with being safe—safer than she had felt in a long time, safer even than she felt in the motel with her mother.

She didn't want to wake. She wanted to stay right there beneath those soft covers for another week, so she rolled over and buried her face underneath the pillow until her stomach groaned. She tried to ignore it, but it groaned again, and she decided it was time to pull herself out of bed and see if there was something to eat.

It was early morning, and the house was quiet. How long

had she slept? Ten, maybe eleven hours?

The door to Marvin's room was closed

She used the restroom and went to the kitchen.

She found some coffee and set the pot to percolate, then lined up on the counter some butter, eggs, cheese, a loaf of granary bread, a bowl, a fork, a wooden spatula, and a frying pan.

She couldn't remember the last time she had cooked. It must not have been since the townhouse. She liked cooking. Playing with the food. Trying new things. The smells. The flavors. Finding some unique combination of something delicious that she would usually share with her mother. But she hadn't had the chance to do any of that in a long time and getting to do that now filled her with a renewed sense of comfort and ease.

She clicked on the front burner as it sprang to life and set the pan. When it was hot, she peeled back the waxy paper covering the butter and rubbed the end of the butter stick onto the pan, coating the hot black surface with a thin bubbling layer the way her mother had shown her, which released an aroma that only cooking butter can produce. Her mouth began to water. There's something deeply comforting about the smell of cooking butter, she thought to herself and smiled. Then she cracked two eggs and gently let their clear whites and yellow yolks pour into little piles on top of the sizzling, creamy pads. She added a dash of salt, a handful of grated cheese and stirred the eggs with the tip of a wooden spoon.

As the eggs began to slowly bubble, she dropped two pieces of granary bread into the toaster and poured herself a large mug of coffee, which she held up underneath her nose to smell the moist, rich fragrance. Her mother had taught her how to pull apart the flavor notes in the aroma, and she could smell chocolate, cherry, and citrus.

There was something so comforting about this home. Where the world outside felt so brutal and unrelenting, the world inside here felt cozy and comforting, like the thick threads and fading fabric of her grandmother's quilt.

She stirred the eggs again as the toast popped up in the toaster.

She quickly wiped the dripping and melted end of the butter stick across the dry toast like a glue stick until the crisp bread was buttered and laid them on the plate.

Before the eggs cooked too far, she scooped them from the pan onto the toast and sat at the small kitchen table. Signs of love and family hung all around her. Magnets adorned the side of the fridge and a single crayon drawing, yellowing at the edges, hung on the front.

She wondered whose room it was she had slept in. It looked like a little girl's room from fifty years ago. But why would they have kept a room like this in such a small apartment? Wouldn't they have had a better use of the space? And why had it been locked?

She scooped the cheesy eggs onto her toast and tried not to absolutely inhale the entire meal without tasting it, but she was hungrier than she had realized, her hunger stirred up by the smells and sight of the food.

When she finished, she toasted two more pieces of bread, plying them with a thick layer of peach preserves she found in the fridge door.

She wondered if Marvin might want something to eat, but when she peeked around the corner, his door was still closed, and she didn't want to bother him. So she finished her toast, cleaned up the dishes and the pan, and carried her second cup of coffee in both hands as she walked around his tiny but cozy home.

Photos in old frames adorned the walls, but they were not dusty. She ran a finger along the top of one and was impressed by the total lack of dust.

She stepped into the living room and looked at the old television set. It didn't look like anything she had seen before. It didn't even have an on button or remote control. *Peculiar*, she thought, looking at the round dials. Then she turned and sat down in Marvin's plush chair. It was comfortable, like a warm hug, and she sank into it.

She laughed at herself, thinking how odd she must look sunken deep into the chair, her feet slightly off the ground. Then she looked at the wheelchair marks rubbed into the carpet next to Marvin's chair.

They loved each other, she thought to herself, imagining them sitting together in front of the news or some television show, laughing at the same jokes for years—for decades. It made her lonely.

She stood and went back to the hall wondering when Marvin would wake. She wanted someone to talk to.

She stood in the hall for several minutes, carefully listening to see if she could hear him moving around, but it was only silence.

Samantha returned to the bathroom and found a stack of soft towels under the cabinet, so she decided this was the perfect opportunity to take a hot shower. She rubbed the cotton-soft fabric against her cheek and remembered home; not the motel, but her real home—the townhouse where she and her mother were happy. As the steam filled the yellow-tiled room, she read the labels on the soap and climbed into the shower. She had never seen a shower with a seat before but knew immediately what it was for and imagined Marvin straining to help his wheelchair-bound wife in and out of the shower. The thoughts of his gentleness made her wonder if she was finally safe. Could she finally let her guard down—really be herself?

How long is he going to let me stay? she wondered, squeezing a pile of pearlescent soap into the palm of her hand and washing her hair. The bed was lovely. Breakfast was lovely. Having a cupboard full of food was really lovely. But, access to a hot shower? This was a luxury she couldn't quite describe. There was nothing like a hot shower to wash away all of the dirt and grit of the street, the soap smells and hot steam intoxicating to a degree that left her feeling like she might still be dreaming. She breathed in the steam and felt it fill and enrich her lungs. Then she opened the chair and sat down. Leaning back, she put her hands behind her head and stretched her long legs out in front of her. *Wow, I need to shave those!* she thought to herself. But, she could get used to a chair in a shower. Yes. It was decided. If she ever had a shower of her own again, she would have a chair installed. Maybe there was somewhere she could buy waterproof books and just sit in the shower and read all day. That would be a dream, wouldn't it? An absolute dream. All of this was an absolute dream. But how long would this dream last? The thought of leaving, going back out there—out into the world—stung. Maybe she could stay long enough to find some answers. Answers to what? She had no idea. She didn't even know what questions to ask, much less where to find any answers. What she did know was that she didn't want to leave. She sighed as another thought began to settle in: She had to get the watch back. But how? She didn't have any money. Johnny said that if he saw her again, he would call the cops. Maybe it was an empty threat, but probably not. Did he even still have the watch? Maybe not, but maybe. It had only been a few days. Maybe he hadn't had time to sell it yet. But even if he hadn't moved the watch yet, every day—every hour—that she waited decreased her chances of ever getting it back. Maybe she could break in.

She leaned forward in the chair, letting water spill down her face.

The lock on the back door wasn't complicated, and she hadn't seen any cameras in the back office. But, it was a twenty-four-hour pawn shop. It was open all day. It never closed. When would she get the chance to get in to find it? And what if he had a gun? He wouldn't use it on her, would he? She was starting to like the idea of a silent entrance until the idea of a gun came to mind. She knew he had guns in the shop; she had seen them in the back case.

As her skin glowed red from the hot shower and her fingers pruned, she decided it was time to climb out.

She didn't want to put her dirty clothes back on, but she didn't have much choice, so she dried her hair and got dressed as another idea came to mind about how she might get the watch back. She didn't like it, but maybe it was time she started thinking about someone other than herself; she owed Marvin at least that much.

Finding the house still quiet, she walked back to the shelves of books in the living room and ran her finger along old worn cloth spines in Greek and Hebrew with titles like Septuagint and Unger's Bible Dictionary. Then she pulled one of the books off the shelf with a red cover and thick as a dictionary labeled Strong's Exhaustive Concordance. The pages were onion-skin thin. Notes were scribbled in the margins between columns of Hebrew.

Then she recognized the name of one of the authors: Dr. Marvin Johnson.

There were four books with Marvin's name on their spines: Communing with the Holy Spirit, Prayer Like Incense, Still Small Voice, and No More Secrets.

She pulled Prayer Like Incense from the shelf and looked at the back cover. A photo of a younger Marvin looked back at her, and she read the back jacket blurb:

Dr. Marvin Johnson is the head of the Boston chapter of Pastors Fellowship with a Masters of Divinity from Boston Seminary. He has served inner-city churches for more than twenty years.

"Sometimes it feels like I wrote that in another life," Marvin said from the living room doorway.

Samantha turned. "I'm sorry," she said. "I didn't mean to pry."

"It's okay," He told her with a gentle smile.

"What are all these books?" she asked.

"Remnants of a past life. I tried to donate them to Boston Seminary several times, but Margie wouldn't let me. I think she figured I'd come back to them one day."

Samantha held up the book she was holding. "Is this you?"

He only responded with a slight grunt. Then he walked over to her, took the book from her hand, and looked at the back cover. "Another life," he said quietly under his breath, then put the book back. "Something smells good. Did you cook?"

"Yes! Can I make you something?"

"I don't usually eat breakfast, but it does smell nice," he told her, and they went to the kitchen, where she prepared Marvin some of her cheesy scrambled eggs.

"Thank you for letting me stay here last night," she told him.

"It was my pleasure. That room has gone unused for far too long. I recently had a guest use it for the first time in probably thirty years. But he decided he prefers sleeping somewhere else."

Another guest? She wondered what that meant.

She piled the eggs on the toast and set the plate in front of him. "Well, it means a lot. I haven't slept that well in a long time."

Marvin took a bite of the velvety eggs. "You're welcome to stay as long as you like, especially if you can cook like this."

Stay as long as I like. Did he mean that? Samantha sat down on the chair across from Marvin, unsure she could believe what she had just heard. "Could I?"

He smiled and nodded. "Like I said, the room's been empty for too long."

"Whose room is that? That I slept in?"

Marvin wiped the plate with the last corner of his toast. "My daughter's room."

Samantha didn't understand. Why was a little girl's room all locked up and decorated like it was from the seventies? But she wasn't sure she should ask.

Marvin saw the look of concern on her face and appreciated her respecting his privacy but didn't see any reason to keep all of this locked up any longer. So, he set his fork down and told a story he hadn't told in a long time.

"My little girl was killed on September 14th, 1978, only eleven years young.

"It was different back then. Kids ran 'round the streets,

played at the park, went to school on their own, and we never thought anything of it. The world didn't feel dangerous back then like it does now." For some reason, Marvin wasn't feeling the anger or jagged edge of deep sorrow he so often felt talking about Ellie's death. Instead, he smiled, remembering Ellie's tenderness, playfulness, and laugh.

"She was walking home from school one day, and someone choked her to death in broad daylight, right there on those steps in front of our house.

"I was away at a Southern Fellowship conference, and Margaret was home. But she was upstairs and didn't hear anything. Margie's hearing was never great, so it wasn't her fault, but I was angry at her for a long time for not hearing what was happening—not knowing it was happening.

"They found the contents of my little girl's backpack scattered across the sidewalk, so they thought it must have been a vagrant looking for drug money." Marvin shook his head at the senselessness of it.

"She was so beautiful. So innocent.

"I always liked kids, but I had no idea I would become so addicted to that little life. But when she gripped my finger the first time I held her, I was hooked something awful. Absolutely hooked. My little girl.

"Losing her didn't just hurt; it cracked my reality. In so many ways, the best parts of me died right along with her.

"Since it was an open police investigation, they wouldn't let me or Margie touch her—hold her—until I told them I was an ordained minister and had to pray over the body before burial, which is not something I actually believed, but I was willing to say anything just to touch and hold my little girl one more time.

"They still wouldn't let Margie in. She made me promise to take a pair of socks with me to make sure her feet didn't get cold," and he grunted at the memory.

"Strange isn't it, how we process something like that. Try anyways.

"But I did as she asked. I put those warm socks on my baby girl's feet, wrapped her in her favorite blanket, tucked this silly little stuffed butterfly she loved into the blanket with her, and said goodbye.

"I didn't know most of the people at her funeral. I think most of the neighborhood showed up, our church, people from churches across the state, so many people came. Crowds of people stood around her little grave all the way back to the main gates. There were news cameras and all sorts. But I wouldn't let some stranger bury her. I couldn't, so I took off my tie and suit jacket, rolled up my shirt sleeves, walked over to the gravedigger, and asked him for his shovel. Then in front of all those people, I buried my little girl myself, with my own hands. It probably took me more than an hour, but I did it myself. Shovel full by shovel full, I did it myself. Aint no one burying my little girl but me.

"By time I was done, everyone had gone home. The crowds. The newspaper people. Everyone except that gravedigger, who simply took the shovel from my bloody hands and walked away, without sayin' a word."

Marvin and Samantha sat quietly together for a few minutes while she processed the awfulness of what she was hearing.

"I guess I buried God that day, too," Marvin finally added.

"For the first few months, Margie kept trying to talk to me about God, but I wouldn't have any of it. She still prayed and all, but I wasn't having none of that.

"I had been raised believing in God. Singing about God. Teaching other people about God. Shoot, I had even officiated more funerals than I could count, standing over grave after grave reading the same verses they read to me, telling those people how they would see their loved ones again in that great mansion in the sky, but all those platitudes go away when it's your own child you're lying in the ground.

"And now, after all these years, Michael goes and brings God right back into my home," Marvin says to himself almost under his breath.

"Who's Michael," Samantha asked, "Your grandson or something?"

He lifted his eyes to her but didn't respond.

Samantha thought about that for a moment. Michael. She hadn't seen Marvin with anyone, but he *had* mentioned a visitor.

She decided not to push.

Chapter Thirty-Two

eter sat in his police cruiser enshrouded in darkness. He had followed every lead and run out of places to look for Samantha, which brought him right back to where he had first seen her. The Blue Bonnet Diner. He wasn't sure if she would ever return, but he was hungry to see her again, and he was willing to wait.

He took her lip gloss out of his shirt pocket, slowly smelled its sweet smell, and put some on. Then he clicked the yellow tube cap back on and returned it to its spot right above his heart.

He used to be comfortable sitting in quiet darkness, waiting for something to happen, waiting for a call, waiting to find trouble in a drunk biker or teenager defacing property, but the darkness was no longer quiet for him. It had not been quiet for some time. There were now voices in the darkness with him. Voices that would talk to him and sometimes talk to each other. Were they his voice? Were they memories? Were they tired imaginings of his own making after a long fourteen-hour shift? He didn't know. What he did know was how the voices made him feel.

There was his father's voice, always driving him forward,

always pushing him to try harder or work longer hours. It was a relentless voice never satisfied, always telling him that he would never be enough. This voice made him feel powerless, weak, and incapable. This was the voice, more than any of the others, that he always tried to prove wrong.

There was a voice that he only heard in the sleepless hours of the night. A slowly stalking voice that made him feel hunted; made him feel afraid. This voice told him that he was going to die, maybe tomorrow, maybe in a week, but soon. It might tell him that the next person he would pull over for a ticket would have a gun hidden under their seat, or the next homeless person he would question would be carrying a knife they would plunge into his stomach. However it started, it always ended with him dying slowly on the side of a highway somewhere.

Then there was the voice of Hunger. Not for food or drink, but for something he could only get from women. Hunger for something he had to take to be satisfied, and even then his appetite would only be sated for a very short while. This voice didn't speak to him or the others but pulled on strings so deep inside of him that he no longer noticed the nuances of how this hunger made him act. Or maybe he no longer cared. Nuances like how long he would stare at a woman's legs at a cafe or jokes he would tell in the locker room at the precinct. Thoughts he would entertain about girls he would see when parked in front of the local high school.

He was hungry now. He thought he could wait, but his appetite was growing, and he was slowly becoming more and more impatient. He had burned Samantha's things, which felt so good at the time but left an emptiness that only she could fill. Her touch, her smell, her presence.

He glanced up at the mirror and for a moment thought he saw someone sitting in his back seat, which startled him, and he quickly turned and looked behind him. But the seat was empty. He got out of his cruiser and looked around. He even knelt and looked underneath his car, but there was no one.

He felt foolish and decided he could use a cup of coffee, so he went inside.

Marty greeted him. "Coffee?"

He nodded.

As he sat down at the bar, he looked around the diner at the patrons, deciding in a moment whether each person might be trying to hide something, might be suddenly uncomfortable with the presence of a police officer or might just be a general risk, when he caught the long look of a blonde woman smiling at him from one of the back booths where she sat with a female friend. He smiled back and pretended to look at the menu while he thought about her for a minute. She was a little overweight and older than he preferred, but he did like being noticed. He played around with some ideas of how to talk to her when a familiar voice suddenly froze his attention.

"Hi Marty," Samantha said, walking behind Peter and sitting in a booth with Marvin.

"Marv, how you doing, hun?"

"Oh, doin' just fine," he said.

"I see you made a new friend."

Instead of replying, he asked: "How's the pie tonight?"

"Pumpkin's back on the menu," Marty told him.

"We'll have two pieces. You want coffee?" Marvin asked Samantha.

"Yes, please," she replied.

"Make that two cups, if you don't mind," he told her.

Hearing Samantha's voice made Peter swallow hard and listen closely. He didn't want to turn and stare, but there she was. What was his next move? He wasn't sure. The voices in his mind were rising to a cacophony and pushing him to the beginnings of a stress headache. He squeezed his mug of coffee and closed his eyes, trying to calm himself. He struggled to reconcile how her lovely voice made him feel with his memories of her laughing at him, rejecting him, and those hurtful things she had said about him in her journal. He was hungry for her—to control her—to possess her. But he couldn't do anything here, not yet. He already possessed her past, her memories. He possessed knowledge of something she wanted, knowledge of where her mother was. These things gave him power over her, and all he needed to do was connect the dots until he would possess *her*.

"Are you okay, darlin'," Marty asked Peter.

He just nodded and took another drink of coffee. Then Marty filled his mug again and walked away.

He pulled out the ChapStick and put some more on as he listened to Samantha laugh and chat with this old man. Who was he to deserve her attention? Jealousy rose in Peter so much that his hand began to tremble, so he stood, paid his bill, and went back to his car to watch them from the cover of darkness.

Samantha and Marvin sat chatting for more than an hour, and Peter studied their body language closely, trying to infer why they were together and who this old man was. She did most of the talking, but he made her smile a few times, fanning Peter's jealousy. They probably weren't family since they were of different races and were such different ages that he couldn't imagine them being casual friends. Maybe she was acting as some sort of caretaker, but the way she was dressed suggested that was unlikely. Old family friend? Was he a friend of Samantha's mother?

As they left the diner, Peter let his cruiser slow-roll as far behind them as he could get away with while still being able to watch them walk down the road to Marvin's apartment.

Peter knew that a police cruiser wouldn't go unnoticed in this neighborhood and decided to take note of the address and keep driving. Only, as he began to patrol some of the adjacent neighborhood streets, he started worrying that Samantha would leave the house and he might not find her again. He didn't want to take that chance, so he turned a corner and went back to the apartment, hoping to talk to her finally. He had so many things that he wanted to tell her, so many different ways that he could let her know that he had information about her mother, which—he imagined–would probably lead to dinner.

His cell phone chirped as he pulled up in front of Marvin's apartment.

He looked at the caller ID. It was his captain.

"This is Peter," he answered, unsure why his captain would call him on his cell rather than over the radio.

"Are you on a call?"

"No sir, just on my way to grab a quick cup of coffee," Peter lied. "What's up?"

"When can you be back at the station?"

"Thirty minutes?"

"Make it twenty." Then his captain hung up.

Peter looked at the phone. *What was that all about?* he wondered.

Peter stepped out of the vehicle and looked around. Two black teenage boys sat on bikes across the street, watching the clean-cut white cop get out of his shiny police car. When he saw them watching him, he glared at them both, but they didn't flinch or turn away, so he spat on the sidewalk and decided they weren't worth his time since he didn't have long.

He knocked hard on the front door and looked through the living room window. Lights in the living room were off, but he could see some towards the back of the house. After a moment of waiting, he heard several clicks as Marvin unlocked the door and peered out.

"Can I help you?" Marvin asked, eyeing Peter's badge and gun.

"Good evening. I'm with Boston PD. I wanted to ask you a few questions about a Savannah Wilkins. Can I come in?"

Marvin thought for a moment and slowly covered more of the entry with his body. "I would prefer that you did not."

This tiny gesture was not lost on Peter, who was an astute observer of body language. His father had taught him how to watch the small subconscious gestures that reveal what someone is thinking. Now Peter knew that Samantha was still in the house. "Is she here?"

Marvin didn't answer.

"I have information about her mother, Susanne."

"I would be happy to give it to her when I see her next," Marvin replied.

Peter clenched a fist, which was not lost on Marvin, who was also an astute observer of body language.

"It is of a confidential nature," Peter replied.

"Then I suggest you come back at a better time, perhaps tomorrow afternoon? Or better yet, if you have a card, I could see that she gets it and have her call you."

This wasn't a good option for Peter either. He didn't want

to talk to her on the phone or through an interpreter. He wanted to see her and give her the information about her mother himself. He wasn't willing to just give up the little bit of leverage that he had.

"I know she's in there," Peter said, but Marvin didn't flinch.

If information about her mother wasn't going to open the door, Peter would take a different tact.

"What if I told you that she has a record of theft? She befriends the elderly until they trust her and let her into their homes, then she robs them blind."

Peter saw Marvin's nostrils flare and knew he was now getting somewhere. He lifted his eyebrows and changed his posture to that of the concerned citizen. "One lady in the North End lost her entire life savings to this girl. She maxed out the woman's credit cards buying herself clothes, jewelry, and other high-ticket items that she could move quickly for cash. The poor woman was forced to sell her home and try to make up for the losses by moving into a retirement facility for the indigent." Peter put special emphasis on the word indigent.

Marvin wasn't moving. But he was listening. He didn't want to believe that Savannah was lying to him. She had stolen from him, but she had come clean and told him the truth. Hadn't she?

"Let me guess. She said her car was impounded, and all of her things were stolen?"

Now, this got Marvin's attention. *How would this cop know that?* Marvin wondered.

Peter nodded. "She probably said that her mother was gone and that she had nowhere to go. That's her MO. She befriends elderly people she meets at diners, people she can see have a few dollars to rub together, then she makes friends and bleeds them absolutely dry."

This couldn't be true, could it? Savannah was a good girl. She hadn't asked to stay with Marvin. That was his idea, or was it? He couldn't remember whose idea it had been now. But how does this cop know so much if it wasn't true? They *had* initially met at the diner, and she told him that her car was gone and her things had been stolen. Now some of *his* things were gone. Was she just using him or waiting for the opportunity to get access to his bank account and leave him penniless? Feelings of distrust of strangers and memories of being taken advantage of were hot and frothy now in Marvin's mind, even though he kept trying to keep his nerve. He did not trust the police, but too much of this rang true.

Then Peter fixed his gaze on Marvin and asked: "Did she tell you her real name? You *do* realize it is not Savannah, right? It's Samantha. Samantha Wilkins."

This stung.

Marvin squeezed the handle behind the door, trying not to show any lack of resolve to this cop standing on his doorstep. It had to be a lie, didn't it? She had made a mistake, but she had come clean. She wasn't using him. Was she?

Peter repeated it: "She uses all sorts of names, Savannah Wilkins, Emily Wilkins, Mary Smith," Peter was making them up now, knowing that he only had evidence of Samantha ever using the one alias. "But none of them are her real name. Her real name is Samantha Wilkins." Then he shrugged. "But if you don't believe me, just ask her."

Peter was starting to feel the pressure for time. He needed to get back to the station and see what his captain wanted, so he pulled a card out of his pocket and handed it to Marvin. "I can help her. Make things easier for her, and I meant it when I said I have information about her mother."

Marvin took the card and looked at it. It looked legitimate. The uniform and badge also looked legitimate. Why would this officer be lying? What could he possibly want?

"Have her call me, and we can talk." Then Peter turned and went back to his cruiser.

Marvin watched him drive away, then looked at the card again before going back inside and re-locking the door.

"Who was that?" Samantha asked.

Marvin slowly looked up at her. "That was a police officer who came by looking for someone by the name of Samantha Wilkins. You wouldn't know anything about that, would you?"

As he watched her eyes grow big, he knew she had been lying to him all along, and his heart broke.

Chapter Thirty-Three

"Marvin, that's me! I didn't even think to tell you that I use the name Savannah sometimes. I guess to try to protect myself. My real name is Samantha. Samantha Wilkins."

Marvin's shoulders dropped. He felt like someone had just punched him in the stomach.

"That was a police officer come by to talk to you. He said he had information about your mother."

"My mother?" Now she was confused. *What cop? How did he know I was here?* she wondered.

"He said that you were here to rob me."

No. That's not true at all, she thought and shook her head. But she *had* stolen from him.

"He said that you meet elderly people at diners to befriend them so that they let you into their lives—their homes. And then you robe them blind."

That wasn't true, but somehow, it was what had happened, partially. She was starting to get lost in which details were accurate and which were not.

"Please, let me explain," she said.

Marvin's voice was starting to rise. "He said that you stole

291

from a woman on the North End. He said you used her credit cards and drained her bank accounts."

She didn't steal from individual people—well, except for Marvin. This wasn't the truth, but it was starting to sound close enough to the truth that she didn't know how to explain.

"That's not true," she replied. "I never stole from anyone in the North End."

"Just from people in poor neighborhoods?"

"No. No. That's not what I meant. I…"

He tried to calm himself and held up a hand. "What else have you lied to me about?"

"Nothing," she said, shaking her head. "I'm sorry! I should have told you my name. I wasn't trying to keep it from you. I must have just …with everything going on.…"

"Where's my wife's watch?"

That was it. It was over. That question shattered everything. Samantha had tried to come clean, but she had forgotten to tell Marvin the truth about her name, and she had been too scared to tell him about the watch. She might be able to apologize and recover from one mistaken and

forgotten lie, but two? Not two. Apparently, she would be unable to hide from her past or ignore her mistakes, even in this tiny, out-of-the-way apartment.

She didn't reply. Her eyes turned red and aqueous.

Seeing it on her face, he simply said: "Get out."

Shame overwhelmed her, and she wanted to hide. She felt naked. She felt exposed. She gripped the edges of her shirt with both hands and tried to pull it more tightly around her shoulders. She turned, subconsciously looking—frantically groping—for answers. But there were none. Then she turned back to Marvin as a tear slowly crawled down the curve of her cheek.

She tilted her head and whispered: "I'm sorry."

He looked away.

He couldn't feign care. Not now. He didn't have the emotional capacity to protect her from what he was feeling, not just now.

So many people had hurt him and taken so much from him, just because of who he was or what side of the county line he lived on, nothing he could ever control. Hurt that had made him flee into this tiny apartment where he quietly took care of his wife, watched his evening shows, enjoyed a piece of pie at the local diner, and ignored the rest of the world. He ignored all the drugs on his street; ignored the homes in his neighborhood that he once loved being torn down and turned into liquor stores; ignored his people being brutalized on television and spoken down to by the highest levels of government. And now this.

He had trusted her, this girl, this woman, this villain. Maybe it was his fault. Perhaps he had hoped for something that wasn't there. Maybe he had seen something in her that reflected the little girl he had lost so many years ago. Perhaps he just wanted to hope again. But now this.

"Get out!" He screamed, pushing the photos and knick-knacks on his entry table onto the floor with anger, which caused him to stumble and fall to the ground. Samantha reached for him to steady him, but he pushed her away.

"Get out. Get out. Get out," he kept repeating over and over as he sat there on the floor, covering his face with his hands. "Get out."

She went into the bedroom to get her bag, took the key out of her pocket, and realized that she had left her bag unlocked the night before. Apparently, four turns weren't necessary to feel safe here.

He was still sitting on the floor when she returned to the entryway.

"Marvin…" she began, reaching for him, but he jerked away, which startled her. So, she laid the key he had given her on the entry table and left.

PETER KNOCKED ON THE HEAVY WOOD DOOR standing behind the rows of police desks on the second floor of his station building.

"Come," a thick, gravelly voice called from inside the office.

Peter stepped into a room large enough for his captain's desk and a conference table with five chairs. An American flag stood in one corner of the room, and a coat rack hung in the other, which held a cowboy hat and well-loved brown Carhart jacket.

Behind the desk sat a man in his fifties with a grey handlebar mustache stained at the edges. He had BPD in brass letters on his collar and two bars on each shoulder. A brass nameplate on the desk read: Captain Conner Collins. He was reading over some documents in a folder.

"Close the door and have a seat," Captain Collins said, not looking up from the papers.

As Peter sat down, his eyes scanned a set of tall shelves behind his captain's desk. There were books on law and police procedure, photos of the captain with his family, and him riding horses. In the center of the shelves sat a single wooden cross.

"What's all this about?" Peter asked, straightening his shirt.

"We've had a complaint."

Peter shifted in his seat.

"Where were you Monday morning at 8 a.m.?" his captain asked.

Peter took out his pad and flipped back to around that time, but nothing significant was noted. "I was off duty."

"That's not what I asked."

Peter thought for a moment. "I don't know. Probably running some errands."

The captain slowly looked up from the papers at Peter for the first time. "It says here that you were at the Self Storage on Franklin and Traveler. Does that jog your memory?" The captain's voice was a heavy baritone, which grew even deeper with each unanswered question.

Peter rubbed the back of his neck. He was off duty, but he was acting with a badge on, which meant that it didn't matter if he was off duty or not, he was still accountable.

"I was following up on a lead," Peter replied, his mouth starting to go dry.

"Off duty?"

"I do some consultancy work on the side. You know how it is…a few extra bucks."

The captain's gaze narrowed. "So, you were there on personal business?"

"Yes, sir."

The captain looked back down at the report. "This says that you came to the storage units asking for information on a Samantha Wilkins, and when the desk clerk asked for a warrant…" he paused and looked up at Peter. "Which he has a legal right to do…" he looked back at the report, "you threatened him by telling him that you were sure you could find drugs on his person whether he actually had any on him or not. You then proceeded to search and seize the contents of said storage unit." Then the captain slowly turned the page and looked at Peter. "How do you respond to this?"

"It's a lie."

"Which part?"

"I came asking about Samantha, and he gave me a key. I didn't threaten him."

"You did not threaten him?"

"No, sir," Peter lied, shaking his head.

The captain lifted the monitor to a laptop next to the folder and turned it so Peter could see the screen. It was a video of the morning, captured from a back corner of the office facing the front desk, a camera Peter hadn't noticed. Peter silently watched the video play for about three minutes before the captain closed the laptop. In the video, Peter was clearly aggravated, pointed to the clerk's computer, then the boy, and leaned partially over the desk. But, there was no audio, so Peter knew he had plausible deniability.

"Does that look like a threatening situation to you?" the captain asked.

"Maybe."

The captain took a breath. "But you claim that you did NOT threaten him?"

"No, sir. I know it might look like I was being aggressive, but I was only expressing my concern for the girl who is currently missing."

The captain glared at him, knowing with perfect clarity that Peter was lying to his face. "Are you familiar with the Plain View Doctrine?"

"Yes, sir. Of course, sir. It states that when an officer

has justification to search an area, objects can be seized as evidence in plain view of that area."

"And did you have a warrant to search the storage unit or clear justification to search the area?"

"No, sir, but this wasn't a search and seizure situation. I asked if I could have a look in the unit, and the clerk said yes. If he had said no, I would have left." Peter was quietly proud of the case he was slowly building in his defense.

"So, you were given access to the unit?"

"Yep."

"And where did the contents of the unit end up?"

"I collected the contents for Samantha's mother. That's who hired me. She's up at McLean and asked me to help her find her daughter."

Captain Collins picked up the next piece of paper, which had various lines of text highlighted in yellow. "According to this, you ran criminal history checks on both Samantha and Susanne while *on duty*."

Peter shifted in his seat again. This would be harder to align with his growing story.

"I did, yes."

"Probable cause?"

Peter had to buy himself a few moments to think of a response, so he slowly flipped through the pages of his notebook, trying to think of anything close to a plausible explanation of why he was using police resources to stalk a minor. Then it hit him—the stolen license plate tag. Maybe that little metallic sticker would be enough to get him out of this.

"I had reason to believe that the car Samantha was driving had been stolen because the plates had fraudulent registration tags. I also found a quantity of cash inside the vehicle, both of which led me to question drugs or stolen property."

"And did you find any drugs or stolen property?"

Peter shook his head. "No. She had illegally parked the vehicle for more than twenty-four hours, so it was impounded, and the registration was fraudulent, but I did not find anything beyond those."

"You expect me to believe that you were hired, as a PI, to find this Samantha but suspected possession, so you decided to run CHCs on both her and her mother after you came back on duty?"

"All do respect, sir. You believe what you like, but it's the truth."

The captain shifted in his chair, and Peter held back a smile.

"Tell me about the Emily Owens case," the captain said, now with a long unbroken gaze at Peter.

Peter's eyes grew, and he swallowed—his mouth quickly becoming dry again. He hadn't heard that name in more than two years.

"The case was thrown out on that," Peter said, his voice quieter than he had intended.

"Excuse me?"

Peter spoke up. "The case was thrown out on that."

The captain leaned forward in his chair. "That is NOT what I asked you, officer. I would like to hear what happened in the Emily Owens case, in your own words."

Peter bit his lip and turned away. "I have nothing more to add to that, sir."

"You have nothing more to add to that?"

"No, sir."

"Very well." The captain lifted the CHC report and slammed

it down on the desk. "According to this, Emily Owens pressed charges against you for sexual assault. She said that you pulled her over, asked for her L and R, which she presented when you asked her to step out of the vehicle. You claimed to smell drugs in the car. Does that ring a bell?"

Peter pursed his lips, choosing not to speak.

"No? Well, please do let me continue. She said that you then proceeded to frisk her, and during that frisk, you slid your hand up her skirt."

"She was being belligerent!" Peter snapped.

The captain slammed his hand down on the desk so hard it made Peter jump, and the brass nameplate crashed to the floor, but the captain didn't seem to notice.

"She had her two children with her in the car! The oldest of which, a nine-year-old, was forced to give testimony—in a court of law—about how he saw a police officer assault his mother, then left her crying and shaking on the side of the road. And according to this, according to THIS, when you were finished assaulting the woman there in broad daylight, you winked at the boy, then walked away."

Peter took a breath, remembering that this was all behind him. The charges had been thrown out, and nothing had come of it except getting transferred, which was fine by him.

"And now here we are again. You claim to be helping this woman find her daughter, but that isn't it is it? You have been transferred four times, all shortly after allegations of misconduct, three of which were against a minor, and all were women. I think you have a thing for teenage girls, and this Samantha Wilkins is the next name on your list."

Peter's mind ran from one incident to the next, remembering how well his father's name had protected him each and every time. Then he began to remember other situations that had never been reported, sometimes worse than any of the ones that had been, and the knowledge of his escape from consequences gave him a sense of empowerment.

"Here's what I think: I think your daddy got you into the police academy, and every time you were caught doing something that should have lost you your badge, some spineless bureaucrat saw to it that you were transferred rather than brought up on charges.

"I knew your father from my days working as a bailiff, and I didn't like him. He was a bully that used the bench to prove a point."

"Now, wait just a minute," Peter spoke up, unwilling to let someone speak poorly of his now deceased father.

"Shut. Your. Mouth. Or I will have you stripped of your badge and thrown in county lockup faster than you can spell your daddy's first name."

Peter bit his lip and sat back in his chair.

"And I do NOT like you. You are the worst example of what is wrong with the old way of policing, protected for far too long by unions and outdated rules that were *not* created to protect or serve our citizens but to create opportunities for bullies like you to thrive and hurt people. I also know that your daddy isn't around to protect you anymore.

"As officers of the law, it is our job, our duty, or responsibility, to be held to a higher account because we know better! When you chose to put on that uniform, when you chose to put on that badge, you accepted the call to that higher level of accountability. And as far as I am concerned, you are a disgrace to that badge. But I do not have evidence enough to strip you of it and throw you in prison, where you belong. I *can*, however, award you some much-needed time off. Say two weeks?"

Peter's look grew intense, and he leaned forward, not wanting to be put on leave.

"But mark my words. I am watching. And if you so much as sneeze wrong, I swear on the name of my good Lord and savior Jesus Christ that I will put you in handcuffs myself. And you better knockoff whatever it is that's going on with this Samantha Wilkins. You are not to have any more contact with either her or her mother. Am I clear?"

"Yes."

"I can't hear you," the captain barked like a drill sergeant from Peter's academy days.

Peter stood at attention with shoulders tucked back and said loud and clear: "Yes, sir!"

"Now get out of my sight," and the captain slammed the folder closed and turned in his chair away from Peter.

Peter said nothing, did nothing, as he went to the locker room, changed into his street clothes, put his things into an army-green duffle, and drove home.

He played the things his captain had said over and over again in his mind, and fires raged inside of him. His head pounded; his mouth was dry; his hands shook.

The voices in his head laughed and mocked him. Then he looked at himself in his rearview mirror and thought that he could almost audibly hear his father's voice above all the rest reminding him that:

"If a man doesn't command respect, he's worthless. Even the dogs at the racetrack get respect as long as they run well. But do you know what happens to them when their running days are over? They get put down."

Peter arrived at his house, pulled into his garage, and slammed his truck door. He went to a beat-up old fridge in his garage that he always kept full of various flavors of beer, soda, and harder liquors, grabbed an IPA, popped the lid off, and took a long drink. Then he took two more from the fridge and went inside, slamming the fridge door shut so hard he could hear some of the glass bottles inside clanking and toppling over.

He kicked off his shoes by the front door and paced back and forth around his living room.

"I am watching you," he remembered his captain telling him. "I do NOT like you. You are the worst example of what is wrong with the old way of policing. You are a disgrace to that badge."

Peter laughed. *Disgrace? Me a disgrace? Who does he think he is?* Peter asked himself, tossing back the second beer and setting the empty bottle on a small table by the couch.

The voices in his head made him feel like he was in a football stadium with screaming fans, only they weren't there to watch teams play as much as they were there to watch him fail.

He rubbed his temples and leaned forward, putting his head between his knees, trying to breathe. Then he stood up again and drank the third beer back in a single motion. He couldn't remember ever being this angry.

He turned to the kitchen to fetch his next round of beverages when he saw Samantha's dress still draped over the empty seat from dinner the night before. And just then, all of the voices fell silent.

He slowly approached the garment and gently touched the delicate fabric when a single voice spoke to him and said: This is her fault.

Peter went to the duffle he had brought back from the station, which was full of his police equipment. He unzipped the bag and removed his black tactical baton from where it hung from a black metal loop on his equipment belt.

He held the cold device in his hand and cradled its weight. Then he flicked his wrist, causing thirty-one inches of black steel to telescope out into a weapon, which he swung in a smooth arc through the air.

"This is all your fault," he said, pointing the baton at the dress.

"You might not like me, but you *will* respect me," he said calmly, then swung the baton and knocked the chair spinning across the dining room. He calmly picked it up, pulled the dress over the back of the chair, and beat the chair and the dress with the baton until nothing but a broken, splintered pile of debris was left in his dining room.

Peter stood panting over the now demolished chair and tattered dress, rubbing his aching hand and wiping the sweat from his forehead. *That felt good,* he thought as he embraced a rush of excitement and euphoria that added to the mental haze the drinks had created.

"I'm going to get some answers one way or another," he told himself, grabbing his equipment belt, climbing into his truck, and heading to Marvin's house.

Chapter Thirty-Four

As Peter drove over a grassy curb between his townhouse and the main road, trying to remember which exit to take to get to Marvin's, the police scanner in his truck chirped to life. He was having trouble keeping his truck between the lines through his drunken vision.

"All units to 15th and Johnson. Suspect reportedly robbed the 24-hour-pawn shop and was last seen on foot heading Eastbound down an alley behind the store.

"Suspect is a young woman, late teens, six feet, shoulder-length black hair, wearing a black hooded sweatshirt."

Peter turned up the radio dial. The description sounded like Samantha.

"Be advised. Suspect may be armed."

Peter sped up and swerved around a van and onto the shoulder, trying to get around the few cars on the narrow streets. The pawn shop was only a few blocks from that old man's house. *If it's Samantha, that's where she's headed,* he thought to himself, pulling a sharp right and knocking over a trash can.

SAMANTHA KNEW HER TIME HAD COME. She had burned all her bridges and was ready to hop on any bus she could find leaving town, and wherever that bus stopped, she would just get on the next. She had no more plans, so strategy, no idea of what to do, she just needed to leave. Boston was dead to her now. But she couldn't leave without giving Marvin his wife's watch back. All he had done was show her compassion and kindness, given her a place to stay, something to eat, a sense of peace and security. What had she given him in return? Nothing but deceit and heartache. The least she could do was get his watch back, no matter what it took.

Her first problem was that she didn't have the money to buy it back, assuming Johnny would even sell it to her. The second problem was that Johnny had told her that if he ever saw her again, he was calling the police, and she believed him.

She planned to try to trade her mother's necklace for the watch; at first, things didn't seem all that bad. Johnny was friendly and sounded willing to negotiate. It wasn't until the blue and red flashing lights streaked across the pawn shop walls that she knew he had betrayed her. He must have tripped a silent alarm or something similar. So, rather than think, she just reacted. She grabbed the watch, jumped over the counter, and ran through the back office and out the back door. She locked the office door behind her, giving her enough time to get down the alley and around the corner without being seen. At least, that's what she hoped.

Now she walked down Marvin's street with her hood pulled over her head. He would never have to see her face again. She wasn't going to try to talk to him; there was nothing left to say. She was going to just knock on his door, drop the watch through the mailbox and leave.

What Samantha didn't realize was that Marvin had hated himself for kicking her out from the moment she left. He had even walked the streets for nearly an hour, and twice to the Blue Bonnet and back, looking for her.

She had hurt him. She had lied to him. She had probably stolen from him, but truth be told, he really didn't care about any of that, not anymore. He had decided days ago to do whatever he could to help her, help protect her, help take care of her, and now he was even more determined than ever to follow through. Ever since his last conversation with Michael and that night in that church, he just couldn't see any reason to hold onto this kind of anger and bitterness any longer. He was no longer angry at the world, Samantha, Margaret, or even those boys who took Moses away from him when he was just a skinny child, all knees and elbows. Somehow, and he didn't know how, he wasn't even angry at whoever had taken Ellie away from him either. He simply had peace, a peace that surpasses all understanding. And he wanted to share that peace with Samantha. He wanted to tell her how much he loved her. What a strange thing, he thought to himself when he realized it, but he did. He loved her like a father loves a daughter and wanted her to find the same peace and rest that was letting him finally let go.

One way to do that, he had decided, was to get rid of the gun. He never really had the power to control his life or the world anyway, and keeping it around was more a symbol than a tool to him. A symbol of a wrong way of thinking, and it was time to let go of all that nonsense. Tomorrow, he would return it to the pawnshop and let that greasy little man do with it whatever he wanted, but it had gotten late and cold, so it could wait until morning.

PETER PULLED ONTO MARVIN'S STREET and turned off his truck lights, letting his pickup silently drift down the drive, not wanting to draw any more attention to himself than he had to. He didn't know if the police-band radio chatter *was* about Samantha or if Samantha was anywhere near here anymore, but he was going to find out. He would break down that little old man's front door and beat the answers out of him with his bare knuckles if he had to.

As Peter pulled up, Samantha walked up to Marvin's front door from the opposite direction. He watched her knock on the door and reach into her bag for something. Then he climbed out of his truck, put his equipment belt on, and approached her.

"Samantha," he said.

She turned toward the man and tried to shield her eyes with her hands. She couldn't see who it was because he was standing in front of the overwhelming lights of his pickup, but she thought the voice sounded familiar.

"You're in trouble. I came to help you," Peter calmly told her.

"Who are you? What do you want?" she asked.

"You need to come with me," he replied, with assurance in his voice, and began reaching for her.

When she realized who it was, she smiled, relieved that it was him. "Aren't you that guy from the diner who asked for my number? What are you doing here?" she said, but her flirty half chuckle triggered him, and something changed. Then he remembered everything she had said about him in her journal. Things that he thought were hurtful and hateful. And at that moment, his calm and carefully controlled self shattered. The cacophony of voices and memories of the abuse he had suffered as a child came crashing over him like a wave swallowing a small child on a beach.

So, instead of reaching for her, he reached for his pepper spray and yelled: "Get on the ground!"

Samantha was confused. What was he holding? Why was he asking her to get on the ground? She had trouble seeing clearly for the blinding lights of his truck. "Okay? I don't...."

"Get on the ground now!" he yelled a second time, not really to her but past her like he wasn't responding to her more than following some prewritten script.

"Okay, okay. Stay calm," she said, trying to reassure him.

"This is your last warning!"

She held up her hands to show him that she wasn't resisting and that there was no need for force. "I'm on the ground. I don't understand...."

Just then, a stream of liquid splashed against her hands and face, igniting blooms of pain in her eyes, nose, and throat as she tried to shield herself with her hands, and she began to shake uncontrollably. She had never felt something so terrible and terrifying. It was as though bees were attacking her eyes and throat. The burning was blinding, and she immediately lost any sense of where she was or what was happening to her. She wiped her eyes with her hands, but that only worsened her pain. She couldn't see anything now, and the pain was so unrelenting that it took her breath away.

"Do not resist," Peter yelled, with no interest in apprehending her.

Samantha coughed and started crying.

"Do not resist," he said again and showered her with more fiery liquid until his canister ran empty.

She was not resisting in any way, and even if she were,

she was barely a third his size, but he had no intention of apprehending her.

He threw the small canister aside, drew the yellow and black taser from his belt, which looked much like a square pistol, and trained it on her.

"Please stop!" she pleaded, shielding her eyes and coughing violently. Blinded by the pepper spray, she didn't realize the porch edge was right in front of her, and she fell forward onto the sidewalk splitting her lip open, blood pouring down her chin and onto her shirt. "Help!" she cried. "Someone, please help me!" She slowly tried to pick herself up off of the cold concrete. "Please!" she coughed, starting to panic, but her tears only motivated him—her cries excited him. The alcohol and adrenaline ignited his passions so brightly that he was now in what felt like a dream state. He didn't see a helpless teenage girl lying prone on the sidewalk. He saw the personification of those who had disrespected the law—who had disrespected *him*. And he was going to right those wrongs here and now.

"Do not resist, or I will tase you!" Peter commanded, stepping closer to the prone teenage girl who helplessly groped at the sidewalk.

At the word "tase," Samantha froze and sat back on her knees, wiping her eyes with the sleeve of her shirt. "Please stop," she begged. "Please don't do this. I don't understand. I'll do whatever you want."

"Do. Not. Resist!" he yelled again.

"I'm not," she cried back.

Deaf to her plea and blind to her pain, he pulled the trigger.

She immediately fell to the ground convulsing, legs and arms shaking violently.

Only, he didn't let go of the trigger.

Peter squeezed the trigger so hard, it was as though the harder he squeezed the trigger, the more pain he could transfer from himself to her.

Then a cry broke through the night.

"STOP!" Marvin screamed, anger and pain pouring through his voice, veins bulging in his neck and forehead. "You're killing her!" And in that moment, he saw both Samantha and Ellie being attacked there on his sidewalk.

Peter snapped out of his stupor, released the trigger, and turned, the light from inside Marvin's house outlining the chrome of the pistol now pointing at him.

Peter dropped the taser and walked over to Samantha, where he pressed his knee into her back and pulled her arms down behind her. "Stay back. This is police business."

Marvin pulled the pistol's hammer back with the palm of his left hand and spat: "You get away from her!"

Police sirens screamed in the distance, drawing closer, as Peter said: "Now hold on there. She was wanted on...."

"I don't care. You get away from her, you hear me!" Marvin roared, hands shaking.

"Put the gun down," Peter lowered his hand to his sidearm, but Marvin didn't move.

Time slowed for Marvin. A sense of purpose and resolve rose in him as his hands stopped shaking, his shoulders dropped, and he stood tall. He had missed the opportunity to save those he loved so many times, but not this time. In this one salient moment, he felt more present than he had ever felt in his entire life.

Samantha slowly shifted, trying to grasp at the grass, which distracted Marvin long enough for Peter to draw his sidearm, and just then, two shots punctured the night air.

"NO!" Samantha screamed, scrambling to her feet and running over to her friend, who now lay bleeding in his front yard, his eyes wide open. "No, No, NO! Marvin! Please!" She lifted his head onto her lap, trying not to touch his face with her pepper spray-covered hands, and gently covered the blooming red hole torn through his nightshirt. "Help! Someone! Please help us!" She screamed and started rocking him back and forth like she was trying to comfort a small child, not an eighty-seven-year-old man. "Oh, please, Marvin. Hang in there. I'm going to get help.

You're going to be okay. Help! Please help!"

Marvin looked up at her as Samantha pulled the watch out of her pocket and put it into Marvin's hand. He pressed it back into hers, curled her fingers around it and smiled. Then he simply said: "Don't be afraid."

And as his hand slowly released its grip on hers, his head rolled limply to the side.

She closed her eyes and cried out again, so loud and so hard that the veins bulged in her neck.

When she opened her eyes again, she saw that the night was no longer dark, but something like liquid fire covered the ground around her and Marvin. And there, also holding Marvin's head in his hands, was a being of light brighter than the noon-day sun, with hard features and long black hair floating around his head, who she recognized from the night she went into the bar looking for trouble.

When this being looked up at her, she saw in his eyes a terrible fierceness that somehow did not elicit fear in her but instead overwhelmed her with a sense of total comfort like everything was going to be alright. And not just for Marvin, but for her as well. In that moment, she knew in the deepest parts of herself that everything was exactly as it was meant to be.

Then this Lord of Terrible Aspect stood and lifted Marvin to his feet, only it wasn't Marvin's body because his body was still laying on the grass with his head in her lap, but a nearly translucent version of her friend who looked younger and healthier like the Marvin she had seen on the back of his books.

And something resembling the glowing outlined shape of a chariot nearly the size of the entire front porch appeared in the yard next to them, and a younger version of Marvin's wife smiled and reached out for him. Next to her stood a beautiful little girl who ran towards him and reached for his hand. "Daddy! Come and see! I've been waiting for you. He's made a place for all of us, and uncle Moses is there too!" Samantha heard the little girl say.

Marvin picked up the girl and embraced her passionately, and Samantha could see tears of joy streaming down his face.

Then, and for only a moment, Samantha saw a fifth someone standing on the back of the chariot, only He wasn't looking at Marvin or his family. He was looking directly at Samantha like someone who had known her from birth.

Then they were gone. The night was dark again, the world was cold again, and Samantha sat holding the lifeless body of her fallen friend.

As sirens screamed down the road towards her, she saw Peter lying motionless in the middle of the street, the lights of his pickup washing over him. As she watched, something barely visible fled from him into the darkness and disappeared.

Chapter Thirty-Five

Three days after the shooting, Samantha stood underneath the naked branches of a maple tree at Forest Hills Cemetery.

It had been a small and quiet funeral service. Only a handful of the old timers from the neighborhood came, and Marty from the Blue Bonnet was there.

Marvin now lay next to Margaret and Ellie, forever together at last.

As she listened to the minister's words conclude and everyone stood to leave, Samantha saw a young boy, with wispy-blonde hair in a well-tailored black suite, standing near Marvin's grave, but by the time she found her way through the thin crowd to where the boy had been standing, he was gone. And there, already breaking through the freshly laid earth over Marvin's grave was a single purple-blue Mountain Cornflower with its fingerlike petals and silver-green leaves.

Samantha thought about how she might typically feel lost and inconsolable, but she didn't feel either of those things. On that grey and drizzling afternoon, all she could do was remember how fiercely her friend had fought to protect her and how he was now with the people he loved. All of the papers had blamed Marvin for the shooting, but she knew the truth, and that was enough for her. The other things she had seen and the overwhelming sense of peace and order stayed with her. And so, instead of sorrow, she was happy that her friend had found his rest.

"Ms. Samantha Wilkins?"

"Yes?" she said, tired of talking to anyone, including the press.

A man approached her in his late fifties, wearing a finely tailored suit and carefully manicured grey beard with his collar popped up against his neck, trying to avoid the rain.

"My name is Franklin Styles. My firm handles Mr. Johnson's affairs. He called me a few days ago asking if I could look into your mother for you and if I could deliver this to you. Neither of us expected I would be delivering it to you at his funeral." Then the man handed her an envelope. "I'm sorry for your loss," he said, tipping his hat towards her. Then he climbed into a black Lincoln Continental and drove away.

Inside the envelope was a small card. The card read: McLean Psychiatric Hospital–room 317.

On the back of the card was a note.

Dear Ms. Samantha,

Do not let your past dictate your future. You may have made some mistakes, but your past does not define you. Every single morning you wake up with breath in your lungs is another chance to change your life. Don't miss those opportunities, and do not be afraid. Not like I was. Go find your family. Go see the world. Go back to school and find a man and have kids and live. Just live.

Your Friend,

Marvin

THREE MONTHS AFTER THE SHOOTING, Samantha spat salt water out of her mouth and paddled onto the warm sand of Lanai, Hawaii, remembering her friend. She was wearing Marvin's Rolex, which she had adjusted to fit her wrist.

She lifted her long smooth surfboard out of the water and walked up to her mother and uncle, laughing underneath the shade of tall palms.

"When are you going to learn to surf?" she asked her mother, who shielded her eyes as Samantha approached.

"Well, if we're staying, I had better learn some time," she replied.

How to Get Involved

3 easy and FREE ways you can support me and my career as an author:

1. **Follow me via email.** Go to GJDaily.co and join my mailing list. You will receive news and updates and pre-release information on upcoming books and it really helps me in a HUGE way because traditional publishers will gauge the success of my book based on the size of my email list. I will *never* sell or spam your account.

2. **Please, please, please leave a review on Amazon!** Your review *directly* tells Amazon to show my book to more people. The more reviews, the more people will find it. This is so critical to the success of this book and my publishing career. It absolutely makes a difference.

3. **Tell at least 3 people about the book and where they can find it.**

Book Club Questions

Who is the child? Is the child real or a figment of Marvin's imagination?

What was the central theme of the story?

How do each of the three main characters deal with separation and loneliness differently?

Do you feel that Marvin's race was ambiguous? Why or why not? How did that affect the story?

How would you have felt differently about the story if the author had pointed out that Marvin was either black or white?

How did Samantha's homelessness affect her struggle with identity?

Was Peter a villain or a victim? How did his suffering turn him into who he was by the end of the story?

How did the story deal with dichotomies of authority figures?

What were Marvin's and Peter's experiences with religion?

What role did spirituality play in the story?

Who or what was Michael?

What was your perception of homelessness before reading the story? What is your perception after?

Author Interview

STRANGE CHILD clearly works with themes of racial tension, which is a hot-button topic right now. Yet, you chose not to identify Marvin's race. Why?

I feel that books have a unique ability to not just spark conversation but really dig into social topics in a way that neither movies nor non-fiction can by giving the reader a glimpse into how someone feels. By playing with racial ambiguity, I wanted the reader to become attached to the character and begin to see Marvin, especially in the light of their own grandfather before questioning how Marvin might look or what race Marvin might be. I really tried to write it in a way that caused the reader to question Marvin's race so that in their mind he bounces back and forth, and then they can ask themselves, does Marvin's race matter or does it matter more that he is simply a person?

What authors have inspired you?

I really love reading a variety of stories, from bestsellers to indies. However, I am drawn to those stories that portray three-dimensional characters, and in the case of STRANGE CHILD, Mitch Albom, John Irving, and Bryce Courtenay definitely come to mind. Each of these authors have done a great job of portraying characters that feel like real people in a way that rings true to my ear as common people dealing with overwhelming struggles. These authors also don't shy away from incorporating spiritual, religious, and even Christian elements into their work in a way that doesn't feel forced into the common religious tropes.

What inspired you to pursue a hybrid publishing model?

When I published If I Lose Her, the ebook market was very young, and it was almost impossible for the average author to produce a highly polished and professional product. Today, ten years later, the landscape for ebooks has changed entirely. It's now a billion-dollar industry, and a lot of professionals are more than happy to offer their services to support cover design, editing, and the like. As such, I felt that my experience with digital marketing would help to get the ebooks off the ground while traditional print publishers could do what they do best, which is find a spot on bookstore and library shelves. It's a win-win situation.